MW01678904

Prelude to a Warrior

Book 1

of

The Saga of the Warrior

by

Burt J. Keltner

HATS OFF™

Prelude to a Warrior

Published by Hats Off Books™
610 East Delano Street, Suite 104
Tucson, Arizona 85705

ISBN: 1-58736-151-5
LCCN: 2002095694

to all who played a
part in the adventure
of my life,
above all
my wife
and
son

CAVE OF KINGS
Hobgoblins
NORTHERN BREAKS
ELVEN FORESTS
Goblin Tribes
AX
CREEK
DEMON RIDGE
RIVER
WESTERN
WASTES
LITTLE
Hills of the
KELT-RA CLAN
BORDER
LIFE
Goblins
OGRES
WOLF WORSHIPPERS
CREEK
BLOOD
SWAMPS
TROLL CLANS
GNOME CLANS
Goblins

Prelude to a Warrior

Book 1

of

The Saga of the Warrior

THE GATE

The young man's body heaved, struggling to push beyond its mighty limits. His heart pumped like a jackrabbit's, sweat forming a soupy film over his whole form, and his limbs labored heavily, saturated with blood and the fatiguing acid that slows.

Although the young man was a mighty athlete—the strongest hunter of his clan—this test was fast proving to be his better. He had been running for an amazing thirty hours straight, no time to stop for food or rest. This was a race of escape as he followed the sun's path through the dry, desolate wasteland.

Behind the desperate figure, trailing him by barely two hundred paces, was a pack of slavering, mindless Dogs of Hell. These horrors of an insane imagination were black-hided canines easily the size of a small horse. Thick, short-edged horns covered their broken, leathery dog heads. Their eyes held no pupil or iris, but a small, green, unearthly flame that burned with an uncanny intelligence. The pack of ten chased this lone exhausted figure with no thought, their minds bent to the will of another. Once, in a time long forgotten now, these hellish creatures had been free souls; they were souls now forced to servitude in a form unknown to them.

This one frightened man did not know that he had been running for over thirty hours. He didn't dwell on the fact that he now faced this fate because he had escaped certain death at the hands of a mightier foe the day before. He had made no conscious decision to test his physical endurance and prowess against these foul hunters. He hadn't escaped because he thought he could. He had escaped because he had to. His very life depended on it.

The terrain he ran through was desolate and harsh. Hard, dry, gumbo flats covered in cactus and soap weed stretched out in every direction but behind him. The amber-tan plains met the champagne sky sharply, the sun barely peeking over the western horizon, tantalizingly promising a safe haven the young man would never reach.

Fortunately, fate had blurred the man's vision over seven hours ago; his eyes were dry of most moisture. All he could do was run towards the dimming amber haze for now. Even his near-mad mind knew that when dark blanketed the sky completely, he would surely be cut off by the pack. He had done well the previous night, but that had been early in the chase. He would be unsure of a straight path of escape tonight and the Dogs of Hell would easily overtake him.

As fate would, and usually does, have it, though, it never came to that. Twisting sharply, the man's ankle bent sideways, sending him tumbling head over heels. Landing roughly on his side in a patch of brightly flowered cactus, the man's body seemed to seize up on him. His arms and legs refused to move more than an inch or two, rejecting the commands of his mind. His body now heaved even harder, his breathing ragged and desperate, his jaw and mouth fully opened, tongue lolling like a dying cow's. Without the rhythm of his running, his lungs fought for more and more oxygen.

Oddly enough, the stinging sweat dripping into his eyes and the lack of oxygen in his brain seemed to clear his vision. He saw the pack of ten demon dogs bearing down on him mercilessly some hundred paces away. Despite the horrid fate fast approaching, the man seemed to find some sort of honorable solace in his seemingly cowardly escape across the desert. At least he had fought to live, rather than cowering in fear before the chase could begin.

The Dogs of Hell were now under a hundred paces away. Death would be painful and brutal, but would end soon enough. The young man had never expected a short life as most of his people had. He had enjoyed what little he could from his pointless existence and dreamed for a future, despite the knowledge that death would likely come someday in the belly of a hell-born demon hunter.

The dogs were fifty paces away now. Finally, he would know the truth of everything. Once his spirit was free of these fleshy shackles, it would travel past the demons, devils, and hunters of this earth and into whatever Realm of Truth lay beyond this abysmal existence. As the dogs leapt forward to ravage his body, the young man wondered if any spirit realm truly existed.

Suddenly, bolts of searing white energy exploded through the two lead dogs, robbing the man of the answer to his doubt. He looked up dizzily, consciousness slipping slowly from his mind. He saw two beautiful figures, bodies seemingly sculpted in muscular perfection, garbed in kilts of white silk, float down among the pack and destroy every one of them utterly. Gigantic wings of doves sprouted from their shoulder blades and fiery broadswords cut easily through the Dogs of Hell.

"WindBearers," the young man muttered as he slipped into oblivion, sure that they would do the same to him as they had to his hellish tormentors.

*

"Best to hurry, Jehoel."

"Aye, Seraphiel. Darkness must see us at the Cave of Kings for the night. Though I fear not the denizens sure to come this night, 'tis best not to gamble with the gods' unknowing will."

"Ha!" Seraphiel scoffed. "'Tis Hosampsich and the blade he wields I think it best not to gamble against." Jehoel nodded at that, his eyes and hands steady at his work.

The two looked like men, but were not. Both stood over six feet tall and were powerfully muscled. They wore silken kilts that ended at mid-thigh, and white leather sandals with straps crossed around their calves and shins to below their knees. Both had long, curly, blonde locks that spilled down to cover their necks. Their eyes were the hard blue of a winter day's sky.

The most striking feature of the two was the massive dove-like wings that jutted from their shoulder blades. Wings the color of summer clouds that spanned over twelve feet across had guided the two from above to their kills. They now were tucked out of the way entirely, folded neatly behind and nearly unnoticeable.

The two WindBearers had sheathed their long steel swords within the golden scabbards bound around their waists with a like-made chain. Neither the scabbard nor chains were truly golden. If they were, it was a form of gold not of this plane, a metal stronger than the steel of their swords.

"This is the vile part of it, eh?" Seraphiel spat as he skinned the inanimate dogs expertly and quickly. He used a short dagger that had been sheathed at his left thigh.

"Aye," Jehoel nodded, busy at his bloody work. "I am a warrior and a hunter, not a butcher. This is work for another." Seraphiel nodded but didn't lessen his pace. The sun was fast to be gone in the western sky and the Cave of Kings was many miles to the east. The two would need to skirt around the treacherous Demon Ridge and Tower of Hosampsich, and this barren land was the outskirts of the fabled Oasis of Sam'mael. A meeting with Sam'mael brought only death—perhaps worse.

"What of him?" Seraphiel nodded to the inanimate form not ten paces away. "Shall we take his hide, as well?"

"No," Jehoel shook his head, piling the wet dog skins. "We've not a permit for him and I haven't the stomach for poaching."

"Aye," Seraphiel nodded again. It was darkening now that the burning orb had fallen below the skyline. He began to feel a touch of fear. He looked wistfully at the unconscious human, not wishing to waste such a prime prize.

"Here." Jehoel handed his partner a thick package of tightly wrapped pelts. "Let us make haste from here and save our own skins as well as these." Without a second thought, the two

WindBearers spread their downy wings, rose into the air, and flew off into the approaching darkness of the eastern sky.

*

Kael's eyes opened slowly, consciousness slow to follow the burning blur of unfocused daylight. The pain in his body struck him instantly, nearly bringing tears to his eyes. His limbs were like lead, his chest racked with pain from his superhuman feat the day before. His side was raw from the sting of the flowered cactus he had landed on, and his ankle tender from its twisting.

Struggling from his back to lean on his elbows, he was surprised suddenly by the cackle and wing beat of a black vulture. He jerked back, rolling painfully to his hands and knees, muscles throbbing in pain. The feeling was nearly enough to make him pass out, but it didn't. Kael crouched, ready and able, he thought, to fight.

The vulture cackled again, seemed to shrug, and hopped over to where twenty other such birds fed on the remains of the Dogs of Hell. The stench was nearly thick enough to physically touch. The dog carcasses were all cleanly skinned and nearly unrecognizable to Kael. The sight was nearly too much for him to stomach, but he had long ago become accustomed to the base vileness of this earth. This horror was just a daily dose of reality for Kael.

Taking a deep breath, Kael struggled painfully to his feet, standing unsteadily on knot-filled legs and shaky knees. His ankle, though sore, was able. He became aware, almost as an afterthought, that he was completely naked. This fact didn't register as odd to the young man; most of his life had been spent unclad, as had most other humans he had ever known, but he was sure he had started his trek into the wastelands with at least a loincloth.

Kael stood just under two paces tall; his frame was thin and wiry, but heavily muscled. He had trained his entire twenty-three years of life to bring his body to excellent condition. His stature had been more the result of hard physical labor than any strict form of regimental training, his thinness more due to malnutrition than diet.

His wavy hair was to his shoulders, thick and blonde. His eyes were an icy mixture of blue and green—the look of hazy seawater. His jaw was straight and stubble-covered, his features grossly masculine and rugged. That was how he thought and carried himself, as well. In this reality, a man did this or did not survive.

Trying to regain his bearings, Kael turned around to see the bright afternoon sun trailing slowly down to the flat, desolate horizon. It had been dusk when he had lost consciousness. Had a full day passed already? After pulling out the tiny cactus prickles, he absently rubbed his sore, knotted muscles, standing unsteadily and pondering his next move: to the east was home and sure death in the lands of Hosampsich, to the south were dark clouds brimming with electricity. It was legend that it was the realm of Sam'mael, a being of earthly power beyond anyone's imagination. To the north and west was nothing but desert and death. What lay beyond that was anyone's guess.

Before Kael could form another thought, his world exploded in an eruption of fire and energy. He felt his body picked up by the blast and hurled mercilessly though the air. Twisting in midair, Kael managed to land on his hands and knees, the breath rushing from his lungs. The vultures that survived the attack rose into the air noisily, flying for their lives to the north.

Kael's knees and shoulders seemed to roar in pain from the impact, his muscles still shuddering from the previous day's exertion. The vision before him, however, nearly made his spasm-wreaked muscles as still as his breath and his wide-open eyes. Standing in the crater formed from the energy blast where the dog carcasses had lay stood the most feared and horrible being Kael knew existed.

Hosampsich was called the Tiger Demon. He stood well over two paces tall and was built like a war-horse. With shoulders easily four feet across, he had the body of a man, his skin thick and leathery, covered entirely with the pattern of a tiger. Rather than orange, white, and black, however, the colors were brown, tan, and black. His face and bald head were striped as well, covered with hundreds of small, finger-sized tusks, each curled sharply like L's in every direction. He was completely naked in the afternoon sunlight save for one article of clothing: a cloak, the hood drawn, which hung to the calves of his legs. The cloak was made entirely of human skin. The thought of the men and women that had given their hides to the demon's cape and their muscle to his diet made Kael's throat constrict tightly. His lip curled, teeth clenched, and sweat poured in fear and rage of the figure before him. The rage that burned within him couldn't thaw the icy grip of his fear, though.

Hosampsich looked around himself in complete disinterest. As he moved, Kael noticed that a long, golden scabbard was strapped at his right hip. The sword handle that emerged from it was three hands long, with a human-leather band strapped around it. It had a jagged, metal hand guard that ran double-pronged from the pommel to the hilt. The scabbard was ornate, covered in a metal worker's dream of angels, demons, dragons, and a hundred other creatures, swimming throughout the exterior of the scabbard. To stare at the artwork, one could actually imagine the beings moving, as the golden forms seemed to come alive in a tapestry of magic.

"So," the massive horror purred, stepping towards the human. Kael was frozen in absolute terror. It may have been only the fatigue in his limbs that kept him from running, frothing like a deranged lunatic.

"Was it you who did this to my precious mutts?" the demon kneeled down, tracing a finger down the vulture-pecked, bare-skull forehead of a stinking dog corpse. He stood up, licking the rotten flesh from his finger. Bile rose in Kael's throat as his bowels struggled against his fear.

"No," Hosampsich shook his head. "You would not have run if you wielded this sort of power. I would be hard pressed against the being—or beings—responsible for this carnage. Why save you, though?" the demon continued, lazily pacing a circle around his prey. He glanced occasionally to the sky and horizons, almost expecting the human's savior to come again to the rescue. "You are but a human bit of cattle, barely worth the oxygen you waste."

Hosampsich knelt down beside Kael, his rancid breath and nightmarish face inches from the human's. Kael's bowels loosened, the sticky shit oozing down the insides of his thighs. Tears and sweat poured from his face, his fists clenching the dry dirt futilely.

"See," the demon chuckled, "You can not even hold your waste. Disgusting, little creatures, you humans are. Disgusting, but nourishing." Hosampsich, still crouching, began to reach for his mammoth sword.

Suddenly, time seemed to stop for Kael. The sword's handle, pommel, and guards were hard mirrored steel, shining blackness. The only other color was the ruddy peach of the human-leather strap wrapped tightly around the handle, and the color of two shining eye-like rubies slanted upon the hilt.

Grip the blade, Kael.

Kael's eyes opened wide at the thought that permeated his mind. His cowering form seemed to halt its fearful quivering. The jewels of the sword shone, penetrating his brain like living heat. Hosampsich's hand grasped the handle slowly.

Quickly, Kael. Take the blade in your hand. Rise and fight.

"I will be merciful, little flea," the demon scoffed, spit dribbling hungrily from his lip, forming around various boar-like tusks on his chin.

Quickly, Kael.

Before the demon could clear the blade an inch from the scabbard, Kael's hands shot to the handle. Somehow his hands were able to grasp the handle beneath Hosampsich's, as if the sword had moved out of the demon's hands and into the human's.

Kael steeled himself, lowered his jaw, and growled gruffly. The fear in his heart and bowels remained, but somehow he was able to act through it. Whether it was from the weapon or within himself, he found the necessary spirit. Kael drew the sword, in the process slicing off fingers and half of Hosampsich's hand. Both froze, wide-eyed, the demon standing in disbelief, the human crouched in terrifying, unbelieving rage.

"Impossible," Hosampsich gasped, green ichor and steam pouring from what was left of his hand. "I'll eat you alive."

"Nay," Kael growled, the fear draining from his soul with the shit off his legs, the demon no longer a visage of terror, but a target of frustration and vengeance. The point of the jagged, five-foot broadsword hovered for an instant before Hosampsich's chest…then plunged itself into the tiger demon's heart. Kael twisted the sword and brought it down through his target's torso. The demon struck out at his assailant as the sword halted in his heavy rib cage. Kael flew across the crater, but was up on his feet the instant after he hit the ground. He stood, fists clenched, ready for the demon's onslaught.

Hosampsich never made that attack. In fact, his last thought was of disbelief and confusion at the actions of the pitiful human. Then, unspectacularly and completely without fanfare, the demon fell flat on his face, dead.

Kael's heart was pounding furiously, his breathing erratic through clenched teeth and flaring nostrils. It felt as if hammers were smashing into his temples.

This blade is yours.

The forced thought in Kael's brain barely registered before the gravity of the situation quashed his awareness like a grape. He melted to the ground, blackness accepting him for the second time within a single turn of the sun.

*

Kael awakened not five minutes after his disembowelment of the demon lord. His head now throbbed worse than his still-spent muscles. Again he found himself struggling wearily to his feet in the waning afternoon. A dizzying sleepiness assailed him, nearly dropping him back to the ground. He closed his crossing eyes, hands over his face. Kael knew he couldn't succumb to the drowsiness. Hunters in his clan had fallen asleep after suffering head wounds such as this before, never to awaken again.

The carnage around him was gruesome. The deep crater formed from the impact of Hosampsich's initial assault still smoked from the heat of the blast. Mutilated, bird-pecked dog carcasses stank in the hot afternoon sun. Green blood and milky ichor pooled beneath the demon's enormous corpse, the blade of the sword emerging from his back up into the air. The black-mirrored, steel blade was thick, straight on the closer edge, murderously jagged on the farther. The massive demon's life fluid and entrails covered it like a syrupy film.

Kael seemed to regain his bearings after a moment, looking about himself for guidance on what to do next. Desolation as far as the eye could see in every direction save east—home. The smooth rolling hills and slopes of his homeland were a blue haze in the eastern distance. At least the vultures were no longer scavenging. The demon's rancid gut odor kept them circling in the air above. The flock looked to be abandoning their kill and flying for the north.

"Good," Kael muttered. The vultures were no better than the demons and other monsters of the world.

The blade.

Kael stiffened at the thought that crossed his mind. Did it come from beneath Hosampsich's unmoving hulk? For long moments Kael stood, trying to dismiss the random thought, but his curiosity at last won over his tentativeness. After all, hadn't he killed a demon with his own hands?

Stepping over to the tiger-skinned demon's body and kneeling down, Kael gripped the figure by the shoulder and torso and flipped him over on his side. The long black blade dug into the arid soil, keeping Kael from completely turning over the demon's body. The handle, soaked in green-gumbo mud, presented itself, the scowling eye-like rubies leering with a supernatural glow.

Kael swallowed hard, feeling his newfound courage begin to waver. He squeezed his hands into fists to steel himself.

Take the blade into your hands.

Kael's jaw slackened, his eyes slightly glazed. The whiteness in his hands faded as he involuntarily seemed to relax, perhaps hypnotized by the permeating commands. Kael's hands suddenly but slowly reached forward, his fingers wrapping around the handle almost familiarly. Although he had never held a forged weapon before, his mind found this handhold common.

Withdraw and command the power.

Kael stood slowly, pulling the sword roughly from the demon's chest. The jagged side of the midnight colored blade ripped and tore the vicious opening even more, splaying Hosampsich's green fluid and guts on the dusty ground. As Kael drew up the sword, holding it before himself in amazement, he didn't notice the weight of it at all. Kael was powerful for a human man, but this weapon was demon-sized. The blade itself was five feet long, over six feet from pommel to tip. He was so stupefied by the look of the weapon that he didn't even notice its most disturbing trait: the slime and entrails covering the blade slowly and completely dissolving into the unearthly metal. That is, if metal it truly was.

It seemed to be the very color of the blade that mesmerized Kael. The color was truly the color of a midnight, star-filled sky. A black beyond black with a deepness that the human mind could not fully perceive. Kael saw the stars of the nocturnal veil through the heavy night's darkness. His eyes now no longer saw the afternoon desolation of earth around him, but motion through some vastness beyond mortal comprehension.

With a gasp, his hand instinctively thrust the captivating weapon away. The blade landed squarely on Hosampsich's exposed neck, cleaving neatly through, with only the momentum of a short fall. At the strike, the demon's unseeing eyes shot open suddenly, lids resting at across the eyeball's equator. Black ichor bubbled and oozed from his fanged mouth and gaping throat.

Kael's eyes strayed to the human-skin cloak, now loosened from its demonic wearer. The sight of the wretched cape, coupled with a debilitating near-madness, was slowly heating the blaze of his mind, bringing an unsettling ease to Kael's spirit and the sword, again, to his hand. Solemnly and with purpose, Kael fell to work. It seemed impossible to do such a task with such a weapon, but Kael did it in less than an hour.

Afterward, Kael sat quietly, his elbows to his knees, his head in his hands, sweat glistening on his body. The immense tiger patterned hide was nearly the size of a buffalo as it lay staked, drying in the dying afternoon. Kael found peace immediately after skinning his demonic tormentor. He seemed to forget the intruding, overbearing voice in his mind, finding rest for his brain, as well as for his aching body. As the sun ducked past the far edge of the earth, Kael allowed exhaustion to again overtake his fear and his mind. As he slept, his hand rested easily on the handle of the midnight-colored sword, its slant-shaped jewel eyes gleaming a fiery red in the cool, clear night.

*

When Kael woke the next morning his head still ached, but his muscles were already loosening. The soreness still coursed, but slighter now since his escape from the Dogs of Hell. A look at his side showed no infection from the cactus and his ankle held no swelling. His first act of the day was to bury the human-skin cloak that had adorned Hosampsich. It was tough digging—Kael used the demon's own shoulder blade—but he was done soon enough.

Kael wasted not a moment or a thought on his next task. Using the midnight blade to cut a sliver of the demon's bone for a needle, and Hosampsich's own ligament string for thread, Kael went to work on the dried, tiger-striped hide.

In an hour he had fashioned a kilt, secured by gut string and bone buttons carved from the demon's collarbone. In three more hours he had made a perfect cloak, hood and all, from the demon's thick animal-like skin. With a sweeping flourish, Kael donned the cloak, pulling up the hood to cover his head from the sun's zenith. The hem of the cloak fell just below his calves, and it could be pulled around and buttoned in the front if need be. On the inside he had sewn over twenty pockets, now containing only the bit remains of the demonic leather.

"Blasted human cattle scum!" roared a familiar voice from behind. Kael leapt in the air, striking out at the air behind him with the night colored blade. There was only laughter as he stood ready to strike whatever foe dared attack. Both his hands gripped the mystic weapon, white-knuckled, as he saw his enemy.

"Down here, feeble minded bit of cattle!" the voice growled.

Kael looked down at the rotting, tusk-covered, striped skull of Hosampsich and his blood ran cold. His bowels, however, held. It lay there, white from lack of blood, its filed, pointy teeth gleaming in a jagged smile.

"You thought it so easy to dispatch the mighty Hosampsich? I am the lord of this puny reality you know, human prickle! Without my skin or my sword, you will still fill my gut."

"Nay," Kael returned, to his own surprise. "Your slaying of my people ends this day."

Before the head could object, the Midnight Blade made sticky goo of it in two slashes. Kael knew Hosampsich would now no longer be able to make or keep any promises ever again. Just to be sure, Kael cut the skinned, dismantled body of the demon into a thousand pieces.

Kael stood, chest heaving slightly, for a moment. He then picked up the golden scabbard, sheathed the unearthly sword and secured the golden chain to his waist. The sword hung heavily at an angle on Kael's left thigh, and again he didn't notice the weapon's weight or its supernatural thirst. Before he could consider the aspects or possibilities of his newfound fortitude, his attention was distracted by a sudden swirling wind.

Small dust devils—tiny, impotent tornadoes—spiraled around Kael, flitting the heavy, tiger-striped cloak and buffeting him with dry, stinging particles of dirt. Raising a hand against the flying soil, Kael imagined he saw a horseman riding down from the clear, blue sky. He rubbed his eyes momentarily and as suddenly as they had started, the winds ceased.

There before Kael was the "illusion" he thought he had imagined. His left hand absently gripped his newfound weapon, submerged warrior instincts Kael knew nothing about unconsciously manifesting themselves.

Hovering before Kael, some fifteen feet off the ground, was a man astride a magnificent black steed. The horse was the most powerful looking animal Kael had ever seen. Tight, lean, rippling muscles made the mount look more like a panther than a horse. Tiny ear-sized wings flapped at both sides of each shining, obsidian hoof. The horse's hoary eyes had no visible pupil or iris. The pure white shone unearthly against the hellish black of the lithe, powerful animal's hide.

The saddle beneath the rider was carved entirely of bone, a polished white like the steed's eyes. The breast and cinch straps were black leather completely covered and inlaid with runes, artifacts, and totems. Kael saw than even more runes were carved into the polished saddle's surface. If the mid-day sun hadn't prohibited it, Kael would have also seen thousands of the same runes tattooed over every inch of the horse's entire body. The tattoos weren't of ink, but the millennia-aged, black blood of a hell-bound angel.

The look of the rider made Kael grip his weapon even tighter, his forearms beginning to ache. The rider was dressed completely in black. The garments were loose fitting for excellent movement, wrapped tightly at his wrists and shins with red leather bracers the hue of blood. He wore black leather gloves and sandals, as well as dark stockings. Around his head, face, and neck was a black cloth, wound into an enveloping turban and mask. A black cape floated with the gentle breeze, smooth as silk, occasionally covering his steed's hindquarters, occasionally covering all but the man's own head and masked face. All that could be seen of the man beneath the clothes was the bridge of his nose and his eyes. His eyes were the ice-blue color that was nearly white; faint dark pupils surrounded by bluish, cloud white. As the rider's cape blew open, Kael saw an enormous two-handed, ivory-handled scimitar sheathed just below the pommel on the rune-encrusted saddle. The weapon was easily the size of Kael's. The only other color on the unnatural rider was a thick, tightly wrapped red silken sash around his lithe waist.

Kael felt the weakness in his knees, but held himself. Surely this man wasn't the caliber of Hosampsich's demonic might.

"That's not exactly true," the rider responded to Kael's thoughts. The rider's voice had the same silken quality as his cape: smooth, deep, and disturbingly dark and familiar.

"Who are you?" Kael spoke, trying his hardest not to sound meek and insignificant. Part of him wished to draw his weapon, allow the madness of his fear to envelop him, and attack the dark rider, embracing a sure oblivion. Something held him in check, though. Something kept his rationale awake and sane.

"Use wisdom and care, human," the rider voiced smoothly. "You are not near ready to oppose one such as I."

Something in Kael knew the rider spoke truth. He loosened his grip slightly from his sword handle (now wrapped in demon skin rather than human), but did not release it.

"Who are you?" Kael asked again.

"The tusks of Hosampsich," the rider motioned to the sticky mass of goo left of the demon's skull. "I've come for a tusk."

Kael looked down at the remains, surprised by the rider's request. After a moment of reflection, he reached down, picked up one of the finger-sized horns and tossed it up to the hovering figure. The rider snatched the hurled object out of the air with a speed that startled Kael. He inspected it momentarily, then slipped it under the red leather bracer around his right wrist.

"Though I know you do not realize it, human, you have done me a grand service," The rider clicked his tongue against his teeth, his steed turning smoothly in mid-air. "The act will be repaid in due time, human. I sense our meeting in the future."

Kael's mind reeled with questions for the rider. His tongue finally loosened as the horse began to rise into the sky.

"Who are you?" He finally managed to scream.

"The tusks, human," the rider returned as his mount pawed the air currents high into the blue void above. "Save the tusks and reap the power."

Kael stood in awe of the confrontation with the dark rider, his hand finally slipping from the midnight sword's handle. He knew that for the second time in two days he had faced certain death and lived.

*

Kael fingered the hundred-odd demonic cranium tusks that circled his neck, held together with a thin strand of tiger-striped leather. He had arranged the L-shaped points of the skull-teeth away from his body. Neither Hosampsich nor his body parts would ever harm Kael again.

Pulling the hood of his cloak up, he looked to the sun, just past its zenith. The dark rider had headed back to the south. Desolation and the unknown stretched to the west and north. He looked to the east. It was home. The thought of being able to see his home and clan again had never crossed his mind. He had been born in green, hilly grasslands that he had seen in the daylight scant times during his twenty-three summers of life. Hordes of marauding bands of devils, monsters, and foul beings had driven Kael's people below the surface over a century ago. Where once his people lived in peace and harmony with wildlife and nature they now dwelled some hundred paces and more below that in subterranean tunnels and caves. There among the dead of many past centuries, they hid from the harsh reality above.

Kael's people knew nothing of any other living clans or peoples, whether any others had also sought escape from extinction into the very earth they once strode. Kael's people no longer knew anything concrete of their genealogy or history. Early in their new lives underground, the warriors of their tribe sought to drive back the demon hordes. None ever returned. Very few young males remained to copulate with the dwindling number of women, afterward. The result was a clan of barely two hundred after half as many years.

Kael's people now weren't the warriors they had once been. They were now more moles than men. With their only thought of survival, they became scavengers and robbers, stealing away into the danger of the surface every night to search for any source of food. Their existence was a silent, dirty one. They had made a life—a village, even—for themselves underground. The knowledge of the caverns they now dwelt in had been a secret of the clan for hundreds of years. Never had any thought that secret would be the last hope for their people's survival. The labyrinth they expanded and created underground kept the people both in shape and sane. Every excursion above ground was a risk, albeit a necessary one, that the demon hordes would find them out and destroy what was left of their civilization. Many men died hunting for their people, risking eternity in the stomach of a demon. Every year their numbers were fewer. With inbreeding a sure way to extinction or worse, the two hundred that remained would slowly drift away like the smoke of a campfire.

Kael looked down at his left thigh at the heavy weight half-hidden by his cloak. He traced the haunting, night-colored pommel and the leather-bound, foot-long handle with his callused hand. The realization of what he should do suddenly struck him, as his fingers slipped through the two jagged guards, his hand grasping the enormous weapon tightly.

His entire life, Kael and his people had bowed to and hid from Hosampsich and his evil band. The demon had hunted and eaten hundreds of Kael's clan. Now Hosampsich was dead and gone. All that remained of him was a cloak, a belt, and the excrement of a flock of vultures, all at the hands of a puny bit of human cattle.

Without a second thought, Kael buttoned the top two buttons of his cloak, gripped the handle of the midnight blade to keep it from bouncing a sore on his leg, and began to trot to the east, to home, and to the salvation of his people.

*

Kael did not even attempt to match his thirty-hour marathon of over two days ago. He arrived at the Border River that separated the desolate plains and the grassy, rugged hills of his homeland in just under forty-five hours. Home was just fifty miles away from here. The river was wide but barely a foot deep in any place. Kael drew his heavy, murderous sword and crossed the muddy waters slowly, ready to kill whatever dare cross his path.

*

Kael crossed the Border River and traveled only a few miles before finding a shrub-covered cave to sleep out until night fell. He knew that the demon hordes that covered these steep hills and harsh sweeping coulees gathered at night to feed on their daily prey. He knew well the prey of this region's overlords: his people were the mainstay diet of the Spawn of Hell.

Kael awakened just as the darkness of night enveloped the gentle, green hills and creek bottoms completely. He knew that most of the demons were huddled around their nightly campfires, feasting on the flesh of humans and drinking the alcohol of fermented man's blood. Kael rubbed his thick legs as he emerged from his brushy hideout. His muscles were nearly fully recovered from his desperate escape from these very hills. The easy-paced two-day journey back had done much to heal him.

Adjusting the heavy weight at his thigh, Kael buttoned the top four buttons of his thick cloak. There wasn't a cloud in the starry sky and the moon was barely peeking over the eastern horizon. Its incredible size this night held Kael's attention for a moment. His people respected the power of the moon, believing it was a crystal-orbed chariot housing the god of death—Gabryl. The god of death was not theirs to worship, but his power was undeniable.

Kael shrugged and made his way east towards the entrance of the underground tunnels of his people. He cared not for the gods, no more than they for he. All that mattered now was his people's survival, and Kael was sure he held the power to assure that.

The moon's slow trail across the sky to the west was a contrast to Kael's easterly journey. He made the fifty-mile journey in less than six hours, a good three hours before the sun would begin to rise. The short trek had been uneventful until now.

As Kael crested the hill above the entrance to his home, he was held in check at the sight nearly a half-mile below: a party of eight demons sat laughing and cajoling around a high burning bonfire. Male and female demons rolled about in drunken sex play, as well other same-sex couplings. The dripping, gutted carcasses of some thirty humans lay strewn about like a dog's scraps. The body's genders were impossible to recognize.

Kael's sharp, hawk-like eyes saw the bodies easily from his hidden vantage above the demon's sinful play. He didn't recognize any of them, but that disturbed him. This land was inhabited by only demons. Any other humans would have to have hidden as Kael's clan had, and he knew of no other such people.

Only six days ago Kael would have seen this scene and ran as hard as he could for his life. The running and digging that had characterized his entire life and people, however, had ironically blessed him with the stature and skills he needed to stop running. He couldn't stop the tears that formed at his eyes and ran lonely down his chiseled, jaw-clenched face, but he showed no other trace of emotion save his white-knuckled left hand, which dug into the midnight blade's handle.

Kael didn't realize that he had changed. The idea of running for his life had somehow been replaced with an all-encompassing, noble sense of self-worth and…was that…honor? His father had spoke of honor and the deeds of mighty warriors from their people's past. Men that had met with steel the first demons to appear. Able men of strength, purpose, and above all, honor—men that had died and slept their final sleep as the excrement of the Spawn of Hell. Kael knew that he would never had been born if his people had not sought sanctuary in the earth, but he now knew he could no longer live that way. He had felt the light of a full day's sun on his face and was sure he could never give that up ever again.

Kael stood straight, drawing the vicious weapon at his thigh silently and slowly. Stepping forward, he began down the hill to the orgy below. He no longer needed to steel himself to action. No more did cowardly doubts invade his mind with reasons to grovel rather than stand. He didn't know if it was madness or foolhardiness that urged him on, but on he walked. These demons were lackeys of Hosampsich and Hosampsich now clothed Kael.

Let go.

Kael's eyes thinned and his chin lowered. He was barely three hundred paces from them now. The hill flattened out as it approached the creek bottom.

Let go and free yourself. Fear not.

Kael's heart began to pound in his chest and temples; adrenaline began to course through his body. At the anticipation of his first sword strike, his tongue thickened and his veins bulged. His kidneys were already sore from the impending action.

Free the blade and loosen your fear.

Now he was only fifty paces away.

"Look," one female demon yelled from her hands and knees. Her skin was orange with dark, red leopard spots. Human flesh still hung from the facial hair around her mouth. The demon on his knees behind her smacked her hard on the side of the head and buried himself even deeper into her.

"Who goes there?" one who seemed to be a leader barked. He stood up from two prostrate females, gently pushing their hands and mouths from his genitals. He stood straight and defiant to the approaching figure, his bat-like wings still folded behind him. "Who goes there? Hosampsich? Master, is that you?"

"No," Kael rattled from deep within his throat, the fury of the gods within him. He was seething like a chained wolf. With a toss of his arm he flipped the left side of his cloak behind him, revealing the mighty weapon he held.

"No!" the demon gasped, unbelieving. He tried to turn to retrieve his own sword, stumbling over himself.

"Yes!" Kael roared, grinning with insanity. The firelight glowed in his face, his cloak spreading behind him as he leapt forward, giving him the appearance of the forms he attacked. He cut the tripping demon in two with one fell swoop, completely separating his upper torso from the rest of his body. Green demon blood exploded over the avenging human.

Stepping straight into the orgy, Kael was a tornado of steel and the demons knew not what hit them. Two of the hellish warriors fell dead, their upper bodies intertwined in lust, their lower bodies stuck forever in the throes of sodomy. Two more fell to the earth in over twelve pieces, their open bellies no longer trying to digest the man-flesh contained within.

Although his attack had been aided with surprise, Kael would not be denied his justice. As the sun peeked timidly over the eastern ridge, Kael slumped to his knees in physical and mental exhaustion. All eight demons were dead. Hopefully gone to the spirit realm forever, Kael thought

*

The dawning amber glow of the sun found Kael feasting on a snared rabbit he had cooked over the dying embers of his enemy's bonfire. He sat straddling a heavy log he had drug up from the nearby creek bottom. Five full demon hides were staked out to dry in the upcoming daylight, as well as three other smaller ones. Kael had recovered about five hundred tusks and horns from the bodies, most half the size of his smallest finger. He had bored holes through them, fastened them together with ligament, and they now crisscrossed his chest and back as two heavy belts.

It had been over two days since he had eaten a bite and it would take more than one rabbit to replenish his energy, but right now it seemed like the greatest meal he had ever eaten. He had set ten snares up and down the creek. By afternoon he would eat like a king.

Kael discarded the bare leg bone, retrieved another from the spit above the embers, and sat back down. He still wore the tiger demon's hide as a kilt and cloak, the golden scabbard chained around his waist and slung behind him. The midnight sword lay across Kael's lap, slanted jewel eyes seeming to smolder now where earlier they had blazed. Kael tried to dismiss their eerie glow but found it impossible. It made his soul shiver when he saw the blade absorb, literally swallow, the thick gooey blood of the beaten demons. He would barely touch the pooled life-blood with the tip of the jagged-edged blade and the plasma seemed to pour up and into the very steel of the weapon.

Kael couldn't understand what he had seen. His mind couldn't believe what his eyes had witnessed. The basest part of him feared that the sword still housed something of Hosampsich's spirit, but that same part of him couldn't relinquish such power. Yet, if the weapon could absorb the fluid of demons, what would it do to the hand of a human? He hadn't felt any ill effects so far, but it had been only a few days. His thoughts were of Hosampsich's spirit housed within the blade, biding its time, waiting for Kael to falter.

To hell with it, Kael thought. He knew the weapon was magical. Surely, this was how it retained its enchantment. Sorcery was no different than anything else in nature, he reasoned. Fires died just as men did. Trees toppled just as armies. The earth governed all things equally in the end; even the earth eroded in the wind and washed away in the rivers.

Kael finished his meal and gripped the midnight blade. Regardless of its effects on him, he would never be able to discard the weapon. The very chance of it falling into the hands of one like Hosampsich made that impossible for Kael. He accepted the sword's thirst and vowed to let it drink deep from the well. A man that had once cowered beneath the earth in fear of a fate worse than death had killed nine of the beings responsible for that possible fate. He wasn't sure whether he would hunt the creatures, but he did know he would never again bow to or hide from them again.

Sliding his sword easily into its scabbard, Kael walked down to the creek bottom, took a drink, and turned to what used to be one of the concealed entrances to the house of his people. Where once thick brush and berry vines had covered a small, rocky opening, now a gaping blast hole yawned. The demons had somehow found this tiny cave and used some sort of sorcery to gain entrance for their hulking forms.

Kael paused for a moment, his thoughts dwelling on the half-eaten corpses he had buried not an hour ago. He hadn't recognized one of the thirty bodies, although he knew each to surely be a clansman to him. He didn't know if even one of his people still lived. Would the tunnels and rocky caverns below reveal the same scene of destruction? If so, perhaps some escaped as he had. Kael had seen no other sign of any Dogs of Hell, the thought making him scan the hillside for a moment.

No. If any lived, they had survived by hiding below. Of course, there could be demons—or worse—down there, as well. Kael tossed back his heavy cloak hood and quietly unsheathed his weapon. Let it be worse, he thought. He was ready.

With a newfound courage that had now seemed to become first nature to him, Kael stepped forward into the enveloping darkness of the cave.

He hadn't gone a hundred paces and he wished he had brought a torch to light the way. The torches that normally lined the walls were all burnt out or gone.

Let the blade burn for you.

The voice that was his own, yet always unexpected, crossed his brain again. Before he could question it, the blade began to glow an unearthly blue. The haunting light bathed Kael, as well as a good fifty steps ahead and behind him. Kael breathed out slowly, both hands clenching the sword painfully, a moment of his forgotten fear streaming down his spine. He hadn't expected that at all.

Kael stepped slowly but surely down the familiar tunnel. He had walked this stretch many times every day of his life since he was old enough to do so. Many were the nights he would sneak up to see the countryside, even from the creek bottom, stealing time with the girls in the clan that were his age. Even a few times he had stolen away with the older widows that were his father's age. Kael knew such action was necessary to keep the clan alive, but soon he worried some newborn would share his hair or eye color. Oddly, something within his soul cried against using his own body as that of a stud. Perhaps now, sadly, there was no longer any need to worry.

Making his way down the long descending entrance, Kael stepped slowly and warily. The dirt tunnel dropped sharply over one hundred and fifty paces into the earth, then opened into a vast meeting cave of such. The open area was domed and supported by aging timbers. This cave was the first constructed by Kael's ancestors that century long ago. From here tunnels ran to separate family caves, over fifty, and to a wide expanse directly below the entrance cave. It was hewn and chiseled from a mountain-sized underground rock. The clan used this enormous cavern for formal meetings and gatherings.

Kael spent over four hours searching through the labyrinth of tunnels, through the dirt, rock, and stones he knew well. He didn't find one trace of his people. What little his people had in the way of material possessions—hides, tools, basic writing materials—all of it was gone. Eventually, after giving up his search, Kael made his way to the meeting hall. Entering sword first, Kael was stopped dead at what he saw.

The entire hall that was originally the tan color of sandstone was scorched completely black. The floor was covered with burnt and charred refuse, garbage still smoldering from some previous attack. The smell of carrion and sulfur was trapped in this area, stagnant and fetid. Kael moved into the room then saw what truly horrified him: over seventy bodies crucified to the walls and ceiling. Among the garbage on the floor were another hundred mangled corpse-pieces. Every body was gutted and dismembered, rotted body parts splayed haphazardly. Those crucified were staked to the rock walls by lances crooked up through their ribcages. Some of the leg-less forms still grasped the lances in an eternal effort to pull it out. Those in the smoldering garbage created a nauseating odor of burning flesh and hair.

Kael's throat constricted and froze at the sight—the horror—before him, chilling his soul to the core. His blood iced and his grip tightened around his newfound weapon. He felt a slight breeze into the rock cave as the smoldering embers pulled oxygen into the cave with no ventilation. The top half of the enormous hall was purely smoke. Surely it was hiding the rest of Kael's clan. The ghostly blue light shed by his blade gave the scene an even more evil look, bathing the hell-born scene in a winter's contemptuous and uncaring view.

It was nearly a minute before Kael could find his breath. His legs weakened and he stepped back against the Hall's entrance. His sword dipped to the hard floor as the strength drained from his body. Stars and flashes burst before his eyes as he felt his knees buckle and bowels grow cold. Even after all he had been through, after all that had seemed to steel his ire and form a semblance of courage within his heart, all of that was waived aside before this holocaust horror.

Suddenly, the light emanating from his sword stopped, flooding Kael in darkness. The hazy glow of torchlight appeared from the tunnel behind him. Clenching his teeth achingly, he fumbled to wrap his left hand onto his sword's handle above his right. He struggled closer to an upright position, the cave entrance wall all that kept him from the floor. As the torchlight got closer and brighter, Kael's chin dropped to his chest. He clenched and unclenched his sweaty grip, trying to work what little strength he had back into his weightless limbs. Whoever came, whether man or demon, would taste cold steel before standing over Kael's dead body.

"Who…who goes there?" a slight tremulous voice whispered into the darkness where Kael hid. The soft wavering pitch perked his head and hearing both.

"Who goes there?" he rasped harshly, still struggling to both stand and hold his weapon. The torchlight halted for a moment then advanced around the corner. Kael looked up and saw a surprisingly welcome sight.

"Alique!" he breathed, choking on the name, the relief of the vision before him as debilitating as his fear and horror a moment before.

There before him stood a raving beauty. Alique stood nearly one half foot over five and was built like the athlete she was. She had shapely legs, curving hips, and a waist Kael could nearly ring with his hands. Her firm, ample breasts were barely contained by her tanned leather jerkin. A similar leather loincloth covered her nether regions, as well as what little she had for a posterior. Her beauty was unquestionable, smooth skin, high cheekbones, and slightly hawkish nose. Her eyes were a brown rarely seen in nature, and her wavy, dark amber hair, streaked dusty by the sun, spilled down the middle of her back like a water fall.

"Kael," she sighed in relief, her eyes widening at the sight of her former lover decked in the kilt and cloak of demon's skin, Hosampsich's dreaded mystical blade in his hands.

"Alique," Kael muttered, stumbling forward to his knees before his former love. The midnight blade fell from his hands as he filled them with her firm hips, pressing her to his face. Alique dropped the torch and filled her hands with his long, dusty blonde locks. She forced his head down and into her downy nethers, pushing aside its tan cover. Lust exploded between Kael's ears and his soft full lips met hers.

The enormous clash of emotions within finally broke him. As a gasp of pleasure escaped Alique's mouth, a groan slipped through Kael's. A pulse of conscious energy, then a blackening...then...nothing.

*

It was a dream and Kael knew it. At the same time, he was startled by its frightening reality. He found himself in a star-filled void, an endless, clear night sky, levitating in the nothingness. All around him were demons, winged warriors, WindBearers (he thought), wizards, barbarians, and creatures Kael had never even imagined. All were doing battle with one another. It was a war of a million beings with a million differing intentions for an unachievable supremacy.

Kael ducked in horror at the power surging around him; bolts of energy and massive sword swipes barely missed their mark. He was helpless to save himself and his fear was freezing him. He was immobile, unable to breathe from the cowardice that gripped his heart like a vise. It was beating near the point of explosion, his fingers and toes curled painfully. Blasts and bursts singed his body, but none ever cleanly connected to kill him

Kael's eyes glazed over as he accepted his certain death with a sigh. His life would end now as it ran its entire course: on his knees before the might of others, a helpless flea on the back of a cosmic buffalo.

Then, as the war reached its pitch, a battle sword appeared before Kael. The blade was over five feet long, the opponent's edge jugged so that when exiting a wound more flesh would be on the steel than the body. The handle was over a foot long, two thick, jagged prongs acting as hand guards running from the hilt to the handle's base. The handle was wrapped in tiger-striped demon flesh and the blade was the color of the surrounding space. The size of the weapon was god-like, creating a presence greater than any man could.

Grab the blade and rule this mass, Kael.

Kael knew it was the weapon speaking. He also knew that the only courage, the only fortitude he had ever experienced, came from the sword. It was this sword that had finally made him a man. Without the feel of the midnight blade in his hands, he was nothing more than food for demons

"Yes," Kael whispered, reaching forward, teeth clenched in determination—determination to be more than fate had demanded. "Yes!"

Yes, Kael. The blade can make you more than fate. It can make you a god.

Kael didn't care about that, barely even heard it. All he knew was that he was nothing. That single, heaven-sent weapon made him something.

Kael gripped the handle with both hands and felt the anguish and fear drain from his bowels, seemingly through the toes on his feet. He spun in midair and began to deal death to the creatures of this meaningless crowd of a demon abyss.

*

Kael jerked awake in a sweat, his hand filled with the handle of the Midnight Blade. It took him a moment to realize exactly were he was. No endless void filled with battling figures surrounded him. He sat up, taking account of his surroundings as he slowly woke. His fist was still unconsciously gripped around his powerful weapon.

Alique lay still asleep beside him, her lithe form still curving around his hip. The tiger-striped cloak, as well as two thick animal skins, were their cover from the summer night's chill. Sunup was over an hour away but Kael could easily make out the environment around him. The two had set their camp just below their clan's hidden entrance, near the little finger of a creek that wound through the Kelt-Ra clan's land. There was danger being in the open sky, but the desecration below was just to great to be near. Kael's eyes were wide with wonder at the golden-red glow over the eastern horizon that was slowly lending color to the rolling hills and grass-covered ridges. It was only his fifth sight of the coming of day and it convinced him even more that he would never again return to the earth's moldy claws. Towering cottonwood and thin ash trees were still, akin to their human neighbor in their profound reverence for the approaching orb of life.

Kael's people were indifferent to the daytime. They hid from the sun and its revealing power. It was, for the most part, daytime that the demons seemed to hunt. It was then that they searched for any trace to the whereabouts of this land's original tenants. The Kelt-Ra clan had been safe—or lucky—for over a century. Now, though, it was all over.

Kael turned, placing his free hand on Alique's neck and ear, brushing her blonde-streaked brown hair from her peaceful sleeping face. They were the last two, at least for now. He had not yet asked his lover how she had survived, or whether she knew of any one else that had.

Suddenly, a twinge at the base of Kael's brain caused his left hand to clench tightly around the Midnight Blade's handle and another vagrant thought permeated his mind.

Quickly! Behind you!

Kael spun away from Alique's sleeping form, gripped his weapon with both hands, and crouched ready to strike.

"Not bad, meal sack," a voice laughed.

"Who is it?" Kael hissed, his eyes narrowing to see the hulking form. The form stepped up, some twenty feet from Alique's still sleeping form. "That's far enough."

"Quite right," the mystery creature chuckled again. Kael stood up slowly, his knees still slightly bent, stepping between Alique and the intruder. He saw now, his eyes fully adjusted to the dawning darkness, the figure before him.

It was obviously a demon. He was over seven feet tall, but wiry and muscled. His skin was a yellowish color, nearly orange in this amber light, and enormous red batwings were folded behind his back. He was covered with hundreds of banana-sized tusks and horns. They sprung from his chest, arms, legs, and torso. Some were drilled or pierced, gold and jewels hanging ornamentally. Platinum chains wrapped around many. The treasures on this creature could easily buy a small kingdom.

The massive creature wore a red, silken kilt and thick, black leather sandals. They were expertly tooled with runes that reminded Kael of the turbaned horseman he saw in the wastelands. The same runes were threaded into the red silk with glistening silver thread.

The surprising thing to Kael about the figure was his face. It was nearly perfect. Every demon Kael had ever seen or even heard about had been at the very least ugly if not completely putrid. This demon had long black hair to his shoulders parted down the middle. Some twenty golden rings lined each ear. A black, rune-tooled headband crossed his smooth, yellow forehead.

"What form of demon are you?" Kael hissed at the imposing figure. He felt little fear now as he had in his dreams. The Midnight Blade, the great equalizer, had cured that.

"Actually," the figure purred, "I am not completely a demon." His hand rested easily on the thick red steel broadsword at his left hip. A black leather belt tooled like his sandals and headband held a like-made scabbard. "I am the product of a prince devil of the highest order and one of his demon harlots from Erebus. My name is Imamiah."

"Move on, devil," Kael growled. "You want nothing to do with me." Talk helped quell his fear of the horror before him.

"I see," Imamiah nodded, his right hand moving to his chin. "That is a fine weapon you wield. I knew a demon who held one of the same make." Imamiah gestured at the bands of tusks and leather garments that lay near Alique's still sleeping form. "I would imagine that is him. At least what is left of him."

"Devil," Kael's mind was near delirious in madness at this conversation. To speak to such a creature was straining his sanity. "Very soon a necklace is all that well be left of you."

"Quite," Imamiah nodded in response. "You've obviously much battle savvy to have usurped such a powerful artifact."

"Enough," Kael roared, his hatred of the devil destroying his reason. He rushed forward to destroy the figure before him, beserker bloodlust fogging his vision. Alique jumped awake, startled to see her naked lover rushing to attack some behemoth demon.

"Kael!" she screamed, jumping to her hands and knees, unsure what was happening.

Kael swooped down to chop through Imamiah … and struck only the soft, grassy earth. Dirt and vegetation exploded up into Kael's face from the force of the blow, momentarily blinding him. A lazy, well-placed kick by the devil struck Kael full in the ribs, sending him spiraling down the short slope and into the shallow creek water.

"Well, damnation, human," the elegant demon pouted, carefully picking his way down the bank. "Do release the weapon to me. It will make you and your mate's death easier."

"You can take easy, demon," Kael rose out of the water, teeth clenched, sword raised, "and shove it right up your ass."

"Hardly prophetic, meat sack," Imamiah shook his head. He held his hand out as if a parent to a disobedient child. "The sword, little one, please."

Kael's eyes flared wide, the whites making his iris and pupils like pinpoints. A guttural roar exploded from his throat as he launched himself at the devil. Imamiah stood yawning at the human's impending attack. Kael threw himself in rage at the monster's uncaring form.

"Please, little one," Imamiah sighed, sidestepping Kael's incredible blow. Another slow and powerful kick to Kael's ribs sent him flying again. He was sure something cracked as he landed roughly against a fallen cottonwood stump. Still, though, he held the midnight blade.

"You've an excellent grip, my little worm," the massive devil stated, one eyebrow raised, as he lazily stepped through the logs and twigs to Kael's bruised form. Kael struggled to his feet wincing, clutching his ribs with one arm. The mystic weapon hung from his weakening grip.

"Not bad for a human," Imamiah stopped before Kael's crouching form. "Truly your species wasn't meant to…"

Before he could finish, a thick log struck the devil in the back of the head, knocking him forward. Kael, seeing his opponent off balance, gripped his blade firmly and brought it murderously up.

The devil was too fast, though. The midnight blade caught him barely, nicking his chin. Imamiah tossed himself sideways, rolling to a crouch, his red broadsword drawn and ready. Alique stood naked before the dawning sun, at the edge of the bank, another dead branch in her hands.

"So, the female has teeth as well. Very good. Two meals are better than one."

"Run, Alique!" Kael screamed, stepping forward to cut off Imamiah. She turned, dropped the branch, and did exactly that, running over the creek bank to what she believed was safety.

"I'll let her go," the yellow-hued monster hissed, raising his massive broadsword to Kael's approaching form. "For now."

"You will never touch her, Hell-spawn!" Kael suddenly felt the pain in his torso alleviate. The sword's two eye-like jewels gleamed from the little black ichor it had drawn from Imamiah's chin. Kael felt his courage rise again, his purpose sure. He had never actually been in a sword fight before. The other two encounters had been little more than butchery. Not only that, but the devil before him seemed to know what he was doing.

"There will be very little left of you to eat, meat sack, after I have made jerky of you."

Kael said nothing. He knew better now than to rush headlong to battle. Three nicely placed kicks had taught him that. The devil was his physical superior, as well as the better swordsman. Kael knew that his survival lay in the defense. Hold off the monster's attack and wait for his one chance to strike. The sword would protect him, and, in the end, the sword would end this confrontation.

Imamiah approached slowly. Apparently the human now had control of his emotions. With Hosampsich's stolen, ancient blade, the human would be formidable. That is, if the puny meat-sack was focused. All the massive devil need do is drive the human into rage and easily slay him. Then the mystical blade and all its untapped power would be his.

"Give up, human," Imamiah circled Kael slowly, pointing the red blade ominously at him. "You look to do the impossible. Slay a devil! Don't be a fool."

"I've killed them before. I'll do it again."

"For your mate's sake, I'll make this deal: give over Hosampsich's blade and I will let her live. You will face oblivion without her death on your hands."

"Come, demon," Kael spat, foolhardiness flooding his veins from the feel of his mighty weapon. "Face me and die."

Imamiah's grin disappeared at the insolence of this lesser being's bravado. Surely, it was a result of the sword's ego on the human's primitive brain. The poor little creature was no more than a pawn to a power he would never be able to understand.

Imamiah made a quick little feint. Kael overreacted and nearly fell over his own feet. The devil smiled slightly, revealing sharp canines as white as new-fallen snow. In one sword stroke, Imamiah would have the power he needed to dominate the endless struggles waging throughout this world. Just one sword stroke, he thought, slowly approaching the human. Then his rivals in the north would bow, or fall, as they should have centuries ago.

You can do this.

Yes, Kael thought, nodding to his brain. I can do this. With this weapon, I can do anything.

Yes, you can. When I say, spin back to the left, stepping to your right and arc the deathblow. Stand ready.

Kael stood up straight, raising the massive weapon up to point toward the heavens. He felt no fear now and it didn't occur to him that he should.

"You are a fool," Imamiah whispered, more to himself, scoffing at the human's unusual, dormant stance. "At least you are a dead one."

The giant devil thrust forward, down on one knee as he struck to disembowel the human.

Now!

Without hesitation or thought, Kael turned left, pushing himself to his right. The Midnight Blade flattened, arcing through the air with an ear-splitting whistle. The sword sped to catch up to Kael's spinning form, much like a ball at the end of a swinging chain.

Imamiah's strike missed Kael's twisting torso by a fraction of an inch and the powerful creature's eyes went wide at the realization he had been bested. Still, his superior reflexes and skill saved his life as he ducked his head and dropped to the ground. His sword flew from his hand in his haste, the murky creek swallowing it completely.

The midnight blade grazed the devil's retracted wings, tearing the red leathery skin at his back and clipped the back of his head, shearing the hair and skin from a palm-sized section of his cranium. Without solidly connecting, the momentum of the strike spun Kael completely around. He thrust down his weapon into the dirt to barely keep his feet.

Before Kael could do anything else, Imamiah struck out with his damaged, bleeding wing. The leathery bat-like appendage unfolded with much force, catching Kael under his calves and knocking him to his back. Kael reacted well while falling back, swinging his blade to chop the devil's wing from his back. Again, Imamiah was quicker. He rolled, pulling his gargantuan limb safely to his back. The mystic blade tasted again only earth.

Kael was up in an instant, his sword held before him defensively. He was too late. Imamiah was airborne, streaking across the amber sky just as the sun peaked the eastern horizon. Kael lost him in the dawning sun, the devil disappearing over the far eastern ridge.

Kael didn't consider the confrontation another moment, scrambling up over the creek bank to where Alique was crouching, covered by his tiger-striped demon cloak.

"He's...he's gone," she stammered, barely able to catch her breath. Her heart was nearly pounding out of her chest. "I...I can't believe it! You beat him!"

"Not exactly," Kael breathed heavily, kneeling to embrace her, letting the midnight blade loose from his grasp for the first time since waking. Their lips met hungrily, the excitement wringing tears from her eyes. Their life had always been one of extremes and the couple shifted from fear and anxiety to lust and passion in an instant.

Kael pushed down Hosampsich's hide from Alique's shoulders and laid her on her back. He took her thighs in his arms and buried himself in her softness. She gripped his blonde locks tightly and let her fears and torments loose with screams of heated passion. She pulled with her hands and bucked with her hips, throwing Kael up and into her. She welcomed his familiar feel and locked her ankles behind his back. Everything dissolved for the couple save their heat and thirst for one another.

*

It was mid-day when the couple finally broke camp and began their journey. They decided to head east, following the shallow creek through their homeland. They knew of nothing else to do. Neither had ever left the rolling hills of the Kelt-Ra clan's land before, and now there seemed to be nothing here to hold them. They did know of the desolation of the west, but nothing of what lay beyond it. They had no wish to find out. Kael's tale of the turbaned horseman had chilled Alique, effectively dispelling any curiosity she had of what lay beyond the desert.

The summer day was unseasonably cool. Kael wore his demon cloak and tusk belts, the mystic blade sheathed at his left hip. Alique wore her leather top and loincloth, as well as one of the thin furs they had scavenged from their tunnels. She wore it as a cloak, clasped with a leather cord under her chin.

"I prayed that you had survived," Alique whispered as they walked, eyes more than occasionally to the sky. The creek bed and numerous cottonwood trees would hopefully cover them from any possible attacker from above. "What caused you to run?"

"The hunting party had been unsuccessful, as surely they reported upon their return." Alique nodded to Kael's words. "I stayed back to lay traps for the next day. Jahn scolded me for it. He was frightened from two near-encounters with demons that night, and was anxious to return to the tunnels. I chided him for his cowardliness, and told him to run home to his mother. He stood up to me as though he intended to fight, but reconsidered. I had bested Jahn in the past, and he thought better of another thrashing."

"Jahn died in tears," Alique interrupted, not looking to see Kael's surprise. "He begged for his life right up to the point that a giant Hell-dog bit his head off whole."

The thought silenced Kael for a moment. Jahn had been a rival of his, but basically a good man. Kael, too, knew what happened to a man when confronted by a creature of such horrific power. He wondered for a moment if he, too, would have begged for mercy had he been caught in the tunnels with the rest.

Kael gripped his blade's handle, letting its solid reality breathe courage over his natural cowardice of the demons. The eye-like jewels gleamed lightly in reassurance.

"Anyway," Kael resumed, pushing the painful memories of his clan away, "I had set some traps and was headed back to the tunnel entrance. I was distracted in my own mind by Jahn's defiance to me and was dwelling on what I would do to him when next we met. The next thing I knew, I had stumbled around a rocky outcropping, straight into a party of demons. They were gathered in a hunting group, Hell-Dogs and all. Without a second thought, I turned and ran. All I knew to do was escape."

"And you did," Alique spoke softly, gripping Kael's left hand in her right. "You did what any human must do. No man can stand face to face with a demon and survive."

"With this I can," Kael said grimly, gripping the Midnight Blade tightly with his right hand. He pulled it a few inches out of its scabbard, and shoved it back again. "I slew the owner of this sword somehow. I still don't know how I did it. Something inside of me was just so tired of being afraid."

Alique nodded, a smile creeping onto her face. She had always believed if any of the Kelt-Ra could retaliate against the demons, it would be Kael. In his veins ran the blood of the Ancient Ones—the Warriors.

"We will make it, my love," Alique smiled. "Surely there are other clans beyond our lands. With them, perhaps, we can again find community and peace. Perhaps they know of lands free of the scourge of demons and monsters. Together we will find such a place—or make it ourselves."

Kael stopped walking, turned and embraced Alique fully. He flooded her face and lips with kisses, embracing her again. Such hope would be his anchor. This love would dispel the fear his heart desperately held on to. With this love and this sword, perhaps he could carve out a new clan, one that would live under the sun and stars, not under the earth.

Alique pulled away, her face beautiful as ever, covered with a loving smile. Kael smiled back, kissing her again before they began to walk again. The two made good time that day, stopping when the sun dropped below the western sky. They camped a short distance from the creek, the cover of a copse of elm trees and snarling chokecherry bushes protecting them from the night's eyes.

*

"What are they?"

"Humans, stupid. Food."

"The demons will eat us if they find out."

"We'll let them have the whore."

"Hore? What's that?"

"The woman, jack-ass. We'll give them the woman."

"They'll want him, you know."

"They ain't gittin' him."

"They're gonna be pissed."

"Shut yer stupid, stinkin' trap and go get Snarl and the others."

"Yer the boss."

"That's right. Don't forget that. Idiot."

*

The night erupted as Kael jerked awake. He felt the weight of three heavy people on him and the smell of pig shit. Was that their breath? Alique's screams were loud, then suddenly silent as she groaned, obviously unconscious. Kael managed to grasp the handle of his weapon as the three figures rained fist after fist onto him. Gripping the Midnight Blade, Kael surged onto his feet, throwing the three larger figures from him. The Blade sang as it exited its golden scabbard, still ringing as it cleaved one of the figure's heads in two. Before he could react, two more figures were on him from behind, bearing him down to the rough, thorny ground and brush. Kael pushed up, turned and struck again with his weapon. Again flesh met steel, sticky fluid exploding all over Kael's upper body.

A barrage of rocks now hailed down on Kael; he struck out blindly, only once managing to find flesh. Where was the blue light of his Midnight Blade to light his way? The rocks were large, as big as his head, and they were finding his skull an easy target. Why wasn't the sword talking to him? Helping him? As the rocks struck, white light burst before his eyes, leaving stars both above and below him in the blinding night.

"Alique!" he screamed, striking out at the fading, laughing voices surrounding him. "Alique!"

It was the twelfth boulder that finally did the trick, striking him full in the face, crushing his nose as well as his consciousness.

*

Kael's grogginess was understandable considering he was awakening from his third concussion in under a week. His entire skull throbbed maddeningly, driving his newfound consciousness to a darkening insanity. His face was tight and heavy with his own caked blood. What hair that wasn't blood-pasted to his scalp hung down annoyingly into his eyes. Tingling needles and spikes coursed through his hands, which screamed for more blood flow. Kael looked down to see tight vines and ropes wrapped around his thick wrists. His hands were white from the lack of circulation. There were cuts and bruises over his entire naked form. The bonds that held him were secured to a massive dead cottonwood tree that still stood despite time's ravages.

It was night still. Kael wondered if a day had passed or not. He doubted it but was unsure. It didn't matter, he realized, as he finally found the strength to raise his head. Horror and fear gripped his heart as never before.

In front of Kael was an enormous woodpile, stacked as a bonfire, around that a ring of flaming wood lighting the hillside in a hellish tapestry of the darkest hearts. The creek bed and surrounding grassland glowed orange and red as though made of flame as well. In the sky above, Gabryl rode his orbed chariot with no regard for the lesser beings below. His twisted goblin followers paid respect to him, however, dancing and twisting lustily inside the ring of flames. They danced around the woodpile and the naked, fragile form tied to the stake within it. It was their sacrifice to Gabryl: Alique.

"No!" Kael roared, his eyes bugging in madness, his veins bulged from his efforts to tear his bonds. Like an animal, he began to throw himself forward against his restraints, again and again. His left wrist popped, possibly dislocating, as did his left shoulder. His right shoulder merely separated. The excruciating pain merely intensified his thrusts against the ties that held him.

The twisted forms that danced and bucked in the midnight fire paid no heed to their male captive. Alique stood limply against the stake. Her nude form glistened in sweat, hundreds of simple symbols painted onto her flesh with goat blood. The goblins had readied their sacrifice perfectly. Soon they would be rewarded for their actions.

One green-skinned, hunched figure lurched away from the orgy of death and stood grinning before Kael's raging form. Kael stopped for a moment, kneeling in rest, his lungs heaving. The whites of his insane eyes nearly drowned the rest of his whole face.

"Give up, little human," the goblin spat, yellow drool dribbling from his jagged, filed teeth. His pig-like features and green leathery skin rose the acid in Kael's throat. The creature, smaller than Kael, backhanded his captive, reopening a cut above Kael's left eye. The thin line of blood trickled down his cheek and across his lips. Kael's tongue slipped out and caught the drop of life, its salty taste bringing a sickening smile to his face.

"Weapon is mine," the goblin chided, raising the Midnight Blade before his captive, careful to stay a distance away. Kael jumped again, gnashing his teeth as though a wolf. The ropes held again, but the goblin lurched backward, tripping over himself and falling back into the ring of fire. His fellow ghouls, hypnotized by their orgy of sex, hate, and demon worship, tore the sword away from him and set on him with their nails and teeth. They tore his skin away from his body. They cut him and bit him. After the lone goblin stilled, the others raised him up and threw him into the bonfire wood before Alique. She made no motion to the offering, slowly writhing in her bonds, as though drugged.

Kael began to seethe again, his teeth gritted in madness, his bowels knotted in fear. He threw himself again and again against his bonds.

"Alique!" he roared as he tore at his wrists futilely. "Alique! What's the matter with you?" She was unable to hold her head up completely. Her glistening sweat began to run the painted symbols over her entire nude form.

The goblin that now held the Midnight Blade roared, raising his new weapon high above the throng. The other goblins rushed to him, throwing themselves down before their new chief. With another roar the goblins emerged from the ring of fire and began to kick and fling the flaming kindling onto the bonfire.

"Alique!" Kael roared, renewing his effort to break his bonds. His lover made no response to his screams, lolling her head drunkenly at the igniting wood and goblin corpse at her feet.

Life now meant nothing to Kael as he redoubled his assault on his restraints. The flames licked up and up to consume Alique's beautiful lithe form. Now her drunkenness was gone as the pain of fire burned awareness. Her screams for Kael split the ears of even her goblin captors. They roared their worship of Gabryl and his obvious pleasure at this most unholy of gifts.

Kael roared as well, his fervor reaching an even more feverish pitch. With every thrust forward, the aged, dead cottonwood creaked and groaned. The twenty-some goblins paid no heed, unable to hear the wooden whispering above their own bloodthirsty antics. The flames now had entirely surrounded Alique's pained form. Her skin seared, the stink thick in the air. Her terrified yells for Kael spurred him on. With one final, body-wrenching pull, the base of the tree cracked and split. Kael continued to pull, his muscles, joints, and veins pushed beyond their limits. The tree bowed to Kael's might. It split and leaned, held defiant for an eternal moment, then surrendered with a shudder.

The enormous wooden weight crushed five of the goblins on impact, the force of its fall sending ten more to the ground, as well as Kael. The human was the first up, though, his teeth immediately to the remaining bonds at his wrists. His teeth chewed and gnawed, futilely, as though a trapped rat.

Kael looked up from his task, hemp and vine in his teeth. The monstrous goblin that now held the Midnight Blade came roaring, sword raised for murder. Kael stood ready, murder's clear reflection in his own eyes. He stepped under the goblins clumsy attack, the sword missing its mark and cutting through Kael's tethers. Kael stepped up to the monster's frame, free now from his bonds, and buried his knee into the creature's groin. The goblin fell to the ground, green face now blue, grip releasing the magical sword. Kael, in his madness, didn't notice that the blade stood upright against gravity for the two moments it took him to reach for it.

Kael's white, bloodless hands could feel nothing, but they gripped the mighty weapon nonetheless. He saw nothing but fodder before him as he rushed to save his love. The goblins clawed and fought to get away, but it was pointless. Kael dispatched them as if straw before a hurricane. He reached the burning inferno, his body entirely covered in yellow-red goblin's blood. With one swift sword strike, Kael released Alique from her bonds and scooped her into his arms. The flames sought but could not touch Kael, or Alique, after he gripped her. Even in his rage, Kael knew this was the work of the Midnight Blade. The two emerged from the hellish scenario to fall to the ground amid what was left of the barbaric goblin flesh. Kael was horrified by what he saw.

Alique was unrecognizable, her flesh burnt and charred to red and black. Her hair was gone, and the features of her face seemed to be skewed. She looked as she had been made of clay, then remolded. Her finger and toenails were gone. Her toes were fused and fingers webbed from the intense heat. Her eyebrows seemed to have withered from the fire, falling down over her eyes. Her mouth gaped like a fish's out of water, struggling to pull oxygen into mortally damaged lungs.

Kael hovered over her in silence, his back and head bent to her in frightened homage. The sticky, putrid blood of over twenty goblin creatures covered the would-be warrior and still he couldn't save his lover from her fate. Both hands, regaining their color from the loosening of the ropes, gripped the Midnight Blade. His head rested on them in submission and loss. A single tear forced itself from his closed eyes.

The ruby-jeweled eyes on the mystic weapon flared, sparking to almost meet the electric impulses of Kael's brain. Suddenly, his head jerked up as he remembered some long-forgotten memory never known to him. For a moment Kael kneeled motionless, unsure whether to believe the image in his mind. As determination overtook lack of surety, motion overtook his whole body.

Kael jumped up, running outside what remained of the flaming ring. There, near where he had been tethered, he found his cloak and scabbard. He rushed back to Alique's unmoving yet still breathing form and quickly wrapped her in the tiger-striped leather. He deftly sheathed the mystic blade, slung the scabbard over his shoulder, picked Alique up to his chest and began to run to the east. Kael sprinted, never slowing, even four hours later as the rising sun crept over the far horizon revealing an imposing ridge and mountains. Atop that ridge rose an even more imposing image: the tower of Hosampsich.

*

Kael gave no thought to the speed at which he had reached Hosampsich's tower. The impressive structure rose up from the jutting ridge like a waterspout from the ocean. Beyond it rose sloped, pine-covered mountains. Kael had never seen mountains before. On any other day they would have made him pause, but not today.

He softly laid his bundle on the rocky ground and searched desperately for an opening to the tower. It was made of the same rocky ground on which he stood, but was clearly not constructed by man. There were no blocks intertwined by the hands and mud of masons. This tower had been formed by will and energy alone. It had been brought forth by a power akin to that which had formed the nearby mountains and trees.

Kael made two desperate circles around the immense tower—some hundred and fifty paces around—and found no sign of entry. There was no door, no opening, not even a notch or foothold. There was no time to look anymore. Alique's breathing was ragged and short. How she had survived this long was a miracle. Kael allowed the gripping madness to consume himself again as he had with the demons and the goblins. Wild-eyed and frenzied, he drew his midnight blade and gripped it tightly with both hands. His only thought was to tear a hole into this structure, be it with sword, tooth, or nail. Kael knew, somehow, that Alique's salvation lay inside.

Just as Kael was to begin his barrage on the unnatural tower, the weapon began to glow its unearthly blue. A similar glow emanated suddenly before the crazed warrior, an outline of a door. Kael stepped forward, touching the blue outlined square with the tip of the jagged blade. The sword, as though a key, fell into the stone and the entrance opened.

Without a second thought Kael sheathed the sword, picked up Alique's demon-wrapped form and hurried into the tower, the entrance sealing behind him.

*

Darkness assailed the duo as the entrance mystically closed. The black was complete, unlike a star-filled night. Kael adjusted Alique's form over his left shoulder and partially drew the Midnight Blade. The half-foot exposed from the sheath glowed blue, eerily illuminating their surroundings.

The floor was stone, just as the tower's walls. There was a heavy stone door with an iron ring latch that led to whatever was below. Stairs spiraled up the wall into darkness, steps emerging from the tower wall as if they grew naturally, not by construction. Before Kael could decide what to do next, a small violet burst of energy materialized in the center of the circular room. Within the flaming energy, a small cloaked figure, hood drawn, appeared.

"Up the stairs," the figure spoke. "Please, make haste."

Kael stood hesitant for a moment, then jetted up the stairs. It mattered not who or what the violet image was. All that mattered was Alique's life and its only hope lay up those stairs.

*

Kael stepped up through the ceiling—so far up—and into the tower's reaches. He had circled the structure's interior countless times, not having any inkling how high he was. Kael held Alique's form even closer. Her breathing had thankfully evened. As he emerged up into the tower's upper quarters, he shifted her again to his left shoulder, pulling a length of his sword from its sheath to light the room.

Kael had never seen any sort of constructed room in his entire life. Many curving stone tables and oak book cabinets circled it, covered with books, jars, and various weapons. There were other circular tables in the room, all heavy and oaken, large simple chairs beside them. There were four thick inner support pillars forming the corners of an imaginary square. Beyond each pillar opened a great window into the barely dawning sky, revealing the terrain from every direction. To the west Kael swore he could see all the way to the desolation into which he had tried to flee days before. At the center of the room was a perfect circle, a full arm-span's width in diameter, open to the dizzying ground over four hundred paces below. The same opening was cut in the point of the conical roof above. Despite the dawning day, it was still night within the room's confines.

Kael slowly laid Alique down near the stairway and drew the glowing blue blade. He gripped the foot-long handle tight with both hands. Whether it was paranoia or good sense, Kael knew another was in this room, another with power akin to his own.

"That is right," a deep voice sounded. A cloaked figure stepped out of the shadows from behind the northern pillar. The blue of the Midnight Blade's illumination made the figure purple in the haunting darkness. Vials and books glowed fluorescent, adding to the room's hellish aura.

"What is right?" Kael breathed through tight teeth. He was able to control his fear so far, but he didn't know how long that would hold.

"I am the house of such power you sense," the figure stated quietly. The figure was well over two paces tall and broad-shouldered. He wore a black knee-length robe, breeches and sandals. Dusty silver runes were tooled all over his robe. They covered the dark purple—nearly black—cloak on his shoulders that concealed a foreboding darkness within the cowl's depths.

"I don't care," Kael hissed, advancing, ready to strike. "I need help. Now."

"Why…" the figure began.

"Now!" Kael roared, barely a step from attacking the figure. "I know you can save my love! Do it now!"

The hooded figure seemed to consider Kael's words for a long moment, then brought forth a long, muscled arm and enormous hand. Kael's grip tightened as did his jaw, his fear rising again at the impending battle.

"Move back," the deep voice commanded. When Kael would not, he added, "Please. I will save your woman's life." Kael narrowed his eyes suspiciously and tilted his head in doubt. "Please."

Kael was hesitant in backing up, but relented. He sensed, either naturally or by the unknown source of his newfound intuition, that the figure before him was whom he sought for Alique's salvation. Kael lowered the Midnight Blade and backed to the western window.

The tall, broad figure stepped to the circular hole in the center of the room. With a grand sweeping gesture and several intricate hand motions, the hooded figure struck out at the barely breathing body across the room as if a conductor to his orchestra. Nothing occurred for long breathless moments.

Suddenly, Alique's form burst up from its demonic wrapping, levitating limply in mid-air. Kael jumped in surprise, nearly stumbling out of the large window behind him. His flesh went clammy and his guts tightened at the display of magic before him. The arcane arts froze him in fear—the flying demon, the levitating horseman in the desert—Kael understood none of it, and wanted that much to do with it. He wanted desperately to strike against this magic user, but knew he didn't dare. Not only was Alique's life held in the balance, but surely his own, as well.

Alique's form, recognizable only as female and human, hovered as though strung up on wires under her shoulders. Her hands were opened forward and her face was slightly upturned. Her melted features not only curled Kael's lip, but also curdled his bile. His left hand shot involuntarily to his mouth, his right still weakly clutching the Midnight Blade. Her floating form reminded him of the old myths of divine ascension that the grandfathers had told in his youth.

The cloaked figure brought his hands together quickly and Alique began to radiate a golden aura. It looked nearly green to Kael as it mixed with the blue glow of his drawn weapon. Slowly, the shadowed man began to draw Alique toward himself, not hand over hand as though she were bound by rope, but finger and thumb over finger and thumb, gently, as though connected by a mere strand of hair.

As Alique's form slowly floated toward the cloaked man, even more surprise crept onto Kael's already unbelieving face. Slowly, hair was forming at Alique's scalp. Her skin seemed to tighten, smoothing the viscious marks and burns. Tears formed at Kael's eyes, pouring over his lower lids to moisten his sharp-boned cheeks. Alique would live despite his ineptitude.

Alique's form came to a halt before the cloaked figure, hovering, still, in open unknowing compliance before the shadowed figure. Kael lurched forward, breathless, gripping his weapon tightly again. She levitated directly above the open hole in the exact center of the stone floor, four hundred paces of air between her and the merciless ground.

"She is fine," the cloaked man held a hand up to Kael, the other hand, palm up, seemed to hold up Alique's unmoving form. "Stay where you are and douse your weapon's gleam."

Kael stood still, unsure what to do. He didn't want to sheathe his blade. Could he control the illumination of the sword? As an answer, the blue light faded then halted all together. Only the golden hue that radiated from Alique lighted the circular quarters now. The shadowed man stepped back from her and she held her place in mid-air above the opening. Already her form had returned to normal, her features seemingly fully healed. Kael's mouth opened in unspeakable thankfulness and wavering disbelief.

"Thank the earth," Kael breathed. "You have saved her life. I..."

"Who are you?" the imposing shadowed figure demanded. "How have you gained possession of the Gevurah?"

Gevurah? Kael thought. Is that the true name of the midnight blade? His eyes involuntarily glanced down at the black jagged sword, then back up on the cloaked figure. Kael was unsure what to do. He felt he could slay the dark figure if he had to, but the man had saved Alique's life. Or had he? Alique's physical form had been obviously restored, but what of her mind and spirit? Kael wasn't fooling himself into thinking he could heal Alique if it came to battle with this dark stranger.

"I asked you a question, human. How did you gain possession of this weapon?" The tall stranger placed his fists on his hips imposingly.

"Why...why don't you read my mind if...if you are so curious," Kael's mouth was betraying his bravado. He clenched his teeth tightly, working his fingers around the long sword handle. He breathed deeply, hoping to control his fear and rage.

The shadowed figure stepped away from Alique's shimmering unconscious form toward Kael. Kael tensed and then forced himself to relax as much as he could. His own body was turning against him. It wouldn't be much longer until his mind followed suit. Kael almost welcomed it. He would either go berserk and attack, or drop his sword and flee.

Kael prayed it wouldn't be the latter.

"Here, human," the dark form stepped closer to Kael. "Let me aid in your decision." Before Kael could react, or even consider any other option, the cloaked man raised a hand and uttered a quick phrase. His hand glowed violet then erupted scattered, liquid energy over Kael.

Wide-eyed and tensed, Kael found himself totally and completely immobile. His pupils dilated and his eyes darted around uncontrollably. Kael tried desperately to move, to speak, to scream. All he could do was think and breathe, and neither of those was working that well either.

"Now we can talk intelligently with you out of the discussion." The shadowed man walked slowly around Kael, his hands folded behind him. "Absolutely incredible. Hosampsich's age-old weapon in the hands of a mortal man. Let me tell you a little story, human. I hope you have the intellect to understand what I am to tell you."

Kael struggled to move, to sniffle, to twitch, to do anything! He could do nothing. Every voluntary muscle in his entire body was frozen as if a statue. Kael knew he had to calm himself or his involuntary muscles would surely follow. He relaxed his breathing and concentrated on the shadow man's deep voice. Not only would it give him something to focus on, perhaps he would learn something—hopefully a useful hint on how to kill this bastard.

"The weapon you hold, little human, is the goal of my existence. I have been apprentice, lackey, and general whipping boy to Hosampsich for over twenty turns around the sun." Kael didn't understand what that was about, but was starting to calm down a bit. He noticed that his toes twitched ever so slightly. Perhaps that was the cure to the wizard's spell. Kael breathed even deeper and slower, hoping to break his cowardice and the spell at the same time. He didn't know how long the shadowed man would talk before Kael would be killed, but he was sure it was inevitable.

"I saw your confrontation with Hosampsich in the wastelands to the far west. The grand scrying window in the western corner revealed that tense little drama." The shadowed man stopped in front of Kael's unmoving form, fists again on his slender hips. "How could you do it, though? It's hard to believe you were quicker than a demon, especially Hosampsich. As foolish a being as he was, he was an unparalleled warrior. I saw what happened out there. The Gevurah force chose you over Hosampsich. I never realized the blade's ego was so powerful. Odd that it would choose a host so easily managed rather than one that actually had a chance of raising it to achievement."

As the shadowed figure turned from Kael, the frozen man wondered again what the dark one meant. Was this Gevurah force he spoke of the power within the sword, or something else entirely? Kael knew that the sword had leapt into his hand from the demon's scabbard. He had never questioned why, knowing he would never fully understand it. Kael knew only that he wanted to live. He had no chance for survival above the ground without the blade, and he refused to return to the life of a worm. That existence had eventually ended in death for Kael's people, just as if they had never tried to escape the demons' hunger. That way of life ended for Kael after his first full day above ground, beneath the warmth of the omnipotent sun orb.

Why didn't this shadowed figure just take the weapon out of Kael's hand, kill him, and be done with it all?

"Because the Midnight Blade cannot usually be forcefully taken from its wielder's hands. That is why it didn't find its mark when the goblin chief had you at his mercy. It didn't let you lose grip when the yellow-skinned devil Imamiah tried to kill you. Only you can relinquish the power of the Gevurah within the weapon, or it you. No amount of sorcery that I know of can overcome that."

Kael sighed, unable to see the shadowed figure at his vantage near the western window. This term, Gevurah, seemed to not be the weapon's name, but the warrior was having difficulty following the cloaked man's words. Suddenly, he felt his toes slightly move. Either the enchantment was wearing off or he was overcoming its effects.

"Probably closer to wearing off, human."

Enough with the mind reading! Kael raged to himself. I must be free. The blade shone bright fluorescent blue. Energy coursed through Kael's arm and shoulder. His left arm and shoulder seemed to turn lighter than air, losing all substance in his mind. The emptiness in his limb gathered itself and then exploded out, expelling the spell's effects with it. Kael fell forward to his knees near where Alique hovered. He kneeled there, crouched like a stricken wolf, both hands wrapped white-knuckled around his weapon's handle. He peered up at the shadowed figure through his hanging hair, sweat and goblin blood matting them messily. His blue-green eyes burned nearly red in magmatic fury.

"Impressive," the cloaked man chuckled.

"You don't know the half of it," Kael seethed, fury effectively masking his fear. "I'll see you torn apart!"

"Hold, human, it is not my intent for us to resort to fisticuffs. Let us not sully our hands with the dirty physicality of this mortal world."

The shadowed man's words struck a chord in Kael. What was this man's motive? Kael felt the demon-wrapped handle in his hands, set his jaw, and drew courage from the Midnight Blade. Regardless of what this term Gevurah was, that was his name for the peerless weapon. The sword hummed eerie blue for the briefest of seconds, as if in direct response to its wielder's thoughts, then darkened to its natural space vacuum color.

Kael stood up, Alique's golden, unconscious form hovering behind him. The Midnight Blade was held level at Kael's waist. The shadowed figure seemed to sigh again. Kael wondered if it wasn't in relief.

"Perhaps, just a little," the cloaked one whispered, turning to face Kael. The imposing figure drew back the hood of his cloak, the golden light emanating from Alique revealing the dark one's features.

He had an oval-shaped head without a stitch of hair on it. His large ears were pointed and his jaw was square. His eyebrows were thick and dark over deep-set black eyes. His eyes held the same deepness that the night did. His features oozed brutality and deep primitive masculinity. They were human-like but also something more—or less.

"You would think less," the imposing figure whispered. "At least your grandfather's grandfather would have."

"My grandfather's..."

"I didn't mean yours directly," the cloaked man chuckled. "I meant humans in general." He stepped slowly away from the western window, arcing a path through the books and tables, toward the southern window. He leaned against the smooth stone opening, resting against his upraised forearm. "Orcen."

"Orcen?" Kael questioned.

"I am half-orc. Your and my great-great-grandfather's clans warred long ago, before the hunters and the permits." Kael didn't follow the last comment but tried not to let on. "Both of our races are near gone since the opening. At least around this corner of the world, anyway."

"Opening?"

"Alas, I shouldn't have expected much from a race of moles." The half-orc turned to face Kael. "My name is Razikyl." He stepped closer to Kael. Kael didn't know what to do.

"I am Kael."

"Yes," Razikyl nodded, "of the Kelt-Ra clan. You were the last 'herd' of humans left in the grassy hills west of here." He gestured at the large western window. "I witnessed Hosampsich and his band as they followed your foraging partners into the coulees and creek beds."

"Followed?" Kael returned. "It was that easy to find our underground tunnels?"

"No, of course not. You had successfully evaded your hunters for nearly a century. No, it was betrayal that ended your clan."

"Betrayal?" Kael didn't follow. "How is that possible?"

"Demons do not take their pleasure only in feasting on humans." Razikyl began to pace again, Kael turning as the half-orc circled. He wasn't about to lower his guard. "Many a human female was seduced and kept, to rear a child not only of power, but of beauty."

"You're saying…" Kael stopped, unable for a moment to grasp the orc's intent. He turned to face Alique's hovering form. Her face was serene and at peace, exactly as Kael had seen her more than a thousand times before. Her beauty had always been hypnotic to Kael. Her golden skin, enhanced now by the arcane energy; her keen brown eyes, a color never seen even in nature, her body shape unmatched by any, curving like a sheet of silk. His sword was now held in only one hand, as Kael held his head in the other, struggling against the emotions Razikyl had stirred. Could it be? Had Alique betrayed the clan to become the thrall of a mighty demon?

"Look, human," Razikyl barked. Kael looked up wearily, head bent. The Midnight Blade was clenched in his hand loosely. Kael felt emptiness in his throat and stomach at what the mage was revealing. With a few gestures and whispering phrases, a glowing disk appeared between the two men. "Here, human. See where your mate's loyalty lies."

Kael was speechless at what he saw: Alique amidst the group of demons Kael had slain days before. She was showing them the way to the entrance of the Kelt-Ra's underground tunnels. Kael saw as the rest of his hunting party disappeared underground, not knowing they were being watched. Suddenly, he saw himself stumble accidentally into the band of demons, turn, and run.

"Wait," Kael shook his head. "I never saw Alique there."

"Oh," Razikyl smirked, "So that means she wasn't there then, since you didn't see her in your haste to shit your own breeches."

Kael watched himself run for his life to the western wastelands. He saw Hosampsich send the pack of HellHounds after him as the enormous demon led his demonic troupe into the depths of the Kelt-Ra's hidden tunnels.

"Didn't you wonder why Hosampsich didn't kill you right away? You actually thought you could outrun the demon? Pitiful."

Kael looked away from the image to glance again at Alique. Was it possible? Had she betrayed her people? Kael was at a loss at what to think or feel. What other explanation was there? How else could Hosampsich have found the tunnels after a century of fruitless searching?

Before Kael could consider it any further, flashing light exploded before his eyes and pain erupted in the back of his skull. A force drove him to his knees, his form teetering dangerously over the dizzying drop. All that held him from dropping was his unyielding grip and the Midnight Blade's tenuous hold on the granite floor.

"Drop, human!" Razikyl roared. He grabbed the sword's handle just below Kael's white knuckled hold. Kael looked up in time to see Razikyl's fist finish the job on his already surely broken nose, tearing the flesh above his left eye. Blood poured down over Kael's face, though his grip was no less tight than before.

"You can't take the Blade from me against my will. You said so yourse..." Kael's words were cut short as Razikyl's powerful hand wrapped around the human's throat. The black-robed orc forced Kael to his back roughly. Kael grappled futilely with his left hand to break Razikyl's hold. With his right he tried to wrench his weapon from his orcen assailant, again, futilely. It seemed to Kael's blood-starving mind that the orc's throat-hold was all that kept him from plummeting the four hundred pace distance below Alique's hovering, seemingly uncaring, form.

"Poor human," Razikyl growled through his sharp and savage teeth. "Soon you will be dead and my lies will no longer trouble you."

Kael's mind reeled at both the orc's words and choking grip, but he struggled to concentrate on survival. He gave up on pulling Razikyl's hand away and began to punch him in the face.

"To hell..." Kael croaked. Rage was finally managing to dispel his natural predisposition to cowardice.

"Aye, human," Razikyl nodded, grinning, "Hell will be a pleasant rest over this fetid shit-globe."

Enough! Kael's near-suffocated brain managed. Gevurah, he called out to the Midnight Blade, hoping to steal power from the newfound word. As if on cue, the ruby eyes on the weapon's hilt flared insanely, the blade again glowing. The hilt glowed violet as the red burning eyes mingled with the blade's bright blue glow. Razikyl glanced over in surprise, the golden glow of Alique melding with the blue to cover his dark form green.

"Nay, Gevurah," the orc sorcerer growled, lowering his jaw and tightening his grasp on both the sword's handle and Kael's throat. "By my hand you will strike, not in the half-witted control of this human. Bow to me, Gevurah."

Kael saw the blue hue dim as he felt his own grasp loosen ever so slightly. Razikyl felt it too and grinned. What the orc did not feel, however, was the tingling and empty feeling stirring within Kael's left shoulder. It began akin to a separation, "filling" his shoulder socket then spreading throughout his entire left deltoid and trapezius muscle. Kael didn't understand where the sensation had come from but, somehow, he knew how to utilize it. He brought his left arm back. Razikyl paid no heed to the human's approaching fist, sure that he would shrug it off as he had the other blows.

The force of Kael's attack tore the orc backward as if he had been struck by lightning. Razikyl flew through the air and landed heavily across the room underneath a heavy wooden table.

With the release of the orc's grip on Kael, he fell backward into the opening below Alique. He reached out desperately, frantically, for anything. What felt like an eternity of hovering above certain death ended as Kael grasped something. He quickly pulled himself to safety, a cold sweat covering his whole body. He looked up at what had saved him. It was Alique's foot he had grabbed. She still showed no sign of awareness, but had unknowingly saved her lover's life.

"Your heart is mine, human," Razikyl growled, dragging himself out from under the heavy table.

"Come and get it, orc," Kael snarled back, his surge of power bringing as much confidence as the formidable weapon in his hands.

Before either could act, a spear of glass erupted through the north window, embedding itself between the combatants. In a hail of energy it exploded, sending Razikyl again under the table and Kael across the room to rest under a stone workbench.

"Quick work, my friend!" A booming tenor voice sounded. Razikyl and Kael tentatively dug themselves out from under the tables to an unbelievable sight: two mighty men dressed in white silken kilts and white leather sandals. Each wielded a gleaming sword; one held a clear glass spear as well. Their builds were like those of lean racehorses, and from their backs sprouted wings of doves, each larger than Kael.

"WindBearers," Kael whispered in awe.

"Right," Razikyl grunted.

"Quickly, Seraphiel," the slightly larger blonde winged warrior pointed. "The orc. He would prove the greater challenge."

"Aye," Seraphiel nodded hurling his crystalline javelin toward Razikyl's unprepared, huddled form. The dark robed orc began to weave a hasty pattern with his hands, mumbling quick arcane words as the spear struck before him. When the weapon struck the stone floor it exploded, sending Razikyl and his oaken table cover splaying. The table was rendered to splinters, the orc very nearly as well. He came to a rest, unconscious, covered in glass, wood, and the remains of several ancient texts.

"An overload of the Netsah, my comrade?" Jehoel raised an eyebrow to his shorter twin, both hoisting their broadswords simultaneously.

"No such thing, my friend," Seraphiel smirked. "And how about you, little human?" Kael rose slowly, the Midnight Blade held low in both his powerful hands. The haunting blue glow of the unparalleled weapon bathed the fledgling swordsman's goblin-blood caked body. Kael stared menacingly through his stringy, blonde bangs. His only thoughts were of maddening anger and survival.

"We've a permit this time, little one," the shorter winged warrior touched a finger to his temple. A tiny orb of green glowed then faded. He gestured to Alique's floating form. "We've plans for her, as well."

The WindBearer's final comment ran ice water through Kael's fiery veins. His eyes glassed over and a fog of homicide settled over his brain. The ruby eyes of the sword's hilt glowed as never before. The emptiness within Kael's left shoulder returned with a fury, this time enveloping his entire arm, from his neck to his fingernails.

"Take me, Gevurah," Kael hissed, bloodlust reddening his watery vision. "Make me yours."

Aye, came the thought across his clouded mind. *You are mine.*

Kael surrendered to the tingling emptiness in his left arm. He opened his mind to the feeling, allowing the powerful will and personality of the Midnight Blade to permeate his entire spirit. A slight dizziness coursed through his mind, only for a moment. A shade of light-headedness remained that Kael mistook as the presence of Gevurah. In reality, the Midnight Blade had opened a gate between Kael's spirit and body. The tingling in his arm matched the corresponding sensation in an exact section of his brain. The imprint of a thousand skilled warriors was on the weapon. With the arcane blade's guidance, instinct bloomed and swelled within Kael. The genetic memory of a hundred forefathers melded with powerful mysticism. He brought up the blade slowly and circled toward the two WindBearers slowly and with purpose.

"Be wary, Seraphiel," the larger one nudged his shorter companion slowly away, moving to flank the approaching human. "Though he be merely human, he wields our hard-sought prize. He made quick work of Hosampsich despite the demon's considerable talents."

The shorter angelic figure nodded slowly, his face a masque of death at the gravity of the situation. This swordsman before them wasn't the same shit-covered sack of cowardice they had left for dead the week before.

Kael stopped, straightening to meet the two hunters boldly. They continued to circle their prey until the human was directly between them. The Midnight Blade pulled the two WindBearers' strategy from their betraying electrical brain impulses. If Kael had been more experienced, he would have wanted to grin at the knowledge relayed to him with an attack plan to match. Instead, Kael lowered his jaw, his eyes still up, and allowed the hunters their advantage.

Silence reigned for long moments within the heights of the Tower of Hosampsich, silence that stretched scant seconds into a near-eternity.

Action occurred faster than thought.

The two winged men brought their swords to level on their prey, both hands gripped to their hand-and-a-half handles tightly. Blood red energy exploded, channeled through the steel to send Kael's life viciously to its final reckoning.

Yet there acted the Midnight Blade. The ancient artifact saturated the fibers of both Kael's muscle and his spirit, pulling his form below the lancing attacks faster than light. The WindBearers struck each other, singeing only the hair of their true target. Kael reacted simultaneously to the attacks with one of his own. He channeled his own essence with and through the Midnight Blade. Star-blue heat met with red fire, finding the shorter hunter its target. The combined attacks, though half-misguided, expelled the lesser warrior through the southern window to plummet not only the height of the mystic tower, but also the tenfold height of the ridge it stood on.

"Well struck," Jehoel nodded, his chest still slightly smoldering from his comrade's inadvertent blast. He shrugged off the attack with a toss of his wavy blonde hair. "Come, little one." Jehoel advanced slowly. "Meet your master."

Kael moved not, still crouched on the stony floor. His weapon acted symbiotically now with his own mind.

Let him come. He is ours.

"Aye," Kael growled. "Ours."

Jehoel came in a furious flurry. His brutal attack was unmatched, faster than human comprehension. Down came his steel blade, glowing with red energy, again and again. There was no mercy in Jehoel's actions, no humanity. He was as far from humanity as any being could be.

Yet for all the unmatched savagery, for all the mind-boggling speed and fury of the attack, Kael felt nary a blow. The blade's jagged edge met every attack.

"Impossible!" Jehoel roared, breaking off his attack for a moment. "Human flesh and blood cannot move this fast!"

"T'hell with you, WindBearer," Kael wasn't even near to being winded. His whole body felt a-tingle now. "Fight or fall on my sword."

"Insolence!" Jehoel spat. "I've a permit for your hide, but it's your heart I shall feast on this morn!"

"Do your worst!" Kael raged.

With a spine-shattering wail, the winged warrior renewed his attack with more savagery than before. Again, Kael met every strike, sometimes barely an inch from his own annihilation. The Midnight Blade glowed mystically, bluer than ever before—nearly white. Kael now, with the guidance of his mighty weapon, launched an attack of his own. Jehoel could not believe his own eyes. Kael could scarcely believe his.

It was now the human who rained down blow after blow. It was the extent of Jehoel's substantial ability to parry and avoid every attack. The assault was quick and brutal and the angelic being knew he had scarce seconds before he felt the sword's cold, jagged edge.

Just as Kael had forced his combatant to the floor, his weapon roared out a warning, painfully resounding in Kael's cranium. Without so much as a thought, he threw himself to the side. Just as he had hurled himself aside, a red bolt of energy filled the space he had occupied, slamming full into Jehoel's chest. The attack blasted the winged one across the room into a stone bench. The bench exploded into a thousand pieces, showering the entire room. Jehoel was slow to get up, regrouping for another attack.

Seraphiel stood at the very window he had been blown out of, his wings folding in again behind him, his red glowing blade in his hand.

"Another fine blow, Seraphiel," Jehoel breathed patiently, standing among the shattered granite ready again for battle.

"Sorry, dear brother," Seraphiel shrugged sheepishly.

Kael backed up a few steps, raising his weapon in defense. He couldn't believe what he had done so far. With the Midnight Blade in his hands, none could stand before him.

"Come," Kael snarled boldly, his cowardice evaporated by the power he wielded. "My hide is here for the taking, as is my heart."

There wasn't an instant between Kael's words and the two angelic beings' attack. Their blades whistled and howled as they cut through the air, desperate to taste the blood of their prey. Seraphiel and Jehoel struck in succession one instant then simultaneously the next. Despite their superhuman strength, skill, and stamina, Kael brought his sword up to meet every single strike. For nearly a full minute Kael kept up his defense. Then, suddenly, he began to feel the wear and strain of the pace.

"Ha! I knew it!" Seraphiel laughed, "Your human limbs cannot match our peerless tempo! Time, as always, works against you, mortal!"

Kael gritted his teeth grimly, realizing the truth in the WindBearer's words. No matter the energy or power the Midnight Blade could imbue, Kael's basic humanity would be his limit. Though he was a physical specimen in his own right, Kael was unused to the effects of magic and it was taking a heavy toll.

"Soon, human," Seraphiel gloated, "You will bring a fine price at the cave of kings."

"Not by your hand, winged one," a deep throaty voice boomed.

"Razikyl," Kael panted, barely blocking the whirlwind of deadly blows.

"Orc," Seraphiel gasped, looking over to see the dark-cloaked figure weaving the air with his hands and quietly mur-

muring. The shorter warrior wished to turn his attack to the newer assailant, but realized, too late, that he was just that: too late. Jehoel cursed the situation, knowing they were defeated, and, if they tarried, doomed. The Midnight Blade knew that, as well.

Kael struck a final blow just as white-hot lightening burst from Razikyl's open hands. Jehoel threw himself backward, though not out of harm's way. The lightning exploded through Seraphiel, opening a hole clean through him as round as a man's leg. The remnants enveloped Jehoel and Kael painfully.

But not so painfully that he could not act.

Kael's final arcing swing sliced halfway into Jehoel's jugular and found its mark squarely through Seraphiel's throat. The shorter hunter's head flew from his body, resting some twenty feet away. Kael fell to the floor not only from the momentum but from exhaustion, as well.

"N…Nay!" Jehoel managed, his eyes on his defeated comrade, his left hand secure around his own throat, his body heavily leaning against the frame of the northern window. Clear, thick life fluid seeped through his fingers, streaking down his heavy chest to stain his silken kilt. "Ser…aph…iel…sor…s…sorry."

"Kill them!" Seraphiel's decapitated head roared, eyes wide open, unseeing. Jehoel tucked his chin to his chest to stem the unearthly bleeding, stepped out the window, and spread his magnificent wings. He pitched his now dim broadsword below and, with both hands at his neck, he flew off the mountains to the east.

"Human!" Seraphiel's head continued to scream, his body "mortally" wounded, yet still standing. "Live a hundred years and I shall see you tortured a thousand more!" Kael staggered to his feet and raised his sword to chop down the WindBearer's headless body. "I shan't go alone, human! Let this sight keep you alive in misery for a century!"

Seraphiel's body raised its arms at Alique's hovering form just as Kael brought the Midnight Blade through the WindBearer's headless form. The winged hunter's body actually siphoned the energy meant to destroy him, added it to his own essence, and expelled it out through his hands. Seraphiel's body evaporated as the energy blew forth into Alique's unprotected body. Kael, physically unable to stop the attack, roared in rage, throwing himself forward to grasp her body. The Midnight Blade was forgotten, thrown to the ground, as Kael launched across the opening in the floor. He rolled to a stop on the other side, Alique's beautiful, naked form in his arms.

Alique had taken the full force of Seraphiel's brutal attack and Kael knew the attack had been fatal. Tears streamed from his tight closed eyes as he pulled her as close to himself as he possibly could. Forehead to forehead, chest to chest, Kael could feel Alique's heart slowing, trying desperately to continue. He brushed her soft hair from her perfect face and tenderly pressed his lips to hers. More tears forced through his lids to moisten her perfect skin. Kael, finally, after a long minute, pulled away, opening his eyes.

"I love you," he whispered, tracing a finger around the round frame of her smooth jaw. Never before had emotion struck him so strongly. Alique, he realized, had been the only light in his entire dirty, gloomy life. His inherit cowardice and fear had always been tempered by the love and need of this one person. He realized he was losing that now. He pushed his ugliness and shallowness away in an effort, somehow, to keep Alique's spirit on earth with him.

"Please," he whispered, a tingling in his fingertips and toes, a purity of true emotion forming in his chest and whole being.

Alique's eyes fluttered open as her heart slowed to barely a tick. Kael's eyes widened, as well, his breath ripped from his lungs in surprise. Time held eternal as their eyes, and more truly, their souls locked.

"Alique," he breathed, a feeling of physical weakness and spiritual strength swelling in his being. She smiled softly, managing to bring her hand to the side of his rugged face. The power of the invincible bond between them brought even more tears to their eyes and proved, ultimately, the final straw for Alique's weakened heart.

There was no breath left for her to speak, but Kael heard the soundless words she mouthed:

"I love you, Kael. Forever."

Alique smiled one final time, hand tracing its familiar path aside his face, and closed her eyes forever.

Only the gentle wail of the soft eastern wind could be heard through the tower. Kael pulled Alique's unmoving form back to his chest and held her as tight as he could. His only movement was a gentle rocking as if soothing a child to sleep.

The very intent and reason of his life up to this point, he realized, was gone now.

Razikyl stood up slowly, pain wracking his entire body. The shield spell he had thrown up before the WindBearer's attack had saved his life, but barely. The attack he had thrown back on them had taken a mighty toll, as well. In his current state he would be no match for the human, nor did he really have the desire to be.

The orcen sorcerer quietly made his way around Kael's mourning form and saw the Midnight Blade lying in the rubble across the room. He paused for a moment, running a hand over his head, then walked over to the powerful artifact. He stood unmoving above the weapon, his deep black eyes blazing. The orc's action had drawn Kael's eyes, but no other reaction from the crushed warrior.

Razikyl bent over painfully, his face locked in a grimace. He gripped the sword's three-handed handle and stood straight again, feeling the sword's reaction to his own will. The shadowed mage turned and stepped over the ashen remains of Seraphiel to the WindBearer's head. Only Kael's eyes moved, following his opponent.

Seraphiel's head still coursed with trace essence, the eyes turned upward, the mouth speaking wordlessly, no lungs with which to draw air to speak. Razikyl moved swiftly, belying the pain in his muscles. He gripped Seraphiel's head by its long blonde locks and sliced Gevurah across the forehead. The head's mouth opened in rage to scream, expelling no sound. Razikyl stood up with Seraphiel's scalp in hand then brought down the

Midnight Blade through the bloody skull. It exploded harmlessly into light, then dissipated to ash.

Razikyl let out a deep, slow breath, turning his head to witness Kael's reaction. There was none. Kael huddled, still holding Alique's unmoving form to his chest. The orc walked toward his adversary, the advantage now clearly in his hands.

"You will be allowed to live, human," Razikyl stopped ten feet before Kael. "You were instrumental in my recovery of the Midnight Blade."

Kael lay Alique's form down gently, standing to face the towering orc. Razikyl tensed, unsure what the human intended. He had offered the human his life. Nothing more could be expected. Kael raised his arm to Razikyl, palm open. The orc raised the Midnight Blade in defense of an impending attack.

"Gevurah," Kael whispered, frightening emptiness in his words and behind his blue-green eyes.

"What do…" Razikyl began, but was silenced by the sword's blue glow and haunting hum. "How…"

Suddenly, the Midnight Blade was tore from his grip by some unseen force. The weapon hurtled, spinning, through the air with a soul-rending wail. Kael plucked the mighty sword from midair. He stood there, his arm still raised, blade held horizontal before him, aglow. The radiant blue was more overwhelming than ever, flooding the entire room completely. Razikyl raised his cloak hood and shielded his eyes from the brilliance. He was sure his own fate was sealed now and was resigned to it.

"Nay, orc," Kael said at last, unknowingly using the mage's own mind-revealing trick against him. "I may yet have need of your services."

"Your mate," Razikyl stated, motioning to Alique's body. Kael nodded, stepping back a single step. The orc shrugged, thinking for a moment, weighing his limited options. He finally stepped forward to kneel by Alique's body. He produced a small, red, jewel-incrusted, porcelain vial. He twisted the shining cap off and held the vial inverted over Alique's open mouth and tapped the bottom softly. Then with a firm hand on her still chest, and a wary eye on Kael's sword arm, Razikyl pressed firmly and steadily, expelling the remaining breath in her lungs. Shrugging again, the orc spun the lid back on the vial, whisking it back into the depths of his robe. He stood up, pulling his cloak around himself.

"What was that?" Kael whispered softly.

"God's-breath it's called, human," Razikyl admitted, meeting Kael's eyes straight. "It is all I have available to combat death. I apologize. She is gone."

Kael nodded, his eyes glassy with emotion. After a moment of collection, Kael adjusted the ornate golden scabbard at his waist and slowly sheathed the Midnight Blade.

"Now what, human?" Razikyl asked, at ease now that the weapon was out of sight.

"My name is Kael."

Razikyl looked up, startled at the levelness and confidence in the statement and voice. Kael's eyes were locked on the beautiful body of his mate.

"The tower is mine, is it not?" Kael asked, still not looking up.

"Aye," Razikyl nodded. There was no use fighting for the stone structure. The orc knew it was an extension of the mystic blade. The wielder of the sword was the master of the castle.

Razikyl walked over to the stairway, where Kael's demon cloak and tusk belts still lay. The orc looked back to see Kael kneel down again to Alique.

"I will return for my belongings," Razikyl stated. Kael didn't acknowledge the orc's words, instead pulling Alique to his chest again and resume his comforting rocking. Razikyl shook his head in pity and began down the stairs.

*

It was late afternoon, not a cloud in the bright, blue sky. The grassy, rolling hills of the Kelt-Ra clan were a hazy blue in the distant west. In the east rose towering mountains, trace drifts of snow still fingering their smooth, easy peaks. A thousand pines, rich, green and towering, covered the gentle, timeless giants.

Razikyl paid no heed to the beauty that surrounded him. He was intent on the bird he had downed and cooked. His small fire traced a faint smoke trail into the clear sky. He had positioned it at the very edge of the extensive ridge. Another step past the smoldering embers was a drop of over two thousand paces, sheer and undeniable. Surely from this lofty perch a soul could see, and be seen, for hundreds of leagues.

"Bah," Razikyl growled, tearing into his meal. Let any come to his camp that dared. They would find their livers in their hands and their scalps in the orc's pouch.

As Razikyl finished his meal, tossing the remains over the cliff, his pointed ears caught the footfalls behind him. The dark-cloaked orc pulled his hood back from his bald scalp, turning to face the figure behind him. From out of the darkness of the tower door strode Kael, master of the tower and wielder of the Midnight Blade. Razikyl's nose wrinkled in disgust. The sword had been his sought-after prize, and he was unsure whether he had forsaken it for good. The weapon obviously favored the human, but in the end it was merely a weapon. The situation was delicate and was to be dealt with accordingly.

Kael wore his two tusk belts across his chest, the WindBearer's scalp attached at the clasp of his tiger-striped kilt. He wore the white leather sandals of the winged warrior he had defeated, forsaking the feel of stone on his bare feet. The sun near-sparkled off of the Midnight Blade's pommel. In his arms he carried Alique's still form, the demon cloak her death shroud. Kael set his stead down gently in the scarce, brushy grass, then stood to face Razikyl.

The orc confidently stepped forward to face the human. There were scarcely ten paces between them as they locked eyes. Razikyl had not healed from the morning's events but was far from incapacitated. He planned his strike to be fast and furious, if needed.

Kael turned to face the enormous tower, seemingly uncaring toward the orc's intentions. Razikyl held his attack. He was unsure if he could overcome the sword's defenses just yet, and besides, with patience came opportunity.

Kael stood for a scant moment before drawing the Midnight Blade and walking before the imposing structure. The opening was sealed shut now, indiscernible from the hard granite of the tower wall. Kael slipped Gevurah again into the invisible keyhole in the wall. This time, however, he didn't search for an entrance.

Razikyl steadied himself as the ground shook. It was as though a giant had smashed his mighty fists to bring the ridge to rubble. The entire structure glow bright blue—the trademark of Gevurah's power. The orc knew exactly what was happening. He had witnessed it before in the company of the Demon Lord Hosampsich.

In a rush of energy and motion too fast to see, the tower fell into the earth as though turned to water. Just like that, the structure was gone. All that remained was Kael, sword held before him aglow in fluorescent energy. With three hard, powerful pulses, the blade fell dark again seemingly a vacuum within the afternoon daylight. Kael sheathed his weapon again, returning to scoop Alique's covered form back to his chest. He stepped up to face Razikyl again. The foreboding black of the orc's eyes locked with the fiery green-blue of the human.

"Keep your magic stifled and keep your life," Kael stated flatly. He didn't back down an inch even though the orc towered eight above him.

"I'll keep my life, human," Razikyl returned. "Be sure you keep good care of my sword while you have it."

"I told you, Razikyl. My name is Kael."

The steel in Kael's voice caught Razikyl by surprise. He had pegged the human weaker of will. Perhaps this was the steel of the weapon's ego more than the human against which the orc dare not trifle.

"Fair enough, uh…Kael."

Kael nodded, turned, and began to make his way down the massive ridge's five-mile decline. Razikyl didn't move toward the human. That was a fight for another day.

Just as the orc was about to follow, something caught his eye near where the tower had stood. Several long strands of Alique's hair lay in the ragged brush. He stooped over to pick up the numerous, thick strands of dark auburn hair. Smiling, Razikyl withdrew the red-jeweled vial from his sleeve and tied the glistening hair around the small bottle's neck.

As he slipped the jar back into his robe, something else captured his eye. Stepping into the slight depression where once the tower stood, Razikyl picked up another interesting item. It was a tiny sphere of energy smaller than a marble. It glowed a green that bathed the shadowed figure.

"A permit," Razikyl grinned, placing the power filled orb at his temple. The sphere disappeared into the orc's temple, only a faint, jade shimmer beneath his thick skin.

"Truly a fight for another day."

*

Kael sat down, exhausted, his arms resting on his knees. He was sweating immensely as the mid-day summer sun beat down mercilessly. He looked over through his drenched bangs at the two large elk hides he had tanned and treated for the last three days. The leather spreads were as soft as a child's skin due to Kael's actions. He had, besides treating them, chewed them to softness over the past fifteen hours. Just past the hides, he had dug a man-sized hole nearly six feet deep. Alique's body was far down below the hill, kept in a cool cave until her burial was ready.

Kael brushed his damp hair back out of his face, taking account of his surroundings. He was sitting on the ledge of a large grass-covered hill, the same that he had crested those many nights ago to murder that first band of demons. The memories of that night seemed a lifetime away as he unconsciously clenched his fists around the demon tusk belts circling his chest. It had been the first true time he had utilized the power he heard called Gevurah.

"Or it utilized me," Kael thought aloud, his eyes falling on the golden scabbard and night-shaded blade beside him. Was it the sword itself that commanded the power, he wondered, or was it something beyond that? He traced a finger around the ornate designs that emerged from the shining scabbard. Demons of unspeakable horror locked in mortal combat with angels of unbelievable beauty. Dragons of every shape, warriors of the human, elven, and dwarven races, all entwined in a deadly dance of death.

Kael looked away for an instant then lazily brought his eyes back to the sheath. Shock widened his eyes at what he saw. The scene of carnage that had covered it now revealed those same figures entwined around each other in an orgy of lust and wantonness. Kael was stunned and confused at the writhing forms heaving and thrusting through and on each other, moving all across the scabbard's surface. Man on woman, monster on man, woman on woman. Then, suddenly, the figures stilled, resuming their static battle.

Kael rubbed his eyes, returning his startled gaze back to the ornate casing. He knew it hadn't been his mind playing tricks on him. More likely it was the sword's doing: the weapon's "ego" opening itself for a moment to his own. But why reveal itself in such a manner as this? Kael felt and understood his own lusts and desires of the flesh, but felt no connection between those feelings and the power he called Gevurah.

Kael knew he didn't understand anything about the power he wielded, but he was determined to try. He knew the opportunity he held in his hands was incredible, and probably inconceivable to him.

Getting up, adjusting the Midnight Blade to hang behind him, Kael brushed the dust from his thick, demon kilt. His cloak of the same make lay folded at his feet.

The view from this particular hill had always impressed Kael. Even though this was the first time he had beheld the scene during daylight, it held much for him. The rounded hills stretched to the north and south. To the east they ran up to the ridge where he had battled the WindBearers and the orcen sorcerer Razikyl. To the west rose a gentle rock-covered ridge. Unseen beyond that were the Border River and desert wastelands. Below trailed the humble life-giving creek, running from the southeast to the northwest.

Kael pushed away the questions that ruled his mind. He had no answers just now, and madness would overtake him in his current state. The memories of his losses, his people, his life's love, still hung heavy on his heart and soul. He could feel nothing but emptiness. Viewing his people's lands comforted him some, but not enough.

Kael started down the steep grassy slope when a shadow crossed over him. Instinctively, he gripped the Midnight Blade's oversized handle, ready for battle. Craning his head upward, he saw a dragon flying far in the sky above him. The creature was massive and beautiful, his flight easy and measured. His color was as red as the fires of hell in Kael's imagination. Tusks and horns as long as a man was tall sprung from his head and jaw.

Kael tensed, ready for a fight against a creature he had never known existed until this very second. The very sight of the blood-colored dragon froze his own blood and very nearly opened his bowels. He steeled his courage as best he could, the strength of his newfound power beginning to open into his hands.

The dragon continued his flight, seemingly oblivious to the possible threat below. Kael breathed a sigh of relief, releasing his hold on the Midnight Blade. He pushed the thought of the horrible creature from his mind with a shiver down his spine, and continued down the hill.

*

The sun was waning, perhaps a couple of hours from setting as Kael set Alique's body in the deep, earthy pit. She was completely covered in the two elk hides he had prepared for her. Kael's people believed the elk to be the carriers and guardians of humans to whatever lay beyond this life. If there was an animal holy to them, it was the elk.

He kneeled in silent solitude before covering her precious form. He did so slowly and sacredly. No tears ran from his eyes during this. He believed he had cried his last tears days before when he lost her for all time.

Finally, Kael began to slowly brush the large pile of dirt onto Alique, a hand full at a time. As the soil landed on her inanimate form, Kael felt his horror and sadness overtake his entire being. He thrust his arms in the dirt pile and began throwing great piles into the deep hole. The mystic energy opened within his left arm surged at the activity, aiding him to fill the pit even quicker.

As the task ended, Kael fell onto the burial mound in despair. The coolness of the earth helped to calm the heated madness welling within his mind. His thoughts wouldn't release the image of Alique and its aim seemed to be to destroy him. Kael felt himself begin to drift off, yielding to the images within.

Awaken!

Kael jerked up, pushing himself to his knees. He swept his demon cloak back and gripped his sword, ready for battle.

"Easy, human," a deep voice sounded.

Kael stood up, drawing the Midnight Blade and boldly faced the figure before him.

"Your name is Imamiah," Kael stated flatly.

"The Gevurah within that weapon is a helpful little tool, is it not?" the enormous devil chuckled, turning to survey the countryside. "Quite a view from here. I would pick a similar place myself to raise the tower."

Kael didn't speak. His only response was the Midnight Blade's slight blue glow. Hatred was filling him at the sight of the towering, yellow-skinned being and soon he knew he would throw himself forward to fell the sickening creature.

"Draw your blade, dog," Kael managed through gritted teeth. "At least meet your maker with steel in your hand."

"No," Imamiah shook his head, grinning, his great black wings opening slowly. "I am a patient one. Time is on my side."

Kael roared and jumped forward to strike down the cocky devil. Imamiah rose above the human's swinging blade and hovered safely above him, his wings flapping out a steady tempo.

"Watch your back, human." Imamiah warned as he rose into the afternoon sky. "I would hate for my weapon to fall into the hands of some other fool demon."

Kael's breath was heavy, his vision red as he watched the flying figure escape to the mountains of the east. There was no intention of vengeance or want of retaliation toward the devil in Kael's mind. Odd, considering when he had drawn the sword, there was little else but murder on his mind.

Kael shook his head and sheathed the Midnight Blade as he turned back to the burial mound of his lost love. Kael thought nothing of the encounter that had just occurred.

In fact, within seconds, he didn't remember it happening at all.

*

"Very nice," Appollyon smiled at his work. Jehoel pushed away from the larger being, his hands at his own throat, inspecting the stitch-work delicately. "This will cost you."

Jehoel looked up at Appollyon menacingly, but wisely kept his mouth sealed as tight as the new stitches at his throat. He was in no condition to refute anything the larger one stated.

Appollyon chuckled to himself as he walked away from the WindBearer, deeper into the reaches of his enormous cavern home. He made his way up a raised dais and onto a plain, stone throne. Behind the throne the cave sloped down into the dark reaches of the enormous mountain. Not even the unparalleled eyes of a WindBearer could penetrate the darkness behind the granite throne. Jehoel wondered if he even wanted to.

"No, Jehoel," the seated being stated evenly. "You really don't." Jehoel hated it when other beings used his own tricks on him.

Appollyon was enormous and appeared to be a man, but was not. He had black hair and eyes and wore simple brown robes as if a hermit. He was also nearly eight feet tall and heavily muscled. He wore no weapon; he had no need for one. His dark hair was pulled up in a topknot that curled behind his right ear and down on his barrel chest. His body hair was darker than that on his head and he was covered by it. He reminded Jehoel of a bear. Another chuckle reminded the WindBearer to be careful what he thought.

"What now will you do to pay for my much-needed services, Jehoel?" Appollyon asked, his face holding no hint of humor. The wounded winged warrior gulped roughly at the bounty master's words. His hand unconsciously fell to the sword handle at his waist. That, too, had been a gift of the larger man after Jehoel had lost his in the battle at Hosampsich's Tower.

"There is very little I can offer," Jehoel said truthfully. "I am a hunter. I hold no possessions."

"True," Appollyon nodded, his gaze falling on everything in the cave but the WindBearer. "A boon, perhaps?"

Jehoel gritted his teeth and grimaced. Perhaps he should have just fell to the human as Seraphiel had.

"A boon." Jehoel started slowly. He turned, subconsciously placing his back to the cave wall. The last thing he needed was a rival hunter to enter the cavern behind him and take advantage of this precarious situation, and suddenly he felt very unprotected.

"Aye, WindBearer," Appollyon rose, standing imposingly over the smaller being. Jehoel tensed for an attack. No being with any sense trusted the bounty master.

Appollyon began to murmur under his breath and thrust out at the WindBearer repeatedly. Jehoel felt the thrusts as physical blows even though he was yards away. After the fifth such sensation, the winged warrior stumbled forward and fell to his knees. His mind clouded as the effects of Appollyon's spell blocked the fore of his brain and implanted the bounty master's intentions. Jehoel stood, finally, his eyes glassy and unseeing.

"Just in case," the bounty-master chuckled. "Just as with devils, I have found I can rarely trust an angel. Whether he knows he is an angel or not."

Jehoel stood motionless as Appollyon's laughter echoed throughout the Cave of Kings.

AN OPENING TO MADNESS

Kael parried the arcing attack easily and countered with a waist-high thrust that opened his opponent's stomach, spilling organs on the ground as the Midnight Blade was withdrawn. The massive red-skinned demon gasped for air as he fell to his knees, sword forgotten, futilely scrambling to hold his guts inside himself with both hands. The demon looked around frantically, seeing only his two other fallen comrades and the unbeatable human swordsman. He tried to spit curses at the frail, pink-skinned vomit-bag, but managed only a mouthful of his own life-blood. Kael showed no emotion and spoke no word as he stepped forward and cut the demon's head cleanly from his shoulders.

Kael stood unmoving for long moments, covered entirely in demon blood. He watched unblinking as the Midnight Blade absorbed the ichor that covered it. The green life-blood of the three massive demons seemed to evaporate in the hot, afternoon sun. Kael knew better than that, though. The weapon was replenishing its power by the absorption. He watched blankly as the demon-blood on his own arms, chest, and legs crept up his body onto his arms, slid over the sword's hilt and disappeared into the void-colored blade.

Kael gave it no more thought as he sheathed the jagged sword, drew one of the fallen demon's curved dirks, and set to work skinning the enormous bodies. In less than two hours three vast demon skins lay staked to the ground drying. Kael tied one last knot in the ligament he held and slipped a new tusk-belt over his head. He now wore seven such belts, each containing over seventy tusks from twenty-five fallen enemies: demon and devil alike. The blonde scalp of the WindBearer still adorned his kilt seam, but now, twelve more scalps, all black and all demonic, lined his weapon's ornate, golden scabbard.

Kael looked down at the dirk he had used to skin the figures. It was almost a foot long and slightly curved. The handle, now covered by demon-skin, was just over one of Kael's hands-breadth. The hilt and pommel were small cylinders. The blade itself was polished steel that gleamed like a mirror.

It was simple and Kael liked that. He scooped up its plain, black leather scabbard and tied it to his thigh, just under his tiger-striped kilt. The scabbard had only one symbol tooled on it and Kael knew not its value. With the imprinting of Gevurah, he had come to recognize nearly every rune and symbol he had seen, but not this one. He shrugged as he unstaked the demon hides, scooped them up easily, and headed back to his tower.

*

The inside of the upper quarters of Kael's tower, save the four windows, was covered with the skins of his defeated demon enemies. His large cloak and kilt lay on the simple cot near the northern window, as did the scalp-covered scabbard. The Midnight Blade hovered above the center opening in the floor, levitating at an angle, and spinning at mind-boggling speed. It appeared to be a florescent blue cone of energy, a line of red circling the bottom of the blurred motion.

Kael sat at one of the heavy, circular tables garbed in an open-chest jerkin and breeches of dark tan demon skin, spotted like the hide of a leopard, white sandals on his feet. He was poring over an immense tome of ancient knowledge. His eyes were glazed but responsive to the information his mind was absorbing. He had completed over ten such thousand-paged books in the past weeks. The ancient sword he wielded had opened the opportunity to him by not only teaching him to read, but to understand.

Kael stopped his studies for a moment, letting his eyes fall on the spinning figure of his weapon. It was the sword's motion that created the protecting barrier around the tower that allowed Kael his rest. It was Kael wielding the mystic weapon that allowed the sword to feed and grow in power.

Kael knew it was a deadly circle, but he didn't care. He knew he could never survive without the weapon, especially after he had slain so many demons. He wouldn't last a moment without this power. The thought of life without the weapon, in fact, had become an impossibility.

His mind wandered as his eyes fell back to the parchment. Kael had always been responsive to learning, even though he had never read anything before. He had quickly learned tracking, wrestling, and trapping from his father and uncles and had added to that knowledge with his own experiences, always improving on what he knew or learned from others.

This type of learning was somewhat different, but Kael gave it no less energy. He knew that it was the power of Gevurah that had opened his mental abilities, dispelling any physical blocks his brain held or any obstacles his heritage had imprinted on him. He had not yet learned the difference between the power called Gevurah and the separate identity of the Midnight Blade, and the weapon did not try to differentiate. Kael welcomed the change that the mystic sword offered. He felt that knowledge would help him dispel his natural tendency of fear or doubt. If he knew what faced him then he would know how to deal with it, be it fighting a demon or building a tower wall.

One thing that had bothered Kael was the lack of history contained within the tomes he perused. He had read of literature, masonry, weapon mastery, strategy, and above all, mathematics, but never of history. Kael's own people had lost much of their history, and what was known had been passed down mouth to mouth, father to son. That was why Kael had always been so curious about history. His people's story began with the defeat of their forefathers in battle against the demon hordes and ended with Kael. All he had ever known of them had always seemed more myth than substance. They had been mighty-thewed, god-like men wielding thunderous weapons and felling immortal beings with single blows; men that had not felled near enough of them, however. Thus the Kelt-Ra clan existed beneath the earth for centuries.

Another thing that puzzled Kael was the fact that he had never written or read before. Were the Kelt-Ra forefathers idiots? Had they no written language? Kael had proved that humans could learn and understand such concepts, albeit with the aide of his newfound weapon, so why hadn't his people formed their own written language or taught themselves a better way to live or anything else? Had the demons destroyed even the thought of hope with all else?

Kael dismissed the thought and dove back into his studies. His ancestors were gone, never to walk the earth again in any form. The present was his only concern now and how he could effectively empower himself.

If Kael could have, he would have considered such thinking absurd. He had always treasured his clan and family, above all else. Above that he had treasured Alique, but since he had buried her, he had not dwelt much on her, not even to grieve.

If Kael had been allowed to, he would have grieved incredibly, possibly endlessly.

If he had been allowed to.

*

Razikyl looked around himself, feeling quite confident. That is, at least, on the outside. The half-orc was garbed in his hardy black robe tooled with silver runes, and he wore black breeches and boots. He held a thick, wooden staff, inlaid with the same runes that covered his clothes. A sturdy deer hide pouch lay against his hip, the strap crossing his heavy chest. His hood was drawn and all that could be seen was his square jaw and pearly-toothed smile.

Standing at the lip of the Cave of Kings, housed far in the reaches of the Eastern Mountains, he was surrounded by twelve WindBearers. The orc was one of the few humanoids that actually stood taller than the winged warriors; regardless, they still looked upon him with disdain.

"You're a brave one, orc," Appollyon smiled, stepping through the circle of serious hunters, "or stupid. Either way you're a fish out of water."

"Perhaps, Bounty Master. Or perhaps I've come to claim a prize."

Appollyon raised an eyebrow at that, the WindBearers around him shuffling in curiosity.

"Speak plainly, orc," the cave master demanded, suddenly very serious. No mortal ventured into the Cave of Kings and lived long, especially not one with a bounty on his own head. "Have you come to claim your own hide?"

The surrounding WindBearers laughed, as did Appollyon, but Razikyl did not miss the larger figure's eyes: they burned with danger. Razikyl's courage nearly faltered at the venomous gaze, but the orc's spine held. He knew this was the most dangerous gamble of his life, but he couldn't back down.

"Laugh, fools!" Razikyl roared, spinning his hands and barking a quick mystical phrase. The glass and feather he had pulled from his sleeve's pockets flared open from his palms and lightening erupted from his outstretched digits. The powerful electricity surged and coursed through the dozen WindBearers, buckling them all to their knees in pain. The sheet of force spared only its enchanter and Appollyon.

The downed hunters were up in an instant, all drawing their red gleaming swords and ready to impale the foolish orc. Razikyl tensed for the attack, fully expecting his gamble to fail.

"Wait!" Appollyon yelled above the deluge of curses. No blade touched the sorcerer, though a few hovered mere inches from his throat. Razikyl breathed out slowly, glad that his bowels had held as well as his courage. "Why should I let you live, orc? What can you do to stop me from issuing another permit on your life right here and now?"

"This," Razikyl stated, starting to move his hand then stopping as twelve blade tips barely pricked his tender neck flesh.

Appollyon waved an impatient hand and nodded for the half-orc to continue. Razikyl straightened his robes as the WindBearers moved slowly back, never dropping their swords. With an exaggerated motion he placed his hand to his temple and, slowly, a tiny, glowing green orb of energy withdrew itself. He pinched the pulsing sphere between his thumb and forefinger, smiling at the reaction it drew. Every WindBearer's jaw dropped to his chest, Appollyon alone masking his disbelief.

"A permit, my friends. A permit for one human male."

"How did you get that?" Appollyon asked after a long silence.

"In the rubble of Hosampsich's tower after the human had defeated his two hunters."

Again there was a long silence. The WindBearers were humbled again by the thought of a human overcoming not one but two of their brothers—equals—in combat. Appollyon crossed his arms, one hand raised to stroke his chin in contemplation.

"You intend to claim the bounty," the cave master stated at last.

"The power of Gevurah is indeed immense," Razikyl admitted. "Yet…"

"Yet," Appollyon mocked disgustedly. "I have found in all my extensive travels that mortals, above all creatures, have more conditions and demands than any other race. Speak plainly, as I said to before, orc. My patience is not without limit."

"Of course," Razikyl agreed. This was playing out perfectly. "I am not such a fool to think that a permit will not be issued on me the instant I leave this place; whether to get the permit from my dying grip or to recover the might of the Midnight Blade itself should I defeat the human."

"You desire something surely, orc," the bounty master interrupted. "I doubt your graciousness reaches that high a level."

"Quite," the dark robed sorcerer agreed. "There is a price for my prize."

"Perhaps we tire of such games and of your life, orc," one of the WindBearers spat at this arrogant mortal. Instantly all eyes turned to this outspoken and rash warrior, eleven other blonde figures subtly backing a cautious step. Appollyon's eyes fell on the brash warrior like a physical assault. Razikyl secretly smiled at the smaller one's precarious situation.

"With...with a....with a permit, of course, dear bounty master," the shorter being stumbled, knowing full well he may have just put a price on his own head. After a very long minute of tense silence Appollyon's eyes calmed and the throng breathed easy again. Both Razikyl and the group of WindBearers knew that the smaller warrior had been instants from destruction; and who knew how many else would have been taken in the wake of the bounty master's fury?

"Your price, orc," Appollyon breathed patiently.

"An exchange, bounty master. I command the power of the Netsah easily. I would be willing to open this gate of power in exchange for a new opening for myself."

"Stupidity!" one of the WindBearers scoffed. "Who would be foolish enough to share any power with a mortal? Mortal flesh can barely contain the power of a single gate of power. Two would be suicide for you, orc. Besides, there are WindBearers already that have mastered the gate of Netsah."

"Not all," a taller winged one stepped forward to confront his brother. "Do you?" The former scowled, turned his back on his bolder twin, and folded his arms in a pout. The taller WindBearer turned to his companions, "Jehoel and Seraphiel were the closest to opening the might of the gate of Netsah, even fashioning weapons to more easily channel the power and see what happened to them. I say let this orc have his few moments of might. The life of one mortal is a small price for the power of the Netsah."

Razikyl was beaming on the inside. He now knew the names of the two that had fallen to him and the human. The orc had found their power of the Netsah wanting, but had been too worn out from his fight with the human to deflect their initial attack. That, plus their mastery over other power gates, had shown their superiority. Not over the human, though. The man's use of the Gevurah energy had either taken the two WindBearers by surprise or it had purely overpowered whatever might they had wielded.

Razikyl knew that all WindBearers inherently commanded the power of Hod, and that most could utilize portions of the Tif'eret and or the blessed Hessed. The orc would take a dewdrop of power from any three of those gates. He could use the Netsah and only that. It had made him more powerful than any other mortal dared dream, but it was no longer enough. More power was needed in order to accomplish what Razikyl intended; and what Razikyl intended was known by him alone.

Still, it would be a chancy maneuver. No man—human, orc, elven or any other—had been able to contain the power of more than one gate opening for countless centuries. Mortal skin and bone, for whatever reason, were just too frail. Razikyl, however, held knowledge gleaned from the memory of an eminent Demon Warlord. That, he felt, was his trump. In order for Razikyl to get what he wanted, though, the WindBearers would have to make him more powerful; and after the WindBearers received the orc's promise, they would be even more powerful than that. That probably sat better on the sorcerer's palate than on the WindBearers.

Still, power was a seductive mistress. Even the illusion of a glance from her could throw the humblest and chastest of beings into a lustful inner struggle of destruction. Hopefully, the orc thought as he looked at the hunters around him, it was happening right now.

"The orc's offer is valid," Appollyon stated, his eyes never lowering from their lock with Razikyl's. "At any time he could have substantially filled the permit he holds. Had he filled the license he would have benefited from the newfound knowledge that the human holds. Instead, he has come to my issue station to offer an exchange of not only one potential source of power—the human's—for one of yours, but his comparable own ability, as well.

"Any WindBearer that wishes may enter into a contract with the orc. I will take no action against either. Whoever accepts the rights of the permit will bring me the human's heart, hide, and testicles by the next face of Gabryl's chariot."

"Testicles, bounty master?" one of the WindBearers contorted his face in disgust. "They are so primitive."

"Primitive or not, I'll have them," Appollyon chuckled. "This human defeated the fabled Hosampsich. Whoever brings them to me will probably need a wagon."

The comment brought a roar of laughter from the cave lord, which in turn brought nervous chuckling from the dozen WindBearers. Razikyl wasn't laughing, however.

He just smiled.

*

Kael.

"What is it?" he whispered, still fully enveloped by the embrace of the night's slumber.

You have finished the tomes within my tower. What have you learned?

"Much," he returned slowly. His breath was still very heavy, his subconscious now reigning over his actions. "I have learned so very much."

Aye. Tactics, mathematics, and literature you now master. You are well on your way to becoming a master warrior-poet, by my designs.

"Warrior-poet," Kael repeated sleepily. "By my des...."

My *designs, mortal!*

The thought assaulted Kael like a thousand fists, his brain exploding in pain and anguish. Still, he remained asleep, the ego of the mystic blade manipulating him with careless ease. A slight trickle of blood trickled from his ear, trailing past his lobe to run through his long, blonde mane.

I am the architect of your power and entire existence! I am the reason you are not demon shit! Never forget that it is I you owe your life and soul to! You are less than a gnat! I am the power!

"You are the power!" Kael quickly agreed, turning over on his hard cot, his hands instinctively going to his face.

Good. It is good that you realize your fitting place on this tiny plane. You shall be my weapon of destruction. By my indomitable will and your necessary, meager physical abilities I will carve myself a sizeable niche in this world as I have in so many others.

"You will rule all," Kael submitted as the arcane weapon allowed him to fall even deeper into the void of sleep.

Indeed I will, my willful lackey. Indeed I will.

As Kael slept, the Midnight Blade intensified its air-warping spinning above the hole in the tower floor, the hellish blue glow turning now to a red color that few had ever witnessed. The red of the sword matched the fiery blood color of the gleaming, slant-eyed jewels at the weapon's hilt. Faster, faster, and faster the Midnight Blade spun, an uneasy hum emitting from the surrounding heated air molecules.

Sleep and let me continue to open the most blessed of powers within you. Every night as you sleep I shall make you more and more powerful. Powerful enough to properly wield me and overcome all that may stand before me.

Slowly and carefully, the sword surged through Kael's brain and opened areas long closed by more than a millennium of physical adaptation, terrestrial evolution, and another thousand natural barriers between the soul and the body. Neuron by neuron, impulse by impulse, the weapon redirected and recreated new pathways for the energy within the human's brain and body to flow.

The weapon wished it had access to the proper technology so that it could create the pawn it needed immediately. Alas, such technology no longer existed, if it ever had on this plane. The end result would be the same, however. When the weapon was done, the human would be the ultimate slaying machine. The power and strength of the very earth he stood on would be in his limbs. Strength that none would be able to stand against would be his to command.

That is, if the sword told him to command it.

Kael slept on, unaware of the manipulations being forced upon him. A familiar emptiness filled an exact section of his brain, as it also filled his entire left arm, tingling with a sensation beyond anything any other mortal could know.

As he slept, he dreamed a dream of glory and power; and of conquest.

*

Razikyl stood up from his campfire at the base of the mountain that housed the Cave of Kings. Turning, he faced the WindBearer that lighted silently before him. The winged warrior was one of the largest the orc had ever seen, looking the gigantic sorcerer square in the eye. He wore the same white silk kilt and white leather sandals as the others, the same large, red steel broadsword sheathed at his left hip.

"I have decided to accept your offer, orc," the WindBearer stated simply, crossing his arms and standing confidently. Razikyl grinned at the figure. Earlier he had magically scanned the powers of the throng of WindBearers the best he could and pegged this one as the second most powerful—and the most dim-witted.

"You're a brave one," Razikyl smiled, "or is it more?" The sorcerer did enjoy tormenting the supposed higher beings.

"Aye," the WindBearer nodded, not catching the orc's sarcasm. "I am the only one brave enough to risk gaining the might of Gevurah."

Or stupid enough, Razikyl did not say.

"I am Soged Hozi, orc," the winged one continued arrogantly, looking around casually, trying futilely to exhume a sense of disinterest and superiority. He leveled his eyes directly with Razikyl's. "Are you prepared, mortal? Are you prepared to witness levels of power you can scarcely comprehend?"

"Witness," Razikyl growled back, stepping up to stare menacingly at the WindBearer. He puffed out his chest and lowered his straight jaw. "And revel in."

Soged Hozi didn't back down any, but neither did he encourage the orc any further. The sorcerer was a large being, even larger than Soged Hozi himself, and his Netsah was not a power to be taken lightly. It was that very reason that the WindBearer would brave this test. Both wanted something the other had.

Soged Hozi was determined that he, at the very least, would get what he wanted.

"Do you know what must be done, orc?" the lithe-muscled winged warrior asked.

"I think I'll catch on," Razikyl snapped back. He knew how to transfer his power, at least theoretically. Hopefully, the other gates could be opened similarly.

Soged Hozi grinned as he reached out to grasp Razikyl above the hips.

"The basis of a WindBearer's power is set in the energy gate dubbed Tif'eret, orc. From there he can effectively draw through and across two of the power triads, linking his innate powers of the Hessed and the Hod."

Razikyl nodded patiently. He knew this already. His power of Netsah shared a leg of one of the power triads with Hod. The orc would have preferred the opening of that gate, but would never let the winged one know that. The ability of the Tif'eret would allow him to branch into an entirely new triad and, hopefully, with the years of knowledge received from Hosampsich, expand from there.

"Netsah," Razikyl stated plainly as he reached down to wrap his enormous hands around the WindBearers right thigh. Even though the warrior's leg was well muscled, the gigantic orc easily circumvented it. He didn't have to explain the power of the gate to the winged one, nor would he have if he had been asked.

The two stood for long moments, Soged Hozi still grasping Razikyl's lower ribs, the orc's hands surrounding the WindBearer's thigh. Each was concentrating to make a connection through the other's body and, in turn, with the corresponding area of the other's brain. They focused mightily to create a bond in the other like they had in themselves.

Each knew that it was at this point that each was at his most vulnerable. At any point either could manipulate the gate within the other's body to try and steal the other's very life essence. It was exactly what each wanted to do to the other, but knew that if he did he would not benefit. One could not steal the knowledge of a gate from another. It could only be given and, even then, it was never a guarantee.

It was that point that had nearly held Razikyl from entering the coupling. It was very possible that he could open the WindBearer's Netsah and end up with nothing in return regardless of the winged one's intentions.

Suddenly Soged Hozi pushed Razikyl away roughly, the orc nearly toppling to the ground as a dizziness he had never felt before assailed him viciously. The WindBearer, too, stumbled back, leaning heavily against one of the monstrous boulders that made up the mountain's rocky base.

"Damn you, cursed hunter!" Razikyl roared, reaching into his robe sleeves to pull the proper components for a devastating attack on the WindBearer. "You'll pay with your life for what you've done!"

"Hold!" Soged yelled back, unable to stand to even defend himself from the sorcerer's impending attack. "It has worked! We have opened the gates within each other!"

Razikyl held the sulfur in his hand gingerly, unsure whether to just destroy the lying bastard if he could or sort through his clouded thoughts. The moment of indecision was just enough to hit the orc full with realization: the WindBearer was right!

"Could it be?" Razikyl asked himself aloud. When he had discovered the power of Netsah within himself it had been much different. It had been more of a mistake than anything else. He had been a shaman's son in his tribe, hundreds of miles to the west of here. His father had recognized his son's inherit power and nurtured open the gate using herbs and countless days of hunger-induced meditation. That had opened the gate. When a horde of demons had come to loot his tribe's lands and his father's life, rage enlarged that opening. From deep inside himself and with the help of mind-altering plants, Razikyl had loosed hellish power from his soul to rain down on the demonic hunters. He had managed to turn back and defeat the unsuspecting attackers, but not before nearly all of his tribe had been killed or carried away.

His tribe, fearing him as He-With-the-Power-of-Demons, exiled him, set fire to their ancient homeland, and set out for unknown lands to the west. Razikyl fled to the east, following the demon's retreat, hoping that within their midst he could find a place for himself with his newfound powers. Here Hosampsich had found him.

"Orc?" Soged Hozi prompted, drawing Razikyl back to reality. "I feel your work within me. You were successful. I now can utilize the power of Netsah, as you do."

"And the Tif'eret, WindBearer," Razikyl nodded back, his own arms pulled tightly against his own abdomen. The sorcerer could feel the tingling emptiness that accompanied the opening of a gate of power. With the Netsah, it was the right leg that was the physical complement that grounded the mystic energies. Every gate corresponded to an area of the body, a humanoid figure the perfect antenna for the arcane power of the soul.

Razikyl looked up at the WindBearer cautiously. The angelic being was regarding the orc coolly, seeming to be fully recovered from the coupling. Did the hunter expect Razikyl to reveal all the secrets of the Netsah? His part of the bargain had been to open the gate alone, no more. He had not expected any more than that for himself.

"No, orc," Soged Hozi smiled, seeming to read Razikyl's very thoughts. "The permit is all the more that I ask."

Razikyl nodded, slowly putting a finger to his right temple. The glowing, green orb housed there pulsated and then fell into his enormous hand. He looked at the marble-shaped object for long moments, prompting Soged Hozi to drop a hand to his sword.

"Here," Razikyl tossed the permit to Soged Hozi's outstretched hand. The WindBearer snatched the glowing orb and touched it to his temple without a second glance. The tiny sphere disappeared into his skull. The hunter stretched out his wings to rise back to the Cave of Kings.

"Wait," Razikyl managed, standing shakily on waveringly legs. The emptiness within his stomach was growing. It was not a pleasing sensation, but the end results, the sorcerer knew, would be. Dizziness began to assail him like an endless wave of ocean water.

"Aye, orc," Soged Hozi grinned, lifting into the air with a graceful flap of his gigantic downy wings. "When I begin the hunt for the human, you may come."

Razikyl tried to grin but could only gasp for air as darkness struck him to his knees. He lurched forward to the ground, his final conscious thought of Kael impaled on the Midnight Blade in the hands of Razikyl the Mighty.

*

Kael was at the edge of slumber and wakening, teetering between the two surreal worlds. The Midnight Blade's constant spinning hummed lonely within the reaches of the tower. The walls and windows were now completely covered with the heavy, tanned hides of many various-colored demons. Monstrous scalps lined not only Kael's golden sheath but the many granite tables arcing around the room's circumference.

The peerless sword had spent the waning summer night as it had all of them: reaching into the depths of Kael's mind and opening the powerful link between his physical mass and spiritual essence. The weapon had also used his abilities for other needs. He had enhanced the areas within the human's brain to stimulate learning, and with startling results. Kael had taken to the tomes with a hunger of his own design; and he had retained a startling amount of the knowledge. It didn't matter that much of the information within the books was propaganda to ensure the blade's ends. What mattered was that the human was a willing sponge to information.

That intelligence, so uncommon with the frail humans, coupled with a remarkable physical prowess, made Kael a fine wielder for the ancient artifact. Despite the human's intelligence, he made a much easier tool to manipulate than the demons and other higher beings that had wielded the sword in the past. WindBearers, bounty hunters, demons, and their like naturally had resistances to the sword's sort of subtle persuasions. The weapon could communicate openly with the higher beings, but could overtly control only a small sliver, a sliver that the blade wanted nothing to do with unless it was to consume their flesh and blood.

It was that very sliver, and their mightier kin, above which the Midnight Blade looked to raise the human, and itself. After it had empowered Kael as much as it could, and folded his brain neatly into its figurative pocket, woe the being to stand before the awful might of Gevurah.

*

Kael heard his name called but could do little to respond to it. His mind let him believe that he had half-lifted his eyelids to try to discern where the sound had come from. The tower room seemed a hazy dream, unsubstantial to his foggy perception. He seemed to stand, teetering on collapse for a long instant, then regaining his spinning equilibrium. The four grand windows were covered by heavy demon hide, masking the outside world. Kael seemed to step to the eastern window, his hand unusually shaky as it reached to push the orange leather curtain aside.

In the east stood Hosampsich's ridge, where the tower had previously stood, and the mountains, a soft, sky-melding blue rising behind them. The sun was an hour at the most from cresting, already lending its aura to the infant morning. A heavy bank of clouds covered the sky, slowly pushing its stormy way to the western wastelands and beyond. In its wake it had left the terrain drenched and muddy. Electricity coursed around the heavy cloud cover, seeming to want to emerge and ravage the foolish earth below; but something held that vast force to the fluffy blackness. Bolts and sheets of energy swooped down to destroy, only to be sucked back up by whatever master guided the motion of the rolling nature.

Kael looked down, seeing enormous, dark scorched patches dotting the grassy hills, dwindling embers smoking harmlessly at the edges of the blackened circles. Evidently the energy did manage to escape its master occasionally, bringing death in its wake to the unprotected land below. Down by the creek far below the hill on which the tower sat, a single tree stood blazing. It had been struck by the energy from above and split evenly in half. One side remained normal, continuing its uncaring green life; the other half lay torn to the ground, blistered and blazing, sure to bring the rest of itself to this dark end.

There again, Kael thought he heard his name.

"Gevurah?" he whispered, the words barely spilling over his questioning lips. It wasn't the voice of the mighty Midnight Blade that had called him. He heard those words only across his mind. This sound had been caught by his ears.

The ancient sword did not react. It continued its methodical spinning, the underlying hum nearly maddening in its consistency. Kael looked around the dark room. Perhaps someone had penetrated the defenses of the sword and entered the tower room. It seemed impossible to the warrior that anything could do that, but he could rule nothing out.

"Show yourself," he hissed, again barely making the words audible. He felt a twinge of fear shudder up and down his spine in the form of a hair-raising tingle. He considered calling his weapon to his hand to steel his courage and then tearing the room apart, but didn't. Something within himself told him that this was not something to fear. This was not something to defeat or destroy.

Suddenly a form appeared before him, hovering near the cot from which had just risen. It was the figure of a beautiful woman. She was fit and perfectly built to Kael's eyes. Her hair was a sun-streaked auburn that flowed like a lion's mane around her exotic, perfect face and down her smooth back. She was facing upward, eyes closed, her arms lifted slightly, hands upturned.

Kael was struck dumbfounded by the unparalleled figure hovering like a dream before him. She was impossibly familiar to him!

"Who…" he started to breathe when she opened her eyes and looked straight at—no, straight into him. Coldness flooded his veins, a familiar, cowardly emptiness opening in his stomach and bowels. His knees nearly buckled as the beautiful, ghostly image floated forward to him, her eyes never leaving his. He tried desperately to move, to look away, to try to reach out for his sword, but nothing would answer his fearful brain's plea.

His teeth clenched and neck tightened painfully. His fists balled uselessly at his side as his fear enveloped him completely. If only he could grasp the Midnight Blade then his courage would return, his power would return. He knew it. Kael was reminded for the thousandth time that without the sword he was helpless. Try as he might, though, the blade did not answer his summons. Perhaps, he thought, the weapon had forsaken him. Perhaps it had seen enough of what lay beneath Kael's soft heart, had seen that he was nothing but a worm in the guise of a man. Perhaps Kael's subconscious knew he was unworthy of the sword's power and strove to undermine his brain.

Kael heard his name again, knowing full well it was the spirit before him that beckoned. He looked up at the amazing figure hovering before him and suddenly felt a tug of recognition at the gorgeous image. Suddenly warmth flooded over the cool fear that had frozen his limbs and mind. He relaxed at the feeling, accepting it as what was surely to be the last sensation he would ever have.

No, the woman-figure mouthed. I need you, Kael.

"What," Kael mouthed back. "Who are you?" Try as he might, he could not recall the figure. Had he known her once? Long ago, perhaps? Why would she come to him even if he did know her? Didn't she see his fear?

Only you can help me, Kael, the woman-figure mouthed. I need you.

Kael dropped his head into his hands, fighting to remember who this was. What was it that he was forgetting? Why did she need him? The effort to remember turned to frustration, which in turn broke into fury and rage. Kael seethed at his failure to remember something that seemed so damned important!

"No," he hissed venomously. He would not be made a fool of by this torturous phantom. He swiped out at the figure with a powerful arm, his blow sailing through the figure. The woman puffed into nothingness as Kael's arm swept through it.

I need you, Kael, the voice remained distantly. Kael dropped to his knees, his hands covering his unwilling ears. The voice sounded one last time, nearly gone, as it wafted back into etherealness.

Kael, I need you.

"No," he finally managed to roar, coming fully awake. He reached out toward the spinning weapon in the tower's center and willed it into his hand. The gate of power within his mind and soul erupted volcanically, painfully. The emptiness flooded his left arm and right brain, power swelled in his limbs achingly.

What is it, Kael? The sword demanded, responding as if awakened from a fitful night's slumber. *What has penetrated my inescapable eye?*

Kael breathed heavily, energy coursing through his body ready to be expelled and destroy any who dared stand before him. Long moments stretched uneasily as he realized it was gone. Whatever it had been, either phantom or thought, it was gone.

Kael held up his sword, willing it back to its spinning in the center of the tower room. The weapon pushed away the human's odd actions. Humans were unstable as a race, usually undependable. Surely this was some sort of reaction to a pitiful delusion, or perhaps a dream. Odd that those very traits were what made the human such an effective tool.

Kael stood unmoving for long moments, trying to recover what was left of his wits. He walked slowly back over to the eastern window, again drawing the hide aside. The virgin day dawned before his squinting eyes as he sat at the vast window's ledge.

The Midnight Blade hadn't seen the phantom. The weapon hadn't even sensed her existence, either through its own faculties or Kael's.

Kael sighed heavily as he fought to understand what had just happened. Obviously whatever power the spirit had, it was concealed from the weapon. Kael had thought the power of the sword peerless. For the first time he was unsettled by the prospect of wielding the powerful weapon. If this spirit held some sort of power apart or over the Midnight Blade, then surely other beings did.

Kael considered this new information for some time as the dawning sun flooded the muddy aftermath of the storm from the night before, helping to dry the world turned to water.

*

Razikyl stood at the lip of the Cave of Kings, looking around at the panoramic scenery that surrounded the immense mountain. The surrounding mountains were majestic to the orc's eyes, bathed as they were in the light of the late summer day's sun. Most of the behemoths were completely covered by towering pine trees; here and there ran a finger of transparent spring water, pooling far below and gradually making their collective way to the grassy hills of the west.

It was to the west that the orc looked next. That was the only direction that wasn't mountainous, breaking easily into deep coulees and rugged hills. The terrain to the west was nowhere near as high, but far rougher. That had been the main reason so many human tribes had lived for so long out of sight from their demonic hunters.

Now there was only one known human left in that area, and though he was now equipped and accustomed to fending off the attacks of the usual demonic predators, a new breed of hunter was taking up the scent.

The sorcerer checked his garb carefully, more suited now to battle than his usual black, stitched robe. He wore a thick, sleeveless, black leather jerkin and pants. Over that he wore a many-pocketed kilt, thousands of runes tooled subtly over its knee-length expanse. Thick, black, leather traveling boots rose to his knees, both housing a double-handful of throwing darts. Two full pouches crisscrossed his torso, both tied down firmly at each hip to his belt. The purses were ornately tooled, as well, leather tassels decorating every seam. At his hips and attached to his thighs were two short, curving dirks. Both were powerfully enchanted weapons, virgin elf-skin leather covering the handles; and instead of a crosspiece, between the handle and blade was a thick round jewel of obsidian carved in the shape of a rune unknown to most that walked the earth. On his shoulders was his heavy leather cloak, the hood unusually drawn back. The existence of anything within the depths of his cloak was knowledge held by Razikyl alone.

On the cliff edge that was the lip of the Cave of Kings were four other hunters, all WindBearers, garbed as they usually were: silken kilts, sandals, and golden-sheathed broadswords. They were milling impatiently, eager to begin this day's adventure, but stood waiting at the beck of one too powerful to deny: Appollyon.

Razikyl kept a distance from the four WindBearers, Soged Hozi among them, as he always did. This morning was the first time he had seen any of them in the two days since he and Soged Hozi had reciprocated each other's power needs. In that short time the sorcerer had made little progress expanding the opening of Tif'eret within himself, even though he hoped to soon be able to wield it as effectively as he did the Netsah. He knew he was far from accomplishing that, but one should always be optimistic. It had taken many years and the helping hand of a powerful demon for him to enlarge the gate of Netsah so far. It would not be so difficult with this newly opened gate, but in the end, time was the determining factor.

Razikyl had not actually expected Soged Hozi to come for him when the hunt was to begin, even though the WindBearer had promised. They had both received more than they had ever reasonably expected from each other from their brief coupling. Obviously, Hozi was not as confident in his ability to take the human as he had been the days before, or perhaps the orc was reading into it too much. For all he knew, this was merely a gloating trip, Soged Hozi rubbing Razikyl's face in the fact that he was about to become the alpha dog in the WindBearer ranks with his acquisition of the Midnight Blade.

The sorcerer's garb did seem to betray this possibility, though. He was dressed for battle. Regardless of what any other expected or did, Razikyl always prepared himself for the absolute worst of possibilities.

"What do we wait for, Soged Hozi?" Razikyl asked after long minutes, tiring of the WindBearers glances over at him and their condescending smirks. The sorcerer was about to comment when the massive figure of Appollyon emerged from the Cave of Kings.

"Well, boys," the bounty master boomed, his deep baritone carrying down the mountainside. "Are we looking for blood this afternoon, or is this merely a preemptive strike?" Razikyl raised his eyebrow at that. Was this to be Soged's first look at the human? Perhaps the WindBearer had spent his time discovering his newfound powers, as the orc had. Razikyl hoped not. He wasn't sure how much he wanted Hozi to know about those newfound powers.

"A scouting mission, bounty master," Soged Hozi replied with a nod. "If all goes well, we may bring back the human's hide."

"Hopefully for you it does go well," Appollyon leveled at the shorter being. "Gabryl's chariot nears full, and you have yet to utilize your permit."

"I've a week until Gabryl opens his full luminance. More than enough time to collect this bounty and my much sought prize."

Appollyon shrugged, then nodded casually. Truth be known, he really didn't care one way or the other.

"Still," the bounty master returned. "I will see that you collect the prize as benefits the honor of a hunter." The enormous being turned and motioned toward the cave entrance. A tall, thick-muscled WindBearer walked out of the Cave of Kings to stand beside Appollyon.

"Jehoel," Razikyl hissed. He instinctively drew his cloak around himself, filling his hands with the proper components to blow the face clean off of this mountain, if need be.

"You recognize him, then," Appollyon chuckled at the orc's actions. Both knew what had happened in the Tower of Hosampsich.

"What is this about?" Soged Hozi nearly whined. "Five is the maximum number of a hunting party. I have chosen the orc to accompany me, not your puppet."

Jehoel started at that comment, but halted as a nagging voice in the back of his mind that was Appollyon's reminded him of his place.

"Jehoel shall be my eyes and nothing else. I wish to view the action as it unfolds, not just hear its ridiculous retelling later."

Soged Hozi wanted to protest, but knew better. He didn't care if anyone came to watch his victory but the permit had been Jehoel's originally. Who knew what the bastard would do once the battle commenced?

Razikyl was wary of the party's newest member, as well. He inherently distrusted the higher beings, especially ones that had once used him as a target. The orc knew that he was nearly in over his head with this situation, but he shrugged away the possibility of running. He would see it through regardless of the consequences. That was his way.

"Gang's all here, then," Appollyon laughed, nudging Jehoel out to join the hunting party. The five WindBearers opened out their massive dove-like wings, settling a steadying hand on their broadswords. All eyes turned to Razikyl.

"You did know that we would be flying, didn't you, orc?" Soged Hozi asked innocently, all of their eyes a dam to a flood of laughter.

As an answer Razikyl grabbed the edges of his leather cloak and began to rise into the air. He willed himself to hover some four feet above the ground, the slight breeze rippling the bottom of his cloak about his ankles.

"I'll try my best to keep up, O Mighty Hunter."

Soged Hozi's face blazed red as the throng chuckled at his expense. Appollyon added to the fire with his own grating roar of mirth. With a scowling pout, the lead hunter rose into the sky, the other four WindBearers quickly following.

"Best to hurry, Razikyl." Appollyon commented, regarding the orc with an interesting gaze, as if reading the sorcerer's mind. Razikyl shared the bounty master's gaze evenly for a few scant moments, not fully sure what was being communicated, if anything, then nodded and rose into the sky behind the speeding hunters.

*

The demon Jeqon brought down his spiked mace, barely missing his intended target. His shorter and frailer opponent retaliated swiftly, bringing his enormous, jagged, three-handed sword up in a sky-splitting arc. Jeqon was just able to block the speeding blow with the gigantic dragon bone shield attached to his left forearm. The heavy shield shuddered from the power of the human's attack, magic older than the wyrm vertebrae nearly unbinding its protection.

Jeqon shook his head and narrowed his eyes as the two broke apart for the first time. The demon had rarely seen this much power housed in any being, let alone in any sort of mortal. Regardless of that, the demon knew he would defeat this puny human. The power of the energy gate Gevurah would soon be all his.

Kael assessed his demonic opponent carefully. They had fought for nearly five minutes and his sword had not suggested any weakness in the demon's attack. He assumed that the Midnight Blade was testing him, allowing him to control the power within the weapon and himself on his own. It was wracking his nerves to think that the weapon would let him face anything like this on his own, but he had to admit, he was doing well. The demon's attack had been furious and brutal, but Kael had met every strike, parried every thrust. He had even managed to counterstrike a few times, twice opening cuts on the demon's sides. Still, those wounds were superficial at best, nothing that would slow the gigantic monster.

"Have you had enough yet, miserable human?" Jeqon blustered, circling slowly around Kael. "Give me the sword and I will kill you before I eat you. You'll not find a fairer bargain than that."

Kael snarled and launched forward without warning, taking the offensive himself for the first time. He brought his blade chopping down on the seven-foot demon. Jeqon raised his dragon bone shield to easily block the expected blow. The red-skinned demon swiped wide, horizontally, with his massive spike-headed mace to crush Kael's ribcage to mush.

Kael reacted faster than the demon could possibly believe. Rather than following through with his overhead chop that was sure to be caught by the dragon bone shield, Kael brought his hands straight down, swinging his sword vertically to meet the rushing mace's strike. The jagged blade caught the oversized mace just below the massive head and just above the demon's thick hand. Kael willed open the gate of power within himself, amplifying the ingrained power of the sword. The Midnight Blade shown fierce blue as the emptiness coursed through Kael's left arm. Jeqon recognized the glow of the power he was fighting to steal but could do nothing to slow his sweeping strike. The Midnight Blade cut easily through the mace's handle, Kael ducking as inertia carried the beheaded spiked head past his own.

Jeqon gasped, throwing the useless handle at Kael and pushing himself away from the conflict. He opened his gigantic black bat wings and began to rise off of the ground with a mighty flap, pulling the dragon bone shield before him with both hands to fend off the human.

"Not a chance," Kael grunted, lunging forward easily to close the distance. The power of Gevurah coursed through his muscles. He brought the Midnight Blade up in an arcing chop, this time with every intent of following through with the attack. Jeqon braced himself for the strike, his wings not yet carrying him out of danger's path. The enchanted shield had held back every other strike the demon had faced before. Surely this time would be no different.

This time was different.

Kael brought his jagged weapon down and through the enormous buckler with a primal roar. With the Gevurah energy saturating his mighty thews, the shield and the demon's thick, flat skull exploded with a sickening splatter, the Midnight Blade passing through Jeqon's brains and body, carrying the demon's guts out with it through his posterior.

The two separate but equal halves of the demon looked stunned for an instant, then looked no more. They fell to the ground to twitch nervously for a few seconds, then fell still as Kael silently regarded them.

Kael wasn't even breathing heavily, considering what he had just accomplished. His weapon had allowed him to control the power within his own body, as well as the power of the Midnight Blade itself, and with exceptional results. A thick sense of pride swelled his chest as he considered it. He was becoming more than just the spineless, sniveling coward he considered himself to have been so many months before, hiding beneath the ground from the hordes of monsters above. There was real power within him now. Was it possible that this power in his limbs was separate from the power of the Midnight Blade itself? Could he dare to hope that he could accomplish such feats even without his peerless weapon?

Kael pushed the thoughts from his mind. He couldn't consider life without the feel of his blade in his callused hands. Regardless of what he could ever do on his own or for himself he could never abandon the dark, jagged sword. It had allowed him to become what he was and Kael, ever the loyal fool, would never betray that gift.

Kael scalped the demon's tangled brown mane and strapped it to his golden scabbard. He adjusted the new shirt he had made for himself as he sheathed his sword. It was a sleeveless garment that he had constructed: a shirt of demon tusks, sewn together tightly and in two layers to make a heavily protected armor mail, much like the chainmail about which he had read. The tusks all lay curled outward, away from his body. A similar tusk mail skirt lay over his tiger-striped demon kilt, as well. The only other material on the tusk-mail was soft elk leather at the armpits to protect his under arms from the bite of the many vicious points. He had inscribed each of the pinky-sized tusks with protective runes that he had found in one of the books in the tower and connected them with triple-bound demon ligament. The shirt had proved its worth many times over, turning death blows aside to the amazement of many a now-dead demon.

Kael wished he had brought his tiger-striped cloak. The hot afternoon sun beat unmercifully on him. The summer was waning and the days were making up for their coolness earlier in the year. Kael shrugged it away, placed a steadying hand on his sword's handle, and began to run the five-mile distance back to his protective tower.

As he made his way across the grassy, rolling hills, many eyes followed his progress. Some were the eyes of the hunted. Some were the eyes of the hunter.

All were the eyes of death.

*

"The human is formidable," Soged Hozi breathed, unable to mask the surprise in his quiet voice and unable to drag his eyes from the receding form of Kael. Razikyl chuckled. The WindBearer might as well admit he had no clue what the hell they were facing. That lone comment said volumes about not only this hunter, but all of his brethren. If they knew so little about the gate of Gevurah, how much did they know about their own gates of power? And if they knew so little about that, then truly, how formidable were WindBearers? Razikyl's smile turned deathly serious at that thought. This expedition might prove to be more profitable than he had intended.

"We need to view the human in action more," Soged nodded to the others in the party as he turned to face them. "We need to plan well for this one. Casualties may by dear."

Sure, Razikyl scoffed to himself. To us maybe, not you. The orc glanced around at the other WindBearers who were nodding stupidly to their hunting leader with much enthusiasm. The sorcerer just sighed. Gods, he thought. If he wasn't careful, he would share the grave with this band of idiots.

"What do you think, orc?" Soged Hozi asked.

"I think that you'll come up with an excellent plan."

The hunting leader nodded at that and turned to watch Kael crest the far southern hills. Soged Hozi was sure that he would wield the power of Gevurah by the end of the next day.

*

Imamiah nearly rolled in laughter at the situation below him. From his vantage he could see the inept WindBearers and their orc plaything carry on their pitiful game. He stood on a high gumbo ridge far to the north of the human's tower and well above his adversaries below. With his ability to hide his aura, he was easily safe from any attack, unexpected or otherwise.

Imamiah turned from the crest of the ridge and sat thinking with his chin in his hands. Surely there was some way to turn this fortunate turn of events to play into his hands.

"Surely," he smiled, turning onto his stomach and inching again to the edge of the ridge. The lead hunter was now barking orders heatedly, his comrades nodding their heads emphatically and wringing their sword handles. Except for the dark garbed orc. He stood away from the others a pace, leaning lazily against a nearby tree.

Imamiah chuckled at that: a mortal after his own heart. The orc had his own agenda; that much was obvious. The lead hunter did as well, the tusk-covered, half-breed devil suspected. Surely, given the little games the WindBearers liked to play in the name of honor, he had a permit from the bounty master at the Cave of Kings. If Imamiah remembered correctly, the bounty master there was still Appollyon. The devil nearly shuddered at the thought of that one. Appollyon had fled from the heat of the Endless Battles to the North years ago and taken root in the towering mountains to the east. Imamiah understood why. He himself hadn't been to the Endless Battle in the North for nearly two hundred years and had barely survived the short time he had spent there.

The Gevurah power would change that, however. All he had to do was find the right tools and couple that with a little self-made opportunity. Then, he would make these hills his own completely, and to hell with the other demons and angels that trod here.

Perhaps, he thought, even Appollyon could be brought to heel under the might of Gevurah. That thought made Imamiah smile immensely.

Imamiah looked below and saw the five WindBearers lift into the air, as did the orc (obviously a sorcerer), and fly off towards the south.

"So," the devil grinned, standing up slowly, opening his monstrous bat-like wings with a flourish. "Opportunity presents itself, I see."

Imamiah rose easily into the sky and followed the hunting party from high above, laughing the entire time.

*

Kael leaned heavily on the sill of the northern tower window. To the east, late summer rain showers hung protectively over the towering mountains, masking their majesty. The surrounding rolling hills and breaks that Kael considered under his protection were still heavy with grass and wildlife. He knew that the leaves were nearly a full moon away from falling to the approaching season; the foliage was dark green and lush. He had spotted a small herd of twenty deer picking their way carefully through the creek bottom, grazing at their leisure.

The wildlife in these lands had never been greatly diminished, even with so many demons and other predators around. Kael suspected that the higher beings fed only on humans, goblins, and other bipedal creatures. Never had he seen a demon attack or hunt any of the deer, elk, or other creatures. Even the bears, mountain lions, and badgers, hunters themselves, seemed to be free of the demons' attention.

Often Kael had wished he had been a wild cat, an elk, a snake, anything to get out from under the eye of the demon Hosampsich and his murdering horde. He had spent many nights at the tunnel entrance watching the animals make their way past, playing out their eternal circle of life, uncaring of anything other than survival.

In a way, Kael thought, he had been just like the deer. Both did whatever it took to keep from being eaten by their hunter, at the same time trying to forage a life for their selves.

"Not now," Kael whispered to himself, pulling an enormous bison hide tighter around himself to defeat the mid-morning chill.

Now he was the hunter, not the hunted. With the power of Gevurah he had become a creature that demons feared. The hides of nearly forty lined the room now, tanned, cured, and tacked up as trophies. That same number of scalps lined the golden scabbard.

Surveying the countryside below, Kael's mind drifted back to the image of the beautiful woman in his dream. Somehow he knew that he should know her, but he could not place her. Her beauty was intoxicating, her form alone raising the lust deep in his heart. He longed for her to become tangible so that he could take her into his arms and rain his passion down on her.

Blood flushed his checks and neck as he recalled her image in his mind's eye. She came to him every night now, calling for him to help her, somehow, to help her. At first he was confused, even frightened by her, but no longer. She was a pleading spirit that came to his bedside every night. It was now the one thing he looked forward to every night: to drift off to sleep, and see the enchanting ghost of a woman he was supposed to know.

For the past two months she had come to him, and not once did the Midnight Blade mention it. Kael considered it odd that the weapon, which could so easily lay bare the thoughts of his mind, couldn't see the vision as well. Odder still was the fact that afterward, Kael's lingering thoughts of the woman were also free of the sword's prying grip.

Kael had found much within his own mind that he could now keep hidden from the ancient weapon. When he had first begun to wield it, the sword could nearly jerk Kael's limbs along like a puppet's. The weapon had shown him the grand possibility of overthrowing the demon claws that gripped this land and making it free for anyone, possibly other humans if they existed. It was a possibility that Kael had embraced eagerly, throwing himself to the sword's designs.

Kael still held those thoughts and possibilities, but now that he had recovered so much of his free will and independence again he considered the blade's "words" carefully.

In the tomes that he had read within the tower, he knew that there were more demons in the land than blades of grass. Even further to the north, beyond the skyline's skyline, was an endless battle, he had read. It was a battle where the land and the very sky were filled with demons, WindBearers, and other creatures he had never heard of. In this endless battle, a thousand million beings fought for a supremacy that was impossible to attain.

Kael recalled a similar vision long ago that his sword had surely given to him. It was a vision where Kael drew the Midnight Blade and brought all the teeming, warring masses to heel, ruling them as a god-king.

The thought of it now nearly made him laugh. He had considered it before, but now, never. He had his hands full handling one demon at a time, let alone an army of them. Perhaps that grounding reality was what had regained for him much of his mental control. Perhaps the weapon had forsaken him and was now waiting for him to face an opponent that was worthy of wielding the ancient artifact.

Kael sighed, looking again to the north, still damp from the cloudbursts now raging to the east. He was tired of thinking about any hidden agenda that might spell his death, whether it by an ancient artifact, a beautiful ghost, or some blasted demon. He had survived longer than he had ever expected to in this world and wouldn't hide in fear as he had for so many years.

Kael knew that fear and apprehension still gripped his heart and soul, but he also knew that he could fight. He wasn't the same shit-covered fool that had cowered helplessly before the might of the demon hunters barely two moons ago; nor was he the same base coward that had stolen the might of Gevurah and ran Hosampsich through, a puppet to the will of the sword.

But neither was Kael the hero he wished to be. He knew he couldn't carve a safe haven for himself out of these grassy hills, even with the Midnight Blade in his hands. If any other human tribes or clans dwelt in these lands, he knew nothing of them. He also knew he couldn't protect them if they did make themselves known. Maybe they too knew that, and that was the very reason they hadn't made themselves known.

Kael snorted at that. It would seem appropriate. His own people afraid that he had become one of those that had once hunted them. Perhaps he had, he thought, looking around the room covered in demon hides and tusk necklaces. Perhaps he was no better than the ones that had once hunted him as food. Did he not do the same thing? Did he not hunt demons merely because they were demons?

Kael pushed it out of his mind with a sigh. It didn't matter really. Whatever he had been was gone, dead and buried with people that had hidden from the light for a hundred years. At least he would die in the open sky, hopefully in the light of the everlasting sun.

Kael looked back into the tower room. His sword was spinning hypnotically in the center of the room above the circular opening. He smiled grimly. If he did die, he would take whoever it was with him, and whoever was left would have to carve the Midnight Blade out of his grip with a dagger.

Suddenly a sound cut through the air and Kael's attention shot back outside the tower room. Streaking over the tower and to the north, leaving a wake of sound-splitting thunderclaps, was a WindBearer. Kael growled, suddenly and unexpectedly, thinking again of the beautiful woman haunting his dreams, and reached behind him into the room. His peerless sword spun whistling into his hand as he stood up, shrugging off his bison blanket. He wore only his demon kilt and white leather sandals. The golden scabbard, covered in demon scalps, hung at his waist. Without a second thought, Kael sheathed the Midnight Blade and leaped out of the tower window.

*

"He took the bait," Razikyl told Soged Hozi, dispelling his scrying image with a wave of his hand.

"Excellent," the WindBearer smiled, drawing his gleaming red broadsword. "Very soon the Midnight Blade and its access to the power of Gevurah will be mine."

The other three hunters nodded back eagerly. Razikyl just smiled.

*

Kael followed the WindBearer easily through the northern breaks, coming to a halt before he delved down into the deep ravine where he knew the winged hunter had gone. Using his sword's powers, Kael had tracked the WindBearer's trace essence that remained in the sky above like a beacon.

The ravine gaped before him as if the earth itself had opened its maw to swallow any that dared enter. The thought wasn't an unreasonable one, considering the geography. Before Kael, the surrounding hills sloped down to meet at the edges of a straight-sided, rugged coulee. The sides of the canyon were over four hundred paces high and nearly sheer, breaking away beneath the topsoil above. Climbing those unstable cliffs would be nothing short of a miracle. At the bottom of the canyon ran a trickling finger of a stream. There were hundreds of slender, clean birch trees scattered throughout the entire ravine. The canyon stretched beyond Kael's eyesight into the hard ridges of the northern forests.

Kael gripped the Midnight Blade tightly, drawing it quietly from its sheath. He was hesitant to follow now. The only visible way into this ravine was slanting there before him. There might not be another way out for miles. That wasn't the thought that disturbed him, though. It was the obvious threat of an ambush.

Before Kael could decide on a course of action, his rage did it for him. Flying down into the canyon nearly half-a-mile before him was a yellow-skinned devil covered by hundreds of tusks.

"Imamiah," Kael spat. He seethed at the thought of his defeat the last time he fought the half-demon devil; even more so at the taunting he had received sometime afterward.

Gripping his sword tightly, Kael charged down the long, steep embankment into the closed ravine.

*

"He fell for it," Razikyl commented.

"Excellent," Soged Hozi chuckled. "Fine touch, using Imamiah's image to draw him."

"Imamiah is probably the only demon left in these northlands that the human hasn't killed yet."

Soged Hozi wasn't listening to the sorcerer, though. He was giving orders to the three other WindBearers that had come with him for the hunt. The three nodded at his orders and flew out of the side coulee into the deep ravine. Hozi turned to look at Jehoel, who stood impassive and emotionless behind the dark-garbed orc. Jehoel's gaze burned into the lead hunter. Soged could not hold the scarred WindBearer's gaze, not because of its intensity or ferocity, but because of its emptiness.

With a shudder, Soged looked back to the opening of the side-coulee in which they stood, and waited.

*

The Midnight Blade was silent. Over the past few months the human had developed an incredible ability to access the gate of power the sword had opened within him completely on his own. On one hand, the ancient artifact was glad—happily surprised—that the human had attained such an aptitude. It was even unheard of in half of the higher beings to access such power.

Still, the weapon was tentative about the human manipulating the power gate that the weapon shared its name and identity with so well. The weapon still implanted the images it wanted to into his dreams, but with less and less effect lately. In truth, the sword could no longer effectively read the human's mind, proving that Kael's brain, and quite probably his muscles, were utterly saturated in the residual aura of the gate of Gevurah.

The Midnight Blade had made Kael into a living, mortal embodiment of itself. It had meant to make the human into a useful tool. Instead, it had created a living weapon.

Luckily the human did not know that. Hopefully, the Midnight Blade would be able to reassert its will over the human before the blasted creature killed itself.

Even if that did happen, though, the weapon would persevere.

The Midnight Blade would survive, thrive, and rule.

*

Kael stepped carefully through the knee-high grass that covered the coulee floor. He walked slowly from one slender, towering birch tree to the next, half-heartedly trying to use them for any sort of cover. Kael had to crane his head nearly straight back to see the top of the sweeping, loose canyon walls. The enclosed area made him squeeze his sword's handle even tighter, both hands white-knuckled.

Kael could discern no tracks whatsoever through the winding creek bed. No animals or men had passed through here for some time. It was the lack of animal tracks that raised the hairs on the back of Kael's neck. Imamiah had flown in here, he knew, so there would be no tracks by him, but still, something felt amiss.

Unknown to Kael, the Midnight Blade was trying desperately to scream a warning across his awareness, but could not break through the fog that dripped from his consciousness.

*

"Now!" Soged Hozi roared telepathically to his hunting party. "Attack!"

*

The canyon floor erupted around Kael like a volcano belching out its hellish fury. Dirt and grass showered down, felling one stout white-barked birch that nearly crushed him. Kael stepped back apprehensively, crouching and bringing his incredible sword to bear before him.

Standing around Kael were four lean, white-garbed WindBearers, red gleaming broadswords held deathly tight. Razikyl was standing behind them dressed in black leather war garb, his dark cloak swirling mystically.

"Orc," Kael growled through his painfully clenched teeth. "So you've brought your motley crew to gain the might of this unparalleled weapon."

"Nay, human," Razikyl stepped up beside the four hunters. "I am merely a spectator in this fascinating turn of events."

"Spectator," Kael hissed, wringing his hands around his sword's enormous handle. "Then watch your own death, orc."

Kael exploded in a flurry of action that few eyes could follow. Launching toward the WindBearer to the left of him, Kael thrust for the hunter's open torso. The winged warrior was barely able to parry the strike, just pushing it wide by crossing his inverted blade before him. He brought his sword up, then quickly arced it down for an overhead chop, but Kael was no longer in the path of his attack. Bringing himself under the hunter's swinging arm and inside the attack, Kael kneed up into the WindBearer's groin and brought the pommel of his weapon into the back of the hunter's neck. The white clad warrior went down roughly, stars exploding in his brain.

The other four attackers were momentarily caught off guard by the human's incredible speed, recovering only as their companion fell to Kael's vicious blows. Razikyl backed away from the fray, pulling a handful of components from his many-pocketed cloak. The two closer hunters threw themselves at the human with a vengeance, anger welling from within them at seeing their comrade disposed of so easily. Soged Hozi, cut off from a direct attack by Kael's offensive to the left of their formation, spread his massive downy wings and raised into the air with a single flap. He held there for a long moment, levitating, amazed at the sight just below him.

The two WindBearers were striking with all of the speed and agility that they could muster from their inherent power over the energy of Hessed, their blades singing through the air. They were brothers, these two, and they fought with a like mind. In tandem they struck at the human, one high, one low, then alternated side to side, then chopping madly at nearly the exact same spot.

All to no avail.

The ringing sound of the Midnight Blade met each and every attack of the identical hunters. Opening the gate of power from within, that now-familiar emptiness saturated Kael's entire left arm, as well as every muscle fiber in his body. That, coupled with the melding of his developing warrior instinct and the extra-sensory perception of the ancient blade, enabled Kael to throw off the two twin hunters with a feral growl and a glancing sword swipe. He sent them head over heels to come to a rest at Razikyl's feet some twenty feet away.

"Impressive!" Soged Hozi roared appreciatively as he swooped down onto Kael, locking blades with the Midnight Blade and landing a foot heavily between the human's shoulder blades. Kael's initial impulse was to shrug off the blow, but instead he decided to roll with it. He added his own leg push to the WindBearer's kick and somersaulted forward. Soged Hozi's blade clipped only the human's long, wavy blonde locks as it filled the space he had emptied.

Kael rolled up to his knees and brought up his weapon horizontally before him before he could even consider the action. Steel sang when two red-hued blades met with the Midnight Blade's deep, starry black. The identical hunters spat unknown obscenities at the cursed human that befuddled them. They were just able to block Kael's sweeping knee-high swipe before beginning their deadly dance with him again. Just as before, the WindBearers realized in disbelief and horror that they were barely equal to the human's maddening prowess.

"Enow!" Soged Hozi roared from behind Kael. He leveled his sword like a lance at the human's exposed back. "Let my newfound power of Netsah open the way to my victory!"

Hozi willed open the well of energy from his spirit through his brain to his right leg, emptiness swelling within his lower limb. A well-known feeling spread throughout his body, melded with the trace auras from the other gates of power he commanded, and channeled into his red broadsword.

"Now, human!" Hozi roared in mad triumph. "Now you will feel power! And then you will feel no more!"

Terror sprang in Kael's chest at the words of the lead hunter behind him. He could sense the overwhelming drawing of force behind him, but was impotent to defend himself from it. The two warriors he faced smirked confidently, knowing that if the human turned to face this new threat, they would run easily run him through.

Kael cried out mentally to the Midnight Blade, pleading for an escape to his impending doom.

But there was no answer.

Enraged at the lack of response from his weapon, Kael drew more energy from the open power gate within his left arm, flooding his legs with power. Soged Hozi cackled with insane glee as he loosed the welling energy within his weapon, shooting the pure force at the helpless human.

Kael was far from helpless, though. Ducking under the twin hunters' duplicate high swipes, Kael gathered himself as if to push against Hozi's impending blast. At the last second, Kael leaped away from the earth, using all of the gate power in his legs to jump as high as he could.

The incredible force of Soged Hozi's blast struck the twin hunters full, hurling them backward and into the broken cliff wall. With two simultaneous, sickening cracks, the WindBearers struck the earth, then fell limp atop the lush green grass. Their bodies were charred and blackened as if they had fallen into the sun.

"No!" Soged Hozi roared, not fully comprehending the power he had just unleashed. He turned to see Kael land gracefully over thirty feet away, unharmed by the mighty strike. The WindBearer that had taken the human's initial attack was now back on his feet beside Hozi, unsure what the lead hunter would command next. Razikyl had moved closer to them, his hands still filled with components for whatever attack he had planned. "What are you waiting for, orc? Help us kill this insolent human!"

Razikyl nodded but hesitated. He had not initially intended to play such an important part of this battle, and after seeing the human in action again, he remembered exactly why.

Kael turned to face the sorcerer's attack, leveling a glance on the orc that sent snow through his veins. Little had ever chilled the massive orc, but the pure animal stare that the human threw on him did just that. Razikyl quickly uttered powerful, arcane words, tossing the components toward Kael. In his haste, however, the dark-garbed wizard-warrior miscalculated his aim. The bolt of lightning that erupted from his outstretched palms only grazed Kael's speeding form. In any other case, he would have been struck fatal by the coursing force, but his Gevurah-soaked muscles exploded into action and he threw himself out of death's way just in time.

"Impossible!" the sorcerer gasped in disbelief, stepping back behind the two powerful WindBearers. Soged Hozi pushed his remaining winged comrade out wide, nodding toward the human.

"It's over, human," Hozi snarled, his blade gleaming as red as his anger. "Your hair will adorn my home."

"Here," Kael growled back, his courage rising with his ire as he pushed his scabbard forward to show the WindBearer. "Take these too when you've had your fill of mine, hunter."

Soged Hozi and his ally's roars were drowned out by Kael's as the three threw themselves together. Razikyl pulled his hood up, shielded his eyes, and backed away from the seething energy that strove to consume them all.

*

"Wow!" Imamiah snorted. "I have never seen a mortal wield that much power and not implode." The half-devil stood with his arms crossed, high above the fracas at the edge of the immense canyon wall. He looked over at the emotionless figure standing beside him.

Jehoel had nothing to say to the yellow-skinned hell-spawn. He hadn't come here at the beck of power, nor at the impeding thrill of battle. Jehoel would care if he could but there was little he was able to care about just now. He knew that it was

Appollyon that had removed his desire for the battle below, but, unfortunately, he didn't care.

Jehoel knew that he could probably overcome the effects of the bounty master's will, but knew that only trouble would come of it. It was easier to bend to Appollyon's wishes now and hopefully regain his wits later. To do otherwise would surely be an idiotic plea for death.

"You know, Jehoel," Imamiah snorted indignantly. "You were a lot more fun before the fall." The devil opened his wings and glided forward, circling down in a wide spiral.

Jehoel's face held a puzzled look for a scant moment, his hand absently tracing the arcing scar on his neck, then fell back to its unsettling mask of nothing.

*

"Yield, mortal!" Soged Hozi roared over the blazing inferno of energy. He was barely able to get the words out of his mouth as his speeding limbs stole the wind from his lungs. The two WindBearers were attacking mercilessly, drawing fully from the inherent power of haste from the gate of Hessed. Their speed was faster than an eye could catch, unmatched as their mere will brought their shining swords down again and again to destroy the pitiful creature before them.

Unmatched, that is, except by the power-filled limbs of Kael.

In truth, Kael's reactions could not meet the winged warrior's speed born from the gate of Hessed, but his power gate, rooted deeply in physical strength, was pulling his arms and legs faster than seemed possible. Unknown to all the combatants, Kael had one other grand advantage: an incredibly sensitive coupling between his brain and his body. Kael's essence was more receptive to his gate of power than the Windbearers were.

Kael also had one grand disadvantage that all the warriors knew about: he was mortal. With his mortality came fatigue, something that WindBearers worried nothing about.

Razikyl backed away from the battle a few more paces, hugging tight to the high, crumbling cliff wall. The ancillary power surges that occasionally missed their mark could take the orc to his grave. Ducking, he pulled a heavy pinch of iron shavings from a pocket in his leather cloak. Razikyl muttered a few scant words, opening the tingling gate between that certain area of his brain and his right leg as he sprinkled the metal flakes over his head. He felt the effects of his spell immediately, the arcane power gate of Netsah covering him in an invisible sheen of protective energy.

Razikyl looked up at the fierce combat, able to see it directly now with his eyes protected. Still, he squinted against the gale that the warriors were creating with their attacks. The orc braced himself as the combat wore on. He knew that the WindBearers would eventually wear the human down, and surely the human realized that, as well. Very soon Kael would be forced to try and overcome the hunters with one last desperate volley, and when he did, Razikyl would be ready.

*

Kael heaved and panted as he worked furiously to fend off the WindBearers' ruthless attacks. They had nearly backed him flat against the cliff wall and were working alternately on his defenses, one after the other, wearing away at his mortal endurance. Kael knew their plan and was defending against it expertly, but in the end his body would falter and their swords would find his body for their scabbards.

Again and again he tried to throw them back, only for an instant, so that he could either escape or stall for a moment to catch his breath, but it was for naught. The winged hunters were far too fast and tenacious to be beaten by physical strength alone.

Kael caught scant glimpses of the dark orc past the hunters, but could spare nary a thought on him. If the sorcerer were to enter the battle now, it would be short-lived indeed, but why hadn't he? It seemed asinine to Kael but he didn't curse his luck. It was that alone that seemed to be keeping him alive.

Finally, Kael could stand no more. He breathed deeply, drawing heavily from his mind and essence, gathering for a final strike. Soged Hozi and his fellow hunter felt the drawing as well, attuned as they were to the rainbow of energy that the gates of power accessed. They, too, gathered themselves, sure that their raw power and superior experience would carry them over the human.

Kael pushed out at his opponents, forcing them on their heels as they danced out of the killing arc of the Midnight Blade. Crouching, he willed open his newfound power source, hoping that the Midnight Blade, too, was adding its ancient energy to his attack. The WindBearers, recognizing the attack, drew up themselves, emptiness filling their torsos as the protecting gate called Tif'eret opened thick within them.

With a roar of pure, animal rage, force and energy erupted from Kael's left arm, channeled through the Midnight Blade. The power surged out of the blade like a cone of nothingness, striking the two WindBearers full and hurling them back like leaves caught in the wind of a merciless maelstrom. The winged hunters struck the far cliff face heavily and landed...easily on their feet.

Kael looked up at them in horror, his eyes wide in disbelief that they had survived his incredible attack. He was barely able to stagger to his feet, his limbs like lead, his very will drained empty. Kael had brought every drop of energy that he could through the gate of Gevurah and hurled full onto the WindBearers. They had taken his best assault. They had taken it and were still very much alive.

Soged Hozi's skin smoked from the bathing of force he and his comrade had taken. They had met the Gevurah power with their combined defenses of Tif'eret and Hessed and had survived. All three knew that the attack and subsequent defense had drained the gates of power from which they had drawn. They all would now stand on equal footing.

"Equal, that is, if it wasn't for my mastery of the Netsah," Soged Hozi spoke unnecessarily to his adversary. Kael had sensed the latent opening of energy when he had flooded his Gevurah over them. Kael knew that it was over.

"Precisely," Hozi grinned, raising his hand. Willing open the Netsah within and uttering a word that he had stolen from one of the orcen sorcerer's books, white, hot energy sprayed from the hunter's open palm. Kael was flung back against the canyon wall with a sickening thud, the Midnight Blade flying from his grip. He slid down the dirt wall slowly, unable to even scream in pain, managing only to drool white bile and blood. Steam rose off of his reddened flesh, blisters emerging instantly as he collapsed to the grassy coulee floor.

"Rare?" Hozi gloated towards his laughing comrade. "Nay. Well done is more to my taste." The lead hunter stepped over to tower over Kael's twitching, struggling form. "Please, human. This is pitiful. You really should just die."

Kael brought his arm out from under himself with a pain-wrenching jerk, lifted it and his head toward where the Midnight Blade lay just feet away.

"Gevurah," he managed to gasp, fear enveloping his body when the blade moved not an inch toward him. Horror gripped his heart and soul at the weapon's betrayal. At the very moment when Kael needed the sword the most, it had abandoned him.

"Don't let it bother you, human," Soged soothed. "Very soon it will matter very little."

"Kill him with his own sword, brother," the shorter WindBearer snidely spat. "Let him feel the weapon one last time."

"A fine idea, brother, but no. I will give him the rest of my gift from the orcen wizard." Soged Hozi braced himself and called open the gate of Netsah one more time, emptiness filling his right leg. "Let him fall to a power that will soon rule the whole of this barren land."

Kael's neck failed him, his forehead falling to rest on his useless forearm. His head lolled to the side as he tried to accept his thrice-damned fate. Just as he thought he was about to feel the brunt of the hunter's spell, Kael saw Razikyl rise up to the side of them. The orc was touching the fingers of one hand to his own scalp and weaving a pattern in the air before him.

"Odd," Kael sighed, sure that it would be the last of a long line of queries he would never have answered. He gritted his teeth and clenched his eyes closed at his imminent destruction. His final thought was that he had never really understood what he had been hurled into, not the power or the situations, or anything in his whole life.

"Now you die, foolish little gnat," Soged Hozi breathed, drawing the full of Netsah with his essence for the final strike. Just when the energy pooled in his form nearly to spilling, he lashed forward with his outstretched hands to expunge the worthless human.

Nothing happened.

"Kill him, brother!" the smaller WindBearer chided at his comrade's supposed play. "Be done with this and let us return to the Cave of Kings."

"Impossible," Hozi muttered to himself, shaking his head in disbelief. No longer could he feel any bond with his own body and the gate of Netsah. He tried again to join his soul with the gate of power, but to no avail. He looked over to Razikyl questioningly. "Orc, why has…"

The words barely escaped his lips when scorching electricity blasted into both winged hunters, sending them flying through the air. They hit the ground solidly, only Soged Hozi able to rise again, albeit slowly.

"What manner of treachery is this, orc?" Hozi growled, his voice the very epitome of scorn and hatred.

"Treachery of the basest sort, hunter," Razikyl calmly returned. The towering orc had pulled himself to his full height, his hood thrown back, the sun shining off of his slick scalp. His bare arms were nearly the girth of the leaner WindBearer's legs. In his hands were his two foot-long dirks, mystic cylindrical runes at the pommels and hilts. "Treachery in the name of power most grand."

"You'll die for this, mortal!" Hozi roared. "I opened the Tif'eret within you! I have given you power above any other mortal!"

"And I used my own vast knowledge of the Netsah to let you believe you shared that very knowledge." Razikyl chuckled as he slowly advanced to where the Midnight Blade lay. "Actually, a surprisingly easy spell once it is mastered. I believe it was the first one that Hosampsich taught me when I was under his tyrannical tutelage."

The wounded WindBearer howled like a maddened dog and threw himself through the air to strike down his mortal adversary with his bare hands. Razikyl brought up his dirks, gleaming with magical enchantment and cut at the flailing hunter. Soged Hozi's own natural quickness was all that saved his life. Spinning away from the attack at the last moment, he bore only two long, shallow slashes across his chest. Razikyl added to the hunter's passing speed with a mighty kick to the back and sent Hozi back to the earth with a tumble.

Soged was even slower to get up this time. He had exhausted his gates of power, which in turn had exhausted him. He had expected only sure victory and had made no concessions for any sort of retreat or flight. He stood on wavering legs, knowing surely that his time on this fetid mud ball had at last come to an end.

Just out of chance, Soged Hozi looked over to where the defeated human lay, still face down in the heavy, green grass. The human's torso still moved from steady breathing and the hunter was sure he saw a glimpse of a fiery green-blue eye.

"Damn," Soged snorted. The human would probably survive this longer than he would.

"Don't count on it," a booming voice sounded through the slender canyon's reaches. Razikyl and Soged Hozi looked up to see a speeding, yellow streak rain fire down upon them. The hunter drew his wings around himself for protection, just as the orc pulled his hood up and cloak about himself. Their actions saved them from the initial assault, but a more concentrated attack on Razikyl's dark form forced him down, then back, to find cover among the thin, snaking birch trees.

Imamiah landed lightly down beside the Midnight Blade, red heat still exploding from his red bladed broad sword. A hasty spell kept any more of the energy from hurting Razikyl, as did Soged's natural resistance to the demon's weapon.

"Very nice," the tall demon-devil chuckled, hurling his broadsword at Razikyl, the blade embedding itself deep into the tree the orc sought protection behind. "Do let us dispense with any pleasantries." Imamiah stooped and picked up the Midnight Blade. The five-foot blade glared bright blue, then red at his touch. "Easy, old gal. You'll come to love my touch as well as that human's."

Imamiah stepped forward towards the humbled WindBearer and the dark-garbed orc.

"Say any prayers that you will, boys. Your time in this world is short indeed."

"To hell with you, Imamiah," Soged Hozi spat, knowing full well his fate.

"You first, old friend."

An instant didn't past between Imamiah's words and his attack on Soged Hozi. The WindBearer crouched to defend himself but his leg muscles, fatigued beyond their unearthly limits, weakened and failed, dropping the hunter to one knee. It was that one weakening moment that doomed the winged warrior. Imamiah dropped down on Hozi nearly faster than an eye could grasp, bringing down the Midnight Blade in a howling downward chop. The downy-winged hunter lifted his arms up instinctively. The tusk-covered demon devil smirked evilly at the blonde warrior's futile gesture. The Midnight Blade roared with red gleaming energy as it cut easily through Hozi's arms, down through his skull, chest and torso, exiting roughly from his silk-covered crotch.

Soged Hozi fell onto the lush green canyon floor in two halves, both eyes still wide in disbelief as they stared blankly at opposing canyon walls.

"Adequate," Imamiah understated with a raised eyebrow and an evil grin, holding the night-colored blade up before himself, running a finger down the close, smooth side of the jagged sword. The red lifeblood of the WindBearer was disappearing into the very metal of the blade as it pulsed red energy.

"And now," the yellow-hued devil turned to face the other two living beings in the deep coulee. "Let us see how mortals fill this dark blade's palate."

Razikyl tried to hide even further into the depths of his dark, leather cloak cowl as he stepped slowly from one white-skinned birch tree to the next. The retreating orc's movement grabbed Imamiah's eyes.

"Hosampsich's little bald-headed plaything," the devil grinned, stepping slowly toward the orc. "I never did see what he saw in you mortals. You were never more than appetizers for me."

"Quite," Razikyl slowly breathed, still making his way through the towering trees. The more distance he put between himself and the towering demon before the action started the better chance he had at survival.

"You have no chance of survival, orc," Imamiah gloated, his pace still measured as he arrogantly toyed with his prey. He came to a stop over Kael's nearly inanimate form, which struggled to breathe. "Pitiful little creature." Imamiah traced a number of invisible random runes in the air above Kael's back with the point of the five-foot blade. "Impossible to imagine that with this very weapon you found yourself a match for even me."

Kael wished he could respond to the dreaded demon's snide words, but Soged Hozi's final burst of false-Netsah had reduced the human warrior to near-helplessness. Kael could feel trace remnants of the power of Gevurah still bouncing around inside his body and soul, but couldn't maintain even the moment's concentration required to pull the energy together. He wished he could muster the strength to sigh in resignation. Instead, Kael lay down and waited for the witty remark that would herald his soul to oblivion.

"No remark, human," Imamiah dropped his head in seriousness, lining his death strike up with Kael's exposed brainstem. "You represented your race better than any could have prayed to. Even I shall not sully that with cruel mocking."

Imamiah raised the Midnight Blade slowly, holding the downswing for a moment more for respect than drama. Razikyl stopped his fleeing for a brief moment to witness the human's death. The orcen sorcerer pursed his lips bitterly at Kael's impending demise. The wizard had no respect for humans, thinking them more bugs than actual beings, but this particular one had shown a side of humanity that Razikyl had never seen. Despite his blinding fear, the human had accomplished much, the greatest act actually staying alive. Imamiah brought down the Midnight Blade swiftly, singing through the air as it approached its exposed target.

The resounding ring of metal on metal exploded throughout the towering walls of the canyon. Razikyl looked on in amazement at the blurring figure that had swooped down to intercept the Midnight Blade's death strike.

"No longer, demon," Jehoel stated plainly, his red-hued sword holding the jagged Midnight Blade mere inches above Kael's neck. "No longer will you terrorize the inhabitants of this plane. It stops here."

Razikyl's jaw fell to his chest as he crouched behind a heavy tree. Everything in his head told him to run away but his feet wouldn't respond. The wizard knew that before him now was a turning point in something big. It was an event that demanded witnessing.

"Be gone, Jehoel," Imamiah spat, his muscles futilely straining to push down for the kill. "You're Appollyon's lackey and no more. Act your part and let me act mine."

"Nay," Jehoel breathed. "No longer am I the thrall of the bounty master. I have the full capacities of my faculties. In truth, it was your cryptic words, coupled with Appollyon's own sorcery, that opened my mind. My powers are again at my disposal and I shall give you a single chance to flee as honor demands. If you do not, I will destroy you."

"Honor demands?" Imamiah snorted, backing many feet away from the deranged WindBearer. "Be smart, Jehoel. Don't make me deepen the scar on your neck."

Jehoel softly touched the pink flesh at his neck then grasped his broadsword with both hands, stepping over Kael's limp form to face Imamiah. Both mighty warriors began to access the tremendous energies from the numerous gates of power each mastered, might coursing around both their bodies and weapons.

"Rush to your death, WindBearer," the seven-foot demon snarled.

"I am not a WindBearer, base fiend. I am Jehoel, a Chief Angel of the Sword, and you are dead."

*

Razikyl was nearly struck blind by the meeting of the two and the resulting explosion sent him and many trees toppling to the ground. The orc sheathed his enchanted dirks, pulled a salve from his cloak, muttered a few phrases, and touched the ointment to his temples and wrists. It would keep him protected long enough to escape this canyon of death. Hopefully.

A final glance back at the clash between god-like powers drew Razikyl's eyes to Kael's still form, covered with burnt grass and brush. The orc was unsure if he was alive or not, honestly not caring at the moment, but the human's form did remind the wizard of something.

Razikyl halted for a scant moment to make sure the container was still in a pocket in his heavy, leather cloak. He nodded to himself with a smile when he felt it within the folds of the cape. The orc turned and began running, making his way out of the towering canyon.

Soon, he would not have to flee beings such as those that battled behind him. Soon, he would crush them beneath his own powerful heel.

That thought alone brought a smile to his face and haste to his frenzied steps.

*

The energy around Kael was so intense that he struggled to breathe. The wind was tearing by him like a tornado and the air that his lungs did manage to pull in was heated nearly to the point of burning. He was an insignificant pawn caught in the crossfire.

Gasping futilely for another breath, Kael managed to roll over to his back. Just as he did a stray bolt of red-hot energy from the Midnight Blade missed its mark and exploded right where he had been laying. The upheaval of grass and soil pushed Kael up against the base of the towering canyon wall, even more deadwood and foliage providing his sure death shroud.

Kael tried to groan but could barely push the air past his lips. He managed to open his eyes and saw through his green covering the two combatants fighting with a ferocity he had never before seen. It would have been more entertaining if Kael knew that he was safe from the occasional stray blast that was sure to soon take him out.

"Kael," a soft nearly inaudible whisper wafted past his ears.

"W…who," Kael managed to whisper back, unsure if he actually heard anything.

Suddenly, the chaotic surroundings around darkened and blurred. Kael struggled to squint into the blackness that was enveloping him. He was sure it was Gabryl come to snatch his soul to the Spirit Realm of Truth. Surely that approaching gleam of light was the death god's chariot.

"No," the whisper sounded softly in his ears again. There was a playful kindness to the voice, one that Kael recognized immediately when the gleam came forward to stand before his near-broken body as a shimmering outline of a beautiful woman. It was the unparalleled beauty of…

"Alique."

"Yes, my love, it's me," the shining outline smiled back.

"Then truly I am lost to this world," Kael muttered, trying to close his eyes to surrender. "I am lost and they have sent you to herald me to the afterlife."

"No, my love. I am no herald to the ever-after. I know not if such a thing even exists."

"Then what? Where does your soul rest now? Is it an evil that can be combated with strength of limb? What need do you have of my broken and busted form?"

"For now you must just survive, my love," Alique's ghostly form pointed above Kael to a small opening where the canyon wall met the lush canyon floor. "There. Allow your wounds to heal and your power to grow. Only then will you be able to save me."

"But…" Kael began.

"Go quickly, my love," Alique's spirit interrupted delicately. "This battle will unwittingly take you if you do not flee."

As she spoke, her form pulled slowly away from Kael, and the darkness lifted like a veil pulled away from reality.

"Quickly, my love," the words were light and the raging tempest nearly bore them away. "I love you."

"I love you," he managed to return to her disappearing outline. Tears, both of pain and emotion, ran down his dirt-covered cheeks as he turned back over onto his stomach and began to drag himself to the small cave opening not ten paces ahead. Kael's legs aided him very little as he pulled himself through the now-burning grass and the mounds of hurled soil. Over a downed birch tree and into the opening, Kael crawled. Just as he pulled his feet the last few inches into the musty, crumbling cave, an explosion at the mouth shot him down the dark shaft.

The concussion wave from the explosion proved to be the final blow to Kael's consciousness as his mind and body joined the safety of the cave's darkness.

*

"Surrender!" Imamiah roared as he brought down the Midnight Blade again and again on Jehoel's swift form. Again and again the downy winged warrior batted aside the demon's attack, biding his time until an opening presented itself. Only then would Imamiah taste Jehoel's steel. Jehoel did not deal out nicks or cuts. Jehoel dealt only death.

Imamiah roared again in rage at his situation. He wielded the power of Gevurah now, even more effectively than the human had, but he could not defeat the angel before him. It had been the demon's own snide remarks, coupled with Appollyon's faulty spell, that had opened the sliver of awareness into Jehoel's soul. Imamiah had doomed himself. It almost made him puke.

Sensing the demon tiring, Jehoel turned the initiative and began to rain down strikes and attacks of his own.

Both knew that Imamiah had less than a minute to live.

*

Razikyl slowed his desperate run as the Tower of Hosampsich came into view.

"The Tower of Imamiah now, I suppose," he grunted. He damned his own luck. He had run right into the gaping maw of danger for a reason, but it had taken him some time. The way his luck was running, Imamiah was probably waiting for him at the tower, using the human and the WindBearer's skulls as goblets for wine.

Before the orc could move to ponder how he would approach, the ground below the tower began to shiver and rumble. Razikyl dropped to his hands and knees, thankful that no rocks or trees were immediately near him, and prayed that the earth itself didn't open beneath him and swallow him whole. On the hill above where the tower stood, the earth heaved and shuddered. In an instant, the tower cracked in a thousand pieces and crumbled to the ground with a thundering crash.

The ground calmed and Razikyl carefully picked his way through the rubble to the top of the grassy hill. His curiosity cared nothing for his well being.

"Imamiah has fallen," the wizard reasoned. The orc knew of only two reasons the tower would have fallen: the wielder willed it so as he touched the blade to the tower wall, or a creature of true virtue gripped the Midnight Blade.

A short distance from the ruins, Razikyl saw what he had come for. The bare dirt area was surrounded by thick grass and out of the ground at the head stuck a single wooden marker. The marker was bare. The human probably didn't know any sort of written language.

Razikyl puffed warm air onto his cupped hands for a brief moment then pushed the heat out of his palms, muttered a choice phrase, and pulled his hands upward as if he were calling for a crescendo from an orchestra. The dirt of the grave exploded out of the hole and a limp, stinking corpse rose out of the ground as if pulled at the joints by invisible marionette strings. Rot had long begun but Razikyl cared not. He knew a way around such earthly shackles.

Pulling the corpse toward himself, the sorcerer withdrew a shining mirror out of his cloak and set it spinning in the air before him. As the mirror's spinning speeded, it also grew. When it reached a size that brought a satisfied nod from the orc's head, the mirror stopped and the corpse slowly levitated into it. The mirror flared bright blue as it accepted the corpse completely, and then began to spin again, shrinking.

Razikyl reached out and snatched it out of the air as it attained its smaller size and slipped it quickly into the folds of his cloak. Looking up into the sky, the orc breathed relief that the new master of the Midnight Blade had not yet come home. Pulling his hood up to block the waning day's sun, Razikyl struck out for Hosampsich's ridge and the towering mountains to the northeast.

*

Jehoel tightened the chain belt of the ornate, golden scabbard and slowly sheathed the Midnight Blade. Looking around, the Angel of the Sword could not see where the human had gone, but was sure he had safely fled. The orc, too, seemed to have escaped. That was fine with Jehoel. It was no longer his intent to harm such creatures, but to offer them the protection they so desperately needed.

Jehoel pondered on the sudden opening within his soul that had clarified his mind so much. It was not a gate of power that had opened; more like a cloud of confusion that had lifted. There was very much that he knew he could not remember, but that would pass. Time would surely bring back his memory, and in the meantime, he would live the life of virtue for which he was sure he was originally destined.

Jehoel spread his enormous, white, downy wings and forced the power of Gevurah to open with the might of the Midnight Blade. The angel now commanded the entire mid-triad of power: the Hessed, the Tif'eret, and, now, the Gevurah. In addition to those he also had access to two of the lower triad: much of the Hod, and an adequate dabbling of the powerful Netsah.

Looking down at the steaming, fetid mass that was once the hated demon Imamiah, Jehoel adjusted the Midnight Blade and golden scabbard at his right hip. A smaller, similar scabbard holding his original red steel broadsword lay between his two massive wings, the white leather strap crossing his lean, muscled chest. At his left thigh was his long dirk, strapped down as well with white leather.

Jehoel pulled a small strip from the bottom of his white, silk kilt and pulled his foot-long blonde hair back and tied it into a ponytail. He kneeled down, tightened the clasps on his sandals then stood silent for a long moment.

Nodding slowly to himself and wearing a slightly victorious smile, Jehoel flapped his wings and rose into the eastern sky.

*

Kael slept peacefully for the first time since he had ran for his life from the demon lord Hosampsich. There were no subtle voices, no demonic visions to haunt him, only sound sleep and rest. In his slumber, the gate of Gevurah opened, filling his left arm with emptiness and working desperately to repair the damage done to his mortal body.

Kael slept on as his own now-innate power healed him. He dreamt of Alique, the memory of their time together, and how he could help her now that she seemed to dwell beyond the realm of reality. Kael dreamt of a gentle, early fall snow that was falling outside of his concealed cave that was covering the still green countryside nearly three months early. Kael also dreamt of one other thing that he hadn't thought of since he had come in contact with the Midnight Blade.

Kael dreamt of happiness.

Appollyon pulled the heavy buffalo hide tighter around him. He leaned at the lip of the mouth of the Cave of Kings, watching the snowfall. It was night but the moon was full. It wasn't yet even the autumnal equinox and the snow was falling heavily. If the storm was this heavy this high up then the foothills below were getting their fair share, as well.

"It's to be a long winter," the seven-foot bounty master mused as he turned to walk back down into the Cave of Kings. The hunting would be sparse until the snow cleared next spring. WindBearers disliked the cold. Appollyon walked slowly down into the cave's depths, his breath a trail in the air behind him. Just as he was about the pass the heavy stone throne into the cave's darkness, a tingle at the base of his neck forced him to look back to the cave's entrance.

A slender figure stood at the cave mouth, the silver moon behind him casting a shadow nearly to Appollyon's feet. The figure shot an unusual shudder down the bounty master's neck. Appollyon dismissed the shiver to the cold and raised his chin to regard the shadow figure.

"Who dares disturb my solitude?" the bounty master demanded.

"I do."

"Ah," Appollyon chuckled. "Jehoel. I was afraid that the human had killed you with the rest. Do you have what I sent you for?"

"I do."

"Good, good. Bring it to me."

Jehoel moved not an inch.

"Do be a good boy, Jehoel. Don't make me quash your mind with your will."

Jehoel did not move. Appollyon reached out with his power of mind control and attempted to grasp the angel's will. The bounty master's attempt grasped nothing.

Appollyon squinted his eyes in surprise. Never before had any WindBearer resisted his mind control.

"What is it, Jehoel?" he shrugged off the buffalo hide. Something didn't feel right.

"Your little reign here is at an end, Appollyon."

"Is it?" Appollyon laughed. "And just how do you think you will accomplish that?"

"With this," Jehoel stated plainly, slowly pulling the Midnight Blade from its golden scabbard. The blade of the weapon was an empty streak of black before the full moon behind the angel. Jehoel placed his left fist on his chest. "And with this."

"With steel and heart," the taller being chuckled. "How quaint."

Jehoel stepped down slowly into the Cave of Kings and Appollyon felt a cold permeate his entire being. It was a feeling he hadn't felt for a very, very long time: fear.

"Arm yourself, bounty master," Jehoel spoke, pulling a tiny, green pulsing sphere from the waist of his silken kilt. He tossed the human's permit at Appollyon's feet nonchalantly and raised the Midnight Blade for battle. "I have come for your bounty."

Appollyon tried to raise the battle rage in his own veins but the gleaming white ice in Jehoel's eyes told another story: a story of the death of Appollyon.

PRELUDE TO A WARRIOR

The snowfall was heavy on the rolling hills. The unsuspecting, waist-high grass was barely able to peek out of its chilling prison. The towering cottonwood and elm trees had not yet forsaken their greenness to the dominating white, so sudden had the winter come. There had been no fall. Late, warm, summer days had given way directly to banks of snow and freezing cold. The thin trail that was Little Life Creek was fringed by thick blankets of dull ice, the cold seeking desperately to stop the chattering life-water for good.

The wildlife of the rolling hills and coulees were caught by surprise but not unawares. Deer, elk, and antelope managed to forage enough for themselves, as did the smaller rabbits, porcupines, and polecats. Even the rougher customers—the wolves, coyotes, and mountain lions—were surviving. After all, the winter, as tough as it was and would become, wasn't the worst it could be, only the earliest.

Kael was watching the heavy snowfall impassively. He had just eaten two rabbits that he had snared and was settled into his small-mouthed cave for the lengthening night. He pulled the thick demon cloak tighter, as well as the immense buffalo hide over that. Kael had a small fire going, enough to warm his modest, shallow cave. The tiny, black trail of smoke that was wafting out of the drifting opening had at first concerned him, but that had been dismissed without a second thought. Kael needed the fire to survive this night and the many more to come.

Anything that it would invite would die.

As Kael was drifting off to whatever slumber he would manage this night, his thoughts turned to the events of the past months and of his lost love, Alique. He could still feel the energy and power that had been opened within his body by the peerless Midnight Blade. He knew that whatever the ancient weapon had granted him, it was permanent. With concentration, Kael was able to find strength within his limbs that would have surpassed that of five men, maybe more.

The concentration was hard to sustain and Kael knew that the reason he had been able to do so well in battle before was due to the jagged-edged weapon's will. He knew that he would have to develop such a will for himself in order to put his newfound power to use.

Thoughts of willpower always drew his memory to Alique.

The Midnight Blade had, for some reason, guided Kael's thoughts away from his lost love. Surely, Kael thought, the weapon had found him an easier puppet without meddling emotion to block anything.

Alique had been the true love of his life; the one soul that Kael had felt mirrored his own. Both had felt such raw emotion for each other, as well as the same frustrations at their situation. Nearly everyone else in their now-gone clan, including the children, had forsaken any hope of anything other than a dirty life destined to end on a devil's trident.

Alique had saved Kael from such thoughts. He had been born four years before her, but it was she that had possessed the indomitable spirit from the beginning. She had taken a liking to him young, even if her father had acted the opposite.

Kael chuckled at that. Their fathers had both been the heads of the two main families within the clan, eager to lord over the clan and each other if the opportunity presented itself. On one hand, though, it had been out of practicality to keep the two apart. Kael and Alique were the youngest and strongest direct offspring of the two clan-heads. The clan's belief was to keep them pure until their maturing as to create the best and strongest offspring. It was bullshit, of course, Kael scoffed. The reason for so called "maturing" was to impose an ancient morality on a people that desperately needed population.

Thinking back, Kael wished he had waited for the "maturing." Alique had. They both knew that they would eventually be together, but Kael had allowed lust to rule his youthful heart. He had stolen moments of sinful pleasure with both the widowed older women and the needful younger ones. He knew at the time that everyone knew of it, dismissing it because he was his father's son.

Alique knew about all of it, too, but not from gossip. Kael told her of each and every time and she dismissed it.

"You love me," she would say every time. "The seed you plant in each of those women will build our people's number, though I know that's not why you do it, so I accept that. No," she would continue, "When you are finally able to be with me for good, nothing will ever come between us. We will join the two families as no one ever was able to and finally rise out the dirt and take our lands back."

Kael had smiled through her words then, focused only on her beauty. It was her mind he should have been focusing on.

With a shiver, Kael was back to the snowy hell he now lived in, alone, his dwindling fire sputtering at the cold wind invading the cave. He tossed a few more thin logs into the tiny flame and it puffed back to a reasonable size, overcoming the chill for now.

Kael closed his eyes and thought again of Alique's unparalleled beauty, joining her in spirit, and remembering how warm her touch had always been even on nights such as this.

*

Jehoel's face was a soaked mask of sorrow as he gently laid Fraciel's now-dead body to the cave floor. Fraciel held a questioning look of resignation and hopelessness on his face. An enormous slash at his chest was the only mar on his slender angelic body.

"Why?" Jehoel whispered to the unhearing ears of his brother. He stood up from the dead body, the Midnight Blade that had ended Fraciel's life still in his hand. Jehoel looked up at the mass of WindBearers grouped at the mouth of the Cave of Kings. None of the hunters moved a muscle toward Jehoel. He knew that they wouldn't.

"So," one stepped forward. "Appollyon is gone now. Are you the bounty master?"

"No," Jehoel shook his thick, golden mane. "I am not the bounty master."

"Then what?" the WindBearer asked. "How do we get our permits?"

"There will be no more permits."

"Then how do we hunt?"

Jehoel sighed. He wished he could make the others see what he now saw. To be sure, it was a fog that clouded his brain, but at least it was the truth. Whatever power Appollyon had exuded over him, crossed with the chance words that the demon Imamiah had spoken, had freed the angel. A horrifying truth was better than a paradise of lies.

Looking down again at Fraciel's inert body as it slowly turned to ash, Jehoel realized that he wouldn't be able to help any of his brethren, not yet. They wouldn't be capable of accepting any reality other than the millennia upon millennia they had lived their lies. Neither could Jehoel kill them all. Even though he knew that death for any of them on this plane of reality was not a final death by any means, such would not be his way. He would not slay for ignorance alone.

"If you wish to hunt and fill your permits, you will find another bounty master. You will find another land."

The band of WindBearers snarled and growled at Jehoel's pronouncement. The talkative one stepped forward, his hand resting on the handle of his broadsword.

"You now wish to force us from our land."

"This is not your home," Jehoel stated back. "You will all be allowed to leave here. If you ever return, you will join Fraciel in darkness. Have any of you ever beheld the banishment of death from this plane?" Jehoel wasn't sure that any of them had or at least remembered if it had. It didn't matter. The fear alone of the possibility would be enough. They shifted uncomfortably. His words had an effect on all, including the loud one. After long moments, Jehoel finally broke the silence.

"Leave and live."

The one that had stepped forward thought for a moment about what to do. He lost all of his nerve when he looked behind himself and saw that his comrades—every one of them—was gone. He turned back to Jehoel completely, unsure what to do. He was convinced that he was dead.

"You may go," Jehoel whispered, sadness in his voice. "If you are ever aware of what you are truly doing, return to me."

The WindBearer was puzzled at that, but nodded. He turned and flew into the sky.

Jehoel stepped forward, sheathed the Midnight Blade, and leaned against the edge of the cave mouth. He lost the fleeing figures of the hunters into the depths of the dark winter clouds.

The snow fell heavily. The angel's daily clearing kept the mouth of the Cave of Kings open from the continuous drifting. He wondered how the human who once wielded the Midnight Blade was surviving. Jehoel was sure that the mortal was fine, but he was curious to see. The wildlife was surviving, albeit with a struggle, and so he was sure the human would be doing the same.

Jehoel stepped out into the chill air and opened his enormous wings. Lifting into the snow-filled air, the angel flew to the west, making his daily watch-flight over his chosen homeland.

*

Razikyl wiped the sweat from his brow and leaned against the heavy workbench he had just fashioned. The bench was of solid rock that grew from the very ground of the stony cave floor.

The orcen sorcerer looked around at his handiwork. The cave was one that he had found when he had first come to this land years ago. That had been a time of trials for him. He had been an outcast from his own people, far to the west beyond the desert wastes, and had sought refuge to the east. His first home had been this very cave.

Situated in the north of the rolling lands of the Kelt-Ra clan's land, it bordered the vast cottonwood and elm forests that ran north with the Border River. Many were the goblin and hobgoblin tribes that inhabited these woods and no orc was a friend to either. Razikyl never had to worry about them, however. Hosampsich had found him soon and used him as an effective tool.

Razikyl snorted at that. He had been a slave to the demon and nothing else. Still, both had benefited from the "alliance." Hosampsich had gained a useful commander for his demon horde and the orc had gained the fine-tuning he needed to utilize the very power that had made him a refugee to begin with. Razikyl had been a faithful soldier for the demon and, in turn, the orc had gained power beyond anything he could have ever imagined.

The wizard shook the past from his thoughts as he turned his mind back to the situation at hand.

Razikyl had used his mastery over the Netsah to mold the very interior of the cave to meet his needs as a workshop. The cave itself was nearly a hundred paces beneath the earth in the very heart of a mile-wide piece of granite. The thin, winding tunnel into the earth was hazardous in itself, without the magical traps Razikyl had set for any intruder.

The bench he had pulled up from the very floor was four feet high, six long, and three wide. He had polymorphed the shape of the cave to a perfect square of thirty-foot sides. Inside the entire perimeter he had raised a four-foot bench-ledge, and above that row upon row of shelves. The shelves would soon be filled with the salves, ointments, and potions he would need to further his studies and power, as would the benches.

Razikyl sighed. This would be his home now. It was a far cry from allying himself (at least in his mind) with a demon and having a mystic tower at his disposal, but it would suffice. Soon this place would be forgotten as he worked again to obtain the Midnight Blade. He looked again at the center workbench he had just finished. Already he was taking strides to increase his power and equip himself with a very powerful ally.

All that remained would be creating that ally.

*

Kael knelt quietly, his hand over his lower face in an attempt to stifle the condensation of his breath. He wore a heavy buffalo hide over his demon cloak and kilt. On his feet he had strapped buffalo hide with his white leather sandals. Over that he wore curious creations that his father had taught him to use in the wintertime. Small tree limbs pulled into a circle of sorts and secured with tree bark and ground vine: snowshoes, his dad had called them.

They were useful, Kael thought, looking back up. Near everything his father had taught him was. Pulling his thoughts back to the present, Kael surveyed what lay around him.

Kael had found a young female deer trying to strip the bark from a lone cottonwood tree some distance from the frozen creek bed. He had crept up on her as quietly as he could and when she had finally noticed him he had been only feet away. He was on her before she could turn and burrow through the heavy snow. It was a simple task to snap her neck given his enhanced strength. He always thought he could have done something like this any other time, but knew that the ease with which he had done it was to be credited to his newfound energy.

Now was the simple matter of keeping the valuable meat.

Kael had quickly buried the deer best he could and now knelt directly over it. Any other time he would have dressed the carcass and carried it to his cave to strip and salt preserve. Any other time, though, he probably wouldn't have been surrounded by fifteen goblins.

Kael no longer had any fear of these green-skinned, short-statured monstrosities on their own, but together they made a cunning and deadly troupe. Goblins had lived above ground among the demons while humans had fled underground. That alone lent to their tenacity. Without looking behind him, Kael knew they had him surrounded. Just like the pack of hyenas that they were.

"Move on, human," one of the squeaking voices croaked at him. Kael turned his head ever so slightly, catching the vocal one in his sights. "We know you have the power to lay many of us to our death bed, but you will not survive our rush. Leave us the deer and you won't share its fate."

Kael smiled ever so slightly at that. The goblin was eloquent for one of his kind. It made the cloaked warrior curious. How could a goblin gain an education in such conditions? Kael chuckled.

"I will share my kill, goblins, but I will not hand it over completely. I will give a healthy share for my life…and for yours, as well."

The goblins shuffled at the human's words. They stood waist-deep in freezing snow around a human they knew would kill at the very least half of them. The vocal one began to nod and was about to speak when a booming voice washed over the confrontation.

"Hand over the kill, human," the deafening bass roared. "Ah, t'hell with it. We'll just eat you, too."

Kael swiveled, swept his cloak back, and turned to the voice's owner. His jaw dropped at the sight before him. It was the largest hobgoblin he had ever seen.

The creature was over eight feet tall and had a hairless, pumpkin-shaped head bigger than Kael's torso. He had no real visible neck, his back rising up to form the top of his cranium. His skin was yellow, peeling and rotted. What teeth he still had left were long and jagged. The horror's build was long and powerful, muscles more like that of an animal than any sort of man. He wore the hides of countless wolves, the heads still attached and covering his whole body. There must have been at least seven. The snow would have drifted to Kael's waist had he not been wearing his snowshoes. It barely grazed this creature's knees.

The creature's repulsive appearance and staggering stature widened Kael's eyes. This mortal was bigger than any demon he had ever seen, or slain, for that matter. The weapon in the hobgoblin's hand was even more amazing: it was a heavy, wooden-handled hatchet with a head of shimmering, blue steel. The hatchet head was of two different sides. One was a slender axehead that flared to a fine-honed edge; the other a thick, flat hammerhead some two inches around and three inches long. There were runes and designs in the metal and wood that reminded Kael of the black-garbed horseman that he had met in the wastelands several months ago.

Something in Kael recognized the magic of the weapon. This was trouble.

"I will kill you if I must," Kael stated, still crouched and unmoving. The enormous hobgoblin threw his head back, roaring in laughter. The fifteen goblins surrounding Kael flinched at their obvious leader's display. Kael noted that.

"You will fill my tribe's bellies, human," the yellow-skinned giant scoffed. "You are one and we are many. You will not survive a fight."

"Just as I told your tribe before: you may kill me in a rush, but many will die with me. Are you prepared to be one of those to fall?"

The hobgoblin chuckled, his blood-shot, black eyes narrowed to a squint.

"You've a spine, human, I'll give you that. I bet there's good meat on it, too."

The yellow monster stepped forward, his green skinned lack eys moving to match his advance.

"No!" he roared, swiping at the nearest, sending that one splaying and the rest of them backtracking more than five steps. They all huddled in anticipation of death from either the human or their leader. "I alone will face this one today." He turned again to face Kael. Kael was still crouched, his eyes on the towering fiend the entire time. This one was cock-sure and for good reason. It was times like this that Kael missed having the Midnight Blade.

"What if he kill you?" the nearby downed goblin squeaked.

The hobgoblin didn't even turn around. He swung his left arm up and back, bringing the shining hatchet to bear on the pitiful little creature. The weapon split him entirely asunder; two unequal goblin halves lay staring at themselves eye-to-eye in the soft, white snow.

Kael curled one side of his nose in respect. It was a worthy blow, one he would have been hard pressed to match even with the Midnight Blade. He wasn't sure if the power lay in the weapon or in the limbs of the putrid monster. Either way, it was a very unfavorable situation.

"Well, human?" the hobgoblin asked, grinning that broken-toothed grin again. "Am I to walk over and simply cleave you as well, or will there be battle?"

Kael didn't move a muscle. The goblins were backing off to let their master step forward for single combat, and that boded well for him. He had learned long ago when watching wolves on the hunt, and later when he had secretly seen demons battle WindBearers: one never gives up an advantage. Fight to survive and fight to kill. If Kael was able to rip this one's head from his gorilla-like shoulders, he just might survive this day.

"Well?" the hobgoblin spat again, this time emphasizing it by spinning his hatchet before him in a dazzling display. The weapon was not a showpiece. He knew how to use it.

Kael stood up slowly, looking around himself one more time. The goblins had formed a loose ring around the two fighters. The ground they would be fighting on was flat, albeit covered by three feet of snow. Kael knew he had the advantage with his shoes on, but that would be lost if the two trampled the snow to slush. He would have to go for the kill and quickly.

A hasty look beyond the goblins showed that the storm was building. Visibility was barely fifty paces and the snow was starting to fall again. Even if Kael did kill the creature, he might not survive the storm. A look at some of the skinnier goblins revealed that they, too, recognized the storm's danger. Kael smiled at that. Breaking through their ranks with his felled deer would be simple after he killed their leader.

Kael opened his arms, palms forward, and threw back his cloak hood with a toss of his head. His long, ragged blonde hair fell around his face and shoulders ominously as he leveled a stare on the hobgoblin.

"Come then, fiend," Kael breathed heavily, his muscles tensing for the fight. His blood heated at the prospect of battle, a tinge of fear heightening his awareness. He had not yet faced off in true combat since he had lost the Midnight Blade and he was unsure whether he could trust in his abilities alone. He had gained much from the arcane sword, both in knowledge and prowess, but this would be his greatest test. A part of him wanted to chance a hatchet in the back, throw himself through the loose ring of goblins, and race for his life. Another part of him wanted to taste the blood of his foe, to revel in the defeat of another by his own hands.

Kael chose the latter.

*

Jehoel hovered high above the conflict with his wings wide open as he floated stationary in the strengthening storm. His left hand steadied the Midnight Blade at his hip as the winds strove to throw him head over heels; but the angel would not be tossed by this storm. He was, after all, bred of the air.

His brow furrowed slightly at the sight below him. The gigantic hobgoblin and the human Jehoel had saved a month ago were locked in mortal combat. Numerous spindly green goblins surrounded the two, awaiting the outcome. Jehoel was sure by the goblins' expressions that they were concerned for their safety not only from the battle, but also from the rising storm. They had cause to be, the angel thought as he glanced around. This storm was one of the largest he had ever seen.

Looking back down, Jehoel pondered interfering. He disliked the tactics of the hobgoblin and goblins. He had seen them ambush and murder other creatures many times; on one occasion he had seen a smaller WindBearer fall to a party of some eighteen hobgoblins. Even so, given what he knew about these creatures, he was hesitant to slay them for something that seemed more of a genetic trait than anything else. In the not-so-distant past he would have blasted them from this plane at his leisure, regardless of their genetic traits, and collected their hides for bounty, but not now. That course of action seemed barbaric, even evil to the angel now. It was something that a WindBearer would do, not an angel.

Even for the human, to whom Jehoel had taken some semblance of a liking, he was hesitant to kill. The man was just a part of this world, as were the goblins. For Jehoel to interfere would be no different than stopping a wolf from felling a deer, or stopping that same deer from eating the grass.

Just the same, a tinge of sorrow crossed the angel's heart. Jehoel felt that he and the human could possibly share the same set of values, but he questioned if the motives of his thinking were pure. Could it be he sympathized with the human because of their likeness of appearance? Both were fair of skin and hair. Both had a warrior's build. Jehoel shook the thought from his head. He would not let prejudice or bias rule his newfound heart. The human would prove himself in Jehoel's eyes before any semblance of justice would be passed. The same would also apply for the goblin creatures. Would Jehoel act any differently than them if there were an intruder in the Cave of Kings?

The thought of an intruder suddenly ran a shudder down the length of his spine and Jehoel slowly drew the Midnight Blade and twisted his wings to turn into the brunt of the rising winter wind. There behind him hovered the most powerful horse and rider Jehoel had ever seen. The horse was magnificent, a color of the starless night sky, covered entirely in a thousand tattooed runes of a thousand unknown cultures. The powerful beast's eyes were the white of the very snow that fell around them.

Sitting on a rune-encrusted bone saddle atop the unparalleled beast was a man—was it a man?—of unquestionable power. He wore black clothing that fit his strong form well. A cape of the same color fluttered in the raging wind behind him, but only as if it were guided by a gentle summer's breeze. The only other color was the red of the silk sash around his waist and the bucklers at his wrists and shins. Cloth from his turban covered his face so that only his eyes could be seen. They were eyes of pure ice; a penetrating blue so radiating that heat was generated.

The rider leaned forward, the reins loose in his hands, resting on the horn of the bone-white saddle. He fingered the long ivory sword handle that rose up beside the pommel. The horse scraped a winged, obsidian hoof across a passing snow cloud impatiently. The rider raised his eyes to meet with Jehoel's.

Jehoel felt the fog of his mind rise for the slightest moment as they locked stares.

"I know you," Jehoel breathed.

The dark rider chuckled, pushing himself up from the saddle horn.

"Everyone knows me."

"Who are you?" Jehoel returned. He couldn't recall anything about this obviously familiar form. "What are you doing here?"

"The same as you, Jehoel. Just watching."

Jehoel hid his surprise at the recognition that the dark one exhibited. The angel's muscles tensed for anything. Never had he felt so exposed, so powerless.

"Put away your fear, Jehoel. I will not harm you. Not today."

Jehoel narrowed his eyes at that. He didn't doubt his own ability, but he didn't know this one's. He saw that the dark figure was now looking down on the combat below with marked interest, paying Jehoel no heed. The angel considered rushing him now while he had the supposed advantage, but then reconsidered. He would not stoop to such tactics any longer. That was the way of a WindBearer, not of an angel.

Jehoel frowned in frustration and looked back down to the mortals below. He couldn't help but occasionally look up at the dark rider.

*

Kael pulled his feet up as he leapt over the hobgoblin's sweeping blow. With a speed belying his immense size, the yellow-skinned creature struck out with his bare hand and caught the human full in the chest, sending him head over heels into a bank of snow. The monster was at Kael nearly before he landed on his hands and knees to spin out of the deadly, shining hatchet's arcing attack. At the force of the hobgoblin's blow, snow erupted as if an avalanche shot from the ledge of a nearby mountaintop.

Taking advantage of the moment, Kael struck out with an upward chop to the monster's jaw; teeth and spittle flew. The blow didn't slow him an instant, however, and a massive paw drove Kael to his knees. Another spin, this time blind, carried the human out of the hatchet's path again. Kael threw himself backward close to the goblins that formed the loose battle ring and gasped to catch his breath. Chilling, winter air rushed into his hungry lungs, freezing him. Vision was now down to hardly twenty paces, barely the diameter of the goblin's circle. The wind had picked up and was swirling the older drifts up with the new falling snow.

"Very good, human," the hobgoblin gasped, not nearly as winded but glad for the brief respite all the same. "What is your name so that I may introduce you properly to my death-god when you meet him?"

"Kael," he wheezed without thinking or caring. "And what name shall I carve upon your tomb?"

"Tamagan," the huge hobgoblin chuckled wickedly, standing tall again, spinning his hatchet, albeit much slower now. "Let's finish this before the snow gods bury us alive."

"Agreed," Kael snarled, kicking off his snowshoes now that the ground was less snow than slush. "Let us finish this." Both warriors roared their last death cry and rushed at each other for the death strike with a beserker's abandon.

Tamagan opened the energy within his enchanted hatchet as he bore down on his smaller adversary, bringing the weapon toward the human in a low, level slash, then arcing up and in viciously at the last moment. The speed of the enchanted weapon in the yellow-skinned behemoth's hand was faster then anything Kael had ever before beheld. Faster even than the deadly attacks of the WindBearers. It would have surely opened him from crotch to nose if the hobgoblin had not used the same attack twice before already.

Recognizing the intent of Tamagan's sweeping arm as he rushed forward, Kael stepped into the attack, then jumped into the air, twisting as he did, diving over the hatchet and under the hobgoblin's arm. Somersaulting as he did, Kael pushed himself up from his knees as he landed and chopped upward with all of the power he could muster. Unconsciously linking, the gate of Gevurah opened within Kael's arm and mind as he struck, lending all that it could to the blow. Tamagan's ribs buckled under the raw power of the attack, the hobgoblin clutching his torso as he doubled over into the muddied slush. Blood exploded from his mouth, and from the deep gash that was now open across his stomach.

Kael stood up slowly, his muscles already tightening from the beating the monster had given him. The wind was so fierce now it was nearly blowing the buffalo hide from his shoulders, vision down to barely an arm's length. Kael stood over Tamagan as the hobgoblin managed to look up. Yellow blood ran freely into the freezing snow.

"Be...be done...with it, human," Tamagan managed to spit.

Kael nodded and raised his left hand, emptiness flooding his power-filled muscles. That blow never landed.

Kael was bore down by the weight of a mass of squealing and kicking goblins. Fingernails and teeth slashed over the warrior's back and legs. Thin, scaly fists rained down on Kael's head and body. He spun and struck out at the closest glob of fighting goblin flesh, smashing two of their heads like melons and sending another two flying, the air blasted from their lungs.

More and more blows smashed down on Kael as he struck out again. This time his fist buried into the chest of a green-skinned little fiend and stuck as he took even more abuse. His Gevurah power was rising but his taxed endurance couldn't maintain it. The hobgoblin had taken Kael's best and left very little for the blonde warrior. It took only two more dead goblins for the dirty little creatures to outlast Kael's Gevurah. They held him down with their sheer numbers as the trampled slush began to freeze against Kael's flesh.

Kael peeked up through a swollen eye and the stinging snow to see the imposing dark outline of Tamagan the hobgoblin rise before him. He stood for a moment tapping the hatchet head on one hand, then rose it for the kill. The gleaming blue weapon arced down through the flying whiteness to cleave the human in twain.

Kael roared in rage, again forcing open the power gate of Gevurah despite his depleted constitution. The hatchet came to an abrupt halt as the human grasped the powerful weapon just below the head. Tamagan's eyes widened in disbelieving horror as he roared his defiance.

"No!"

"Aye," Kael spat. "No longer will this axe spill blood in your hands."

Before either could react, their world exploded.

The hatchet was torn from Kael's halting grasp as Tamagan was bore down in a flurry of hair and howls. Goblins were torn asunder as their comrades shrieked in maddening fright. Kael took full advantage, pulling again on the emptiness of Gevurah and striking out at those who sought to kill him.

Goblin blood poured freely as Kael's might tore through his exhaustion and ripped the pitiful creatures to pieces. The snowstorm became a true blizzard now, freezing air swirling the blowing snow into a frenzied howl.

Yet, not all of the howling was of nature.

Kael reached out in his rage to finish off another of the skinny green beasts, but grasped another sort of creature when the goblin ducked. Hair and thick, heavy hide filled Kael's fist as he pulled the new adversary to him. Snapping teeth, fetid, sour breath, and a blood-curdling growl blasted him straight in the face.

Kael ducked as the figure added its own power to his pull, swiping and biting as it sailed past. Kael looked up just in time to see that the figure was humanoid but with a body as hairy as a man's head. He pulled the demon and buffalo-hide cloaks around himself as he rose back up to his feet. He saw five more figures rise around him as a momentary break in the wind opened the veil of snowfall.

"Werewolves of Thunder!" Kael heard the hobgoblin roar from out of the depths of the blizzard. Tamagan's voice held the same fear that Kael's spine did. They stepped slowly toward Kael, their feral features becoming more and more clear the closer they got. A wave of dizziness washed over Kael as the effects of the previous battle began to take more and more of a toll on him the longer he held open the Gevurah power. He knew that he had to escape, and now. He had no idea how to manage that until the only chance to do so presented itself.

"Die!" sounded the maddening roar of Tamagan as he tore into the werewolves' ranks with viscous abandon. Kael didn't skip a beat as he jumped over the nearest werewolf, shoved his arms into the snow, and ripped the front quarter off of the now-frozen deer carcass. His prize in hand, Kael sprinted into the heart of the blizzard, the snow waist-high as he pushed against it with every ounce of his strength. The Gevurah gate was still open, but was fast waning. Kael wasn't even sure of the direction he was running. He knew only that survival depended on getting away from where he was.

Kael had gotten nearly five hundred paces when he lost his footing and fell into the depths of the consuming snow. Before he could push himself up, a hairy, clawed hand raked his back raw, drawing a scream from his throat. Kael pivoted, swinging out at the wolf man, but proved too slow. The lycanthrope easily ducked the attack and struck with an uppercut that sent the human upside down.

Before Kael could even think or react the werewolf was on him, tearing at his arms and chest, rotten breath filling his face. The beast's attack was so savage it left Kael no opportunity to even let his own instinct to take over.

Just as Kael was about to get his bearings enough to watch as he lost his life, there was a sharp, fluttering snap of cloth and suddenly the werewolf was torn away from atop him. Kael scrambled to his feet and picked up his deer meat just as a sickening crack filled the air, sounding over even the roar of the winter wind. The beast that had attacked Kael fell before him as if dropped from a great height. The werewolf was bent and broken, the back of his misshapen head touching his hairy heels.

Kael looked up for a brief second but could see nothing for certain in the enveloping whiteness.

Without a second thought, he hurled himself through the storm, praying that he would come across a familiar landmark rather than whatever it was that had just saved his life.

*

"Why did you do that?" Jehoel asked as the dark figure rose back up into the higher clouds to hover beside the angel.

"Why didn't you do first?"

"I wanted to, but..." Jehoel paused.

"But, what?" the dark figure pressed.

"I didn't think it right for me to interfere." Jehoel stated at last. "I am not of this world, and despite any being's appeal, it isn't my place."

"Are sure about that?" the figure asked.

"Whether I should interfere?" Jehoel returned with a raised eyebrow.

"Nay," he chuckled, rising up above the storm and out of the angel's view, "Are you so sure you are not of this world?"

Jehoel watched the dark figure ride off beyond his sight, leaving the winged warrior alone in the buffeting wind and snow, yet again with more questions than answers.

*

Razikyl worked meticulously and methodically, careful with every point of his work. The body that he worked on was sustained entirely by his continual inflow of Netsah. The heart pumped, the lungs breathed, and the blood flowed. Granted, the blood that did flow was contributed by the orc himself, but that would work to his advantage in the time to come. This body was in every aspect alive. The only thing that was missing was a soul to inhabit it.

Razikyl's current work was that of tattooing the body with every imaginable power rune he had ever learned. On his own body he had tattooed similar mystic symbols, using a dye that Hosampsich had supplied him that was invisible to mortal eyes. Such supplies were now unavailable to the orcen sorcerer, so he did the next best thing: he stalked and downed a WindBearer, draining his life fluid before sending the winged bastard to an ashen death.

The wizard pulled away, wiping the stinging sweat from his eyes and brow. He had finished another half-palm-sized tattoo that would serve as a compliment to the power this body would one day wield. He stared at the magnificent body as he rested. The woman had a beauty that Razikyl had never seen in a mortal. Her features were closer to that of a WindBearer than a human woman. Her build was lithe and athletic, her breasts and hips round and seductive. Her hair was an amber color Razikyl had never seen in nature. He wondered what color her eyes were. Oddly enough, he had never lifted her lids to see. It was the one surprise he would save for himself when he installed true life into the body.

Then again, it would not be the only secret.

On numerous occasions Razikyl had nearly let the lust in his blood and the loneliness of the snow-buried cave take him over. Her body had been penetrated before in life, he knew, so it would not damage any of his work. Yet, despite the obvious temptation of her delectable femininity, Razikyl did not fold to temptation. He would raise this woman again to life and then bed her with her will, not against it.

Razikyl bent down again with his long, hollow needles and went back to work. Thoughts of a powerful and beautiful mistress at his side and the Midnight Blade in his hand brought a smile to the wizard's face.

*

Slowly now, Jehoel. You must unsheathe me and use my power to rule this land.

"Aye," the lean muscled warrior nodded blankly. "I could do just that."

Jehoel leaned against the mouth of the Cave of Kings watching the violent storm rage outside. The tempest had reached a feverish pitch and had stayed there for the past three days. There seemed to be more than just nature combined with these fierce elements. The proof to that was the fact that Jehoel had lost the human in the storm, as well as the wolves and goblins. He was sure they hadn't completely killed each other, but then again, with this weather, none could be sure.

Jehoel turned back into the cave, pulling his white silken cloak around himself. He wore only a short-sleeved shirt, a knee-length kilt, and his leather sandals, all white as the mountaintops outside.

And, of course, the golden scabbard and the peerless Midnight Blade.

Now is the best time to strike, Jehoel. You are impervious to these elements. Attack now and bring this land to heel!

Jehoel placed his left hand on the sword's three-handed handle and willed open the gate of Gevurah within himself. He pulled and sucked at the seemingly limitless power within the ancient weapon, forcing the energy from the blade against its will. After what seemed only moments, the Midnight Blade forced shut the link between the two that Jehoel had forced open.

The lithe angel pulled his hand away gingerly, his palm steaming from the coursing of energy. Jehoel smiled. He knew that he was immune to the persuasive powers of the Midnight Blade, and he knew if he channeled open the path between himself and the weapon enough times he would be able to open the gate of power within himself alone. Then he would no longer need the weapon to access the strength of Gevurah. That truth was emphasized by the fact that he still could feel the remnants of the energy tingling its emptiness within his left arm and shoulder despite the weapon's efforts to end their coupling.

After Jehoel opened the Gevurah, he wondered what he would do with the weapon. It was a powerful blade despite its arcane properties, able to damage demons and such monsters where earthly steel rarely could. Still, the sword was too dangerous to keep near for an eternity—even more, too dangerous to let fall into the wrong one's hands for an instant. Given time, could even an angel fall to the weapon's wooing and soothing suggestions? Jehoel thought not, but he was unwilling to see. Even if one did not fall to the sword's immediate will, it would find other ways to achieve its wants.

Jehoel looked back into the enveloping nothingness that was the unseeing pit of the Cave of Kings. Perhaps that dark unknown would be a fitting resting-place for the sword. None that the angel knew of, not even Appollyon, had ventured into the furthest of the Cave's hellish depths. Who knew what manner of horror he would be aiding by arming it with the Midnight Blade?

Jehoel turned back to the mouth of the cave to delve again into his own thoughts and wonder exactly what his place was on this plane of existence.

At his hip the red, slanted jewels at the crosspiece of the Midnight Blade glowed with a simmering blaze of the very fires of hell.

*

Tamagan sulked as the feast carried on around him. At least by the standards of a goblin tribe it was a feast. The gigantic hobgoblin had held off the werewolves the best he could until the blizzard became too much for even them. Tamagan had escaped with the remainder of the human's deer kill and only three of his goblin lackeys alive.

He sat now in the tribe's hideout, a construct of loosely-placed timbers set against five towering, downed pine trees. When the snow had started falling two months ago, Tamagan had put the goblins to work thatching the roof of their immense "stronghold" with layer upon layer of pine and driftwood. With the Axe Creek running a short distance away from their enormous teepee, the tribe was safe for the winter. Their only concern was keeping a section of the water open to drink, and finding enough fresh meat to keep from eating each other.

The goblin's "stronghold" was essentially one large room. A small cook fire in the center found a way to push its smoke through a microscopic hole in the ceiling. It was surrounded by towering pine trees at the base of the enormous mountains of the east.

Tamagan looked around at his motley troupe. It now numbered thirty-seven male and eight female goblins. It was an eclectic assembly, most of the little beasts having as much hobgoblin or human blood as goblin. For the most part it was the hobgoblin's roaring voice and unquestioned muscle alone that kept the spindly little green roaches from eating each other. Under Tamagan's rule they had some semblance of society, regular guards, and regular scouting and hunting parties. The hobgoblin truly had no need for such creatures, but they did make his life much, much easier. In return the goblins lived: a wonderful bargain by anyone's measure.

Tamagan chuckled at himself, looking down at the hatchet that he held loose in his large right hand. With this weapon he knew that he could bring death to demons and ruin to whole lands. There was power in this steel and oak that probably went beyond the grasps of the hobgoblin's imagination. All of this power and here he was lording over a den of maggots.

"What a waste," he sighed hopelessly under his breath. It was a breath that was near-filled by dark soot "You," he yelled at the nearest goblin, a spineless little worm of a creature named Lorg. "Go up and clear off the roof opening." The goblin jumped up and ran out the door to do his lord's bidding.

Tamagan fingered the outline of the arcane runes that covered the blue steel hatchet head. It had been one full run of the seasons since he had taken possession of the weapon. It had been when the leaves had first dropped one year ago that he had happened on a well-hidden cave that would forever change his miserable life.

The giant hobgoblin had always been hated by his own people. He had an infuriating ability to enrage nearly any other creature with his brash and brazen attitude. He had always seen himself as a regal figurehead of his people, but they had always seen him as something of a dangerous nuisance. The final straw for his people had been when he had sprung from his hiding place and roared his defiance to a horde of hunting demons passing near. Of the fifty in his former tribe, only himself and five others had survived. Word quickly spread that Tamagan was a curse to be shunned with the greatest of fervor. Whenever he had been discovered lurking at the fringes of a tribe's boundaries, he had been hunted or run off. No tribe would abide an idiot that could jeopardize the life of the whole.

It had been a night when Tamagan had been very near his own death when he had found the ancient cave. He had journeyed to the woodlands of the north along the edges of the Border River to escape the viscious, and probably rightful, persecution of the goblinoid people and the demons of the southern Kelt-Ra lands. It was there that he fell into an area protected by elven rangers and very nearly met oblivion.

The rangers had kept their lands clean of goblinoids for unknown centuries and they intended to keep it that way. Too bad it was a legend that had never filtered into the southern lands.

Beaten and battered, his form riddled with numerous eagle-quilled arrows, Tamagan sought sanctity near the river's bank. As the elves surrounded him he had dug at the loose bank in terror, hoping against hope that he would survive. That prayer had been partly answered when the bank had given way and the hobgoblin had fell some fifty spans. Tamagan had landed roughly, loosing consciousness for the god's knew how long.

The cave bank had collapsed on itself, both hiding him from the rangers and burying him in impenetrable darkness. He had regained his senses in a gradual, surreal way, the darkness being no different than the inside of his eyelids. The cave was knee-deep full of the river water seeping from above and smelled of musty, rotted vegetation. It had been the faintest shimmer of blue glinting in the corner of the darkness that beckoned Tamagan and stilled the fright in his heart.

Tamagan had limped through the river water, ducking stalactites, to crawl on his knees into a shallow inner-cave where a small dais rose from the hard, slick rock. The platform was completely out of place in this dank underground cavern, but the hobgoblin paid that no heed. He was too curious—and careless—to worry about his well being.

Here was the source of the shimmering blue. The tiny altar was covered entirely in deep, green moss, the blue glow radiating from beneath it. Tamagan reached tentatively, cautiously, toward the fierce blue. Any fear that his heart held was dispelled by his insatiable curiosity and innate hunger for the unknown as he pulled the thick moss away from the source of light.

Something else pulled at Tamagan, as well. It was a calling that was made less of words than of a beckoning to the very soul. It both chilled the hobgoblin and warmed him at the same time. It was something the selfish creature had never felt before. Before he could decipher the strange emotions, Tamagan slipped his hand under the blanket of moss and gripped something very solid.

Tamagan's eyes went wide had he slowly pulled the object up out of the moss. It was a hatchet unlike anything he had ever beheld. The steel of the half-axe, half-hammer head shone like that of a sword. The handle was a half-pace-long limb of tooled, solid oak that looked very near to a twig in the massive hand of Tamagan the hobgoblin.

Tamagan backed out of the tiny sub-cave and staggered back to his feet into the pouring water. Wonder filled his widened eyes as his touch opened the slumbering essence within the rune-covered weapon. The gleaming blue of the steel coursed down the thick oak into the goblinoid's very hand and arm. Incapacitating shock filled his mind as emptiness filled his right arm and shoulder. Tamagan gasped in horror at the lack of feeling within his naturally powerful arm. At the same time, he felt something quite different. Though his first impression was that of emptiness, it was merely a mask for the raw, unfettered power beneath.

Tamagan held the weapon before him, his boulder-like knuckles white. He suddenly spun the hatchet in a dangerous, figure eight maneuver that he never knew he knew. The speed that he exhibited was faster than even his own eye could trace. Even Tamagan had enough brains to know that it was born not from his own limbs, but from the power within the axe.

Tamagan cut through the air again with another mind-dazzling display, then grinned an evil, splay-toothed grin as he looked up at the slightest hint of daylight above. It was time to end his role as the hunted and castaway.

Tamagan would now become the hunter.

That was how he had gained this ever-resourceful weapon that long year ago. Tamagan snorted again at himself. He had made quick work of that band of elven rangers and had returned to the south to become the bane of his people's existence. He had come down as a demon would, killing them for their previous judgements of him. In a short time, though, even that became empty for him. He had traded one mantle for an opposite yet equal one. The power that he wielded, he realized, was beyond petty emotion. There was purpose in this unlimited power that he held.

But Tamagan still knew not what that purpose was. For all of his power and skill, he was still just the lord of a pitiful troupe of goblins. He continuously told himself it was merely a stopping point in the trail that would lead to his eventual rule of this land's people, but that had been over seven months ago.

The hobgoblin looked down yet again at the weapon in his hand. The hatchet had opened something within him that long day ago in the now-lost cavern. It was a power that Tamagan had thought was unique and meant to be wielded only by those worthy enough to hold it. He had thought that, until he faced the human only days ago. Somehow their powers were different, but at the same time very much similar. As they had squared off in the face of the roaring blizzard, Tamagan knew that he was undoubtedly the better warrior. Now, though, he wasn't sure.

Tamagan was blessed with the natural strength of a hobgoblin, which was easily three times that of a normal man. On top of that he happened to be bigger and stronger than any other goblinoid he had ever known. He knew that his natural strength coupled with the power of the hatchet made him the premier warrior of these lands.

How then had the human managed to fend off his attacks?

Tamagan's gift from the mystic weapon was speed. The emptiness that had opened and the energy that had flowed so freely from his soul to his body had saturated the whole of his muscles. When he had emerged from that musty cavern beneath the riverbed, he had waded into the rangers with ease. There had been five of them. Normally, any one of them would surely had taken his head from his shoulders, their fighting skill and dexterity was that great, but not against the hatchet.

Tamagan had fell into their midst with a bloodlust. He set on them with a frenzy, wielding the hatchet with one hand, tearing and clawing with his other. It took only fifteen seconds and all five were dead. Great as their speed had been, Tamagan's had been greater. He had parried their attacks with something beyond his own instinct and retaliated with more strikes than the eye could follow. Most of the ranger party had been hit ten times before their dead bodies had hit the ground.

Tamagan had run after that, both in fear of another ranger party and at his own display. It wasn't until later that it sunk in what had happened. Shortly after that realization he had returned to the southern hills to pay back his people for their "kindness."

The hobgoblin sighed as visions of his brutal past faded back to the scene of his goblin followers around him. They were settling down for a long winter night, their bellies full of the food that Tamagan had secured for them. The hobgoblin wondered what would have happened to these worthless little creatures if he hadn't pulled them out of their snowy grave. He also wondered why he had done it and if he really cared.

The least homely of the goblin females stepped up to Tamagan, pulling him down with her to the buffalo rugs near the fire. She cast off the ratty, deer hide shawl she wore and went to work beneath his dirty loincloth.

Tamagan sighed again, resting the gleaming hatchet beside him and folded his hands behind his massive head. Up through the hole in the ceiling he saw the moon break through the thick cloud cover, the brightness of Gabryl's eternal chariot matching the gleam of the shimmering hatchet.

*

Kael was on his feet and set to attack before he was even awake. His body had jerked him from the ground out of his slumber before his mind could respond. The powerful visions of a dream of Alique still flitted at the corners of his scowling eyes.

He recognized the surroundings of his modest cave home: a typical flame surrounded by smooth rocks heating the room from the center. Above that cooked the hindquarter of deer meat that Kael had won. Keeping the winter outside, the lower two-thirds of the cave mouth was covered by limbs and wood Kael had fashioned together with vine and weed to make a door. All was familiar and in place in his home.

All save the man crouching near the fire.

Kael and the man locked eyes. The stranger didn't move a muscle. Kael crouched a little lower in anticipation of the man's possible attack. It didn't make sense that the stranger would enter his home, replace the door to keep out the elements, and then wait for Kael to awaken so he could kill him; but, then, odder things had happened before.

Kael regarded the stranger in a new light, though, given the man's garb and aura. He couldn't tell the man's height since he was crouched by the fire, his forearms on his knees, but the man looked far taller than Kael was. He had jet-black hair that was long. It was pulled into a braid at the back of his skull that flowed down well past his shoulders.

His features weren't very different from Kael's. Both shared fair skin and rugged, masculine features. The stranger's cheekbones were a bit higher and more pronounced, his jaw-line and face slightly less square than Kael's. He wore simple cotton clothes: a long sleeved jerkin and heavy, loose-fitting pants tucked into knee high leather traveling boots. His garb was well made and all of it was a sandy brown. Kael noticed his well-worn boots and the fact that the toes were open, only a strap running between his big and next toe. He wore thick stockings under his boots.

On the stranger's arms, legs, and chest, he wore an unusual set of armor. They were thick, square "boards" of some sort, curving to perfectly form his body. There were four large pieces on his upper arms and legs, and five short ones, two on his forearms and shins and one, circular, dangling at his waist near his groin. The largest one was on his torso strapped with thick leather to a similar piece on his back, the bottom secured both to his belt and back. All of them were covered with runes and symbols. The pieces were secure and didn't slide out of place when the stranger moved, even when he stood. Kael was right about the stranger's height. He was well over two paces tall, at least a spread-hand's breadth taller than Kael was.

As the stranger stood, something fell from his lap to dangle at his left hip: a sword. It was a thin weapon, the blade around three feet long, with a two-handed grip. The handle was wrapped with twisted leather, the pommel and guard were small and simple.

"A warrior," Kael whispered at last, standing up from his wary crouch. The distance between the two was less than ten paces—the diameter of the cave—and only the campfire was between them. Kael was not worried about the obvious skills of the stranger as a warrior. It was the power that radiated from the stranger that Kael noted—his aura. "A warrior...and perhaps...more?"

The stranger bowed his head low, pursing his lips and shrugging his shoulders slightly.

"I apologize for my intrusion into your home without welcome," the stranger stated. His voice was deep, resonant, and powerful. His eyes held the strength of rock. "When I found you in the clutches of the blizzard, you were barely a stone's throw from your destination." The stranger gestured around himself with a hand. "I thought, after surviving the conflict with the goblins and werewolves, that would be a sorry epitaph for you."

"Then, thank you," Kael bobbed his head ever so slightly. He still wasn't sure how he should feel about this tall, dark warrior.

"Please," the stranger gestured at the cooking meat. "After all, you are the one that downed the creature."

Kael snorted and stepped forward to the opposite side of the campfire. After regarding the stranger for a long moment, he sat down, crossing his legs. The stranger nodded again, and pulled a slender knife from behind him, the blade barely four inches long. Before Kael had a chance to consider what the stranger would do with it, the small blade had carved a piece of meat and flicked it to Kael. The blonde warrior caught the meat gingerly and began to cautiously chew at it.

"Please," the stranger chuckled. "I would have cut your throat when you slept had that been my intent."

Kael stopped, considered the words for a moment, shrugged, and continued to eat. The stranger cut himself a piece, sheathed his blade, and sat back onto a raised boulder, his elbows on his knees. Kael kneeled forward, reached over the spit, and held his hand forward toward the stranger.

"The knife."

The stranger looked up in mid-bite, unmoving.

"If I wanted you dead," Kael smiled, "I would have broke your neck when I first awoke."

The stranger squinted his eyes, held for a moment, then pulled the knife and tossed it to his host. Kael caught it deftly and carved both of them another hunk of meat. As the duo took to their second helping, the stranger stopped, raising his head. Kael, too, felt the tremor in the back of his mind.

"How long have I been out?" Kael asked quietly. He looked back quickly behind himself, seeing his long dirk lying where he had awoken. It was the one he had taken from a demon's corpse long ago and it was a good weapon. He reached back and grabbed it in his ready hand. Looking over, Kael saw the stranger had followed his movement carefully, and then replaced his gaze again on the large door. Kael wondered if this man would truly be an ally.

The silence was long and complete save for the popping of the burning wood. The stranger lifted his head, seeming to sniff at the air. He slowly slid his thin blade from its leather sheath and gripped it one-handed with his right hand. Kael's eyes nearly bulged at the sight of the amazing weapon. The blade was long and slender, curving back near the tip so slightly it was nearly unnoticeable. The backside of the blade was thick and flat, the exact opposite of the fore side. It had been sharpened finer than a hair, half-diamond wedges polishing the entire edge. In the firelight the blade truly shone, as if ablaze itself. The polished steel was a veritable mirror.

"Werewolves," the stranger said at last.

"Are you cer…" Kael began. The air filled with the sound of howling.

"Aye," the stranger returned with a nod of his head, covering his top lip with his lower. "Fairly certain."

Before Kael could form a reasonable retort, the makeshift door exploded, sending shards of wood raining down on the duo. The sudden rush of winter wind blew the deer hindquarter into the flames and flared the campfire to twice its size, then doused the flame completely. The air was thick with burnt flesh and freezing cold as five figures stepped out of the raging snowstorm into the mouth of the cave. Gabryl's orb chariot was visible past their massive, hair-covered bodies, shading the black clouds around it in mysterious blue.

Kael felt the fear in his heart rise and decided that he must try to douse it in rage before it froze him like the wind had. Lowering his head to his chest, his long, thick, unkept hair fell around and into his face. He gripped his dirk tightly in his left hand, trying desperately to will open his gate of power. The werewolves looked on his hellish countenance and held for the slightest of a second.

It was a second that Kael took full advantage of.

Letting his fright turn into fury, Kael bathed in the pure ferocity of the moment and hurled himself into the depths of the lycanthropes. He broke through the front two with his onslaught and began to slash and tear at the three behind. Those three dodged his assault easily with a backward step, falling into a triangle around him. The two he had pushed through rushed forward toward the stranger.

"Come," the stranger smiled, gripping his sword handle tight with both hands before him. "Meet your doom." The two wolf men roared their rage and fell onto the warrior.

Kael did not fare as well.

As Kael faced off against the crouching werewolves, his mind took the scant moment to rationalize the reality before him. That instant impulse of thought spun its humanity around the gate of power harnessed by his essence. Kael felt the diminished energy within himself as the familiar emptiness gradually began to fade. Wide-eyed terror gripped his heart and clenched tight around his stomach as he realized he was just a man now. A man facing three creatures that could tear him limb from limb.

The fear of old coursed through his veins now. It was the fear that had run out his bowels and down the inside of his legs when he had kneeled speechless before the awful might of Hosampsich the demon lord. It was the fear that had made his mind blame himself for the death of his true love, the death of Alique. All of this exploded within him in the span of a half-second—the very time it took for a gate of power to seal.

"S-stay b-b-back," Kael stammered as he desperately tried to build his bravado. "D-don't m-m-make me k-kill, you."

"A-a-all-all right, g-g-guy," one wolf man laughed, no growl to his voice. "Sheez, can ya believe this guy?" The two other hairy creatures matched the first's laugh with throaty growling guffaws. "This is a joke. Kill him."

Kael's blood stopped cold at those words, but didn't have a chance to react to them as his back was ripped open from behind. He fell forward from the force of the blow, bent at the waist, his dirk flying from his hand. As he was heading to the ground the one at his flank kicked him in the side of the head. Stars exploded before his eyes as he was plunged into the foot-deep snow. The air sung with laughter amplified by the merciless winter wind. Kick after kick, punch after punch rained down on Kael's struggling, writhing form. One concentrated on raking his long, jagged claws the length of the human's back.

Kael flailed out wildly, desperately, to punch or kick away the savage hunters, but for every blow he landed, they returned threefold. He screamed for his mind to open up his power, but the emptiness would not come. It had never happened like this before. The power had never been so unstable. It had never completely deserted him so utterly. Kael wished to hold the Midnight Blade again and decimate this trash.

The truth of the moment blasted away his wish like a leaf in a tornado as the assault suddenly halted. His back and body was raw and sticky from the raking claws. Already bruises formed on his ribs and arms.

"What a joke," the lead werewolf scoffed. He looked over seeing his other two companions being cut apart by a dazzling display of swordsmanship by the dark haired stranger. "Come on," he flicked his head at Kael's groaning form. "Pick him up and let me kill him so we can save those other two idiot's lives."

Chuckling, the two lackey wolf men gripped Kael roughly and hauled him to his unsteady feet. Kael's mind could no longer focus on the situation, the pain of the beating too great. He hung like a rag doll between the two.

"That's it, boys," the leader smiled, placing one hand on Kael's hanging head and pulling his fist back to strike. "This one is gonna go straight through his rib cage and tear out his heart." The two laughed. They had seen their leader do this countless times before. It was a good show.

"No," Kael hissed, pure rage seething through his fogged and battered brain. The sloth in his limbs drained away, replaced by a sudden surge of very real fire. He abandoned the reason of his mind, the attempts to will open the power within himself. Instead, Kael threw himself into the depths of the familiar emptiness and surrendered to the moment. Free of the shackles of his humanity, his instincts tore open the gate of power. Gevurah opened itself within his soul, seemingly blasting out of his brain and left arm to consume his whole being. Energy bathed over his entire form like a sticky fluid, coating him with an invisible shield of god-like power.

Kael raised his head to face the leader's approaching blow. His teeth were bared and his eyes slits. As the punch came in, Kael lunged forward to butt with his head. His forehead struck faster and harder than the wolf man's approaching fist and they came together with a thunderclap.

Every bone from the werewolf's shoulder down exploded into dust.

"Hey, now..." one of the lackeys gasped. Before either could think, Kael raised his arms up and slammed the two wolf men together over his head. They hit with a sickening snap and both fell lifeless to the ground at Kael's feet. The bones in their skulls and necks were shattered.

"S-stay b-b-back," the leader gasped, gripping his hanging right arm with his left and backing up against the cave mouth. His beserker bloodlust was gone and there was no adrenaline left to sustain his rage. "L-leave me b-b-be."

Kael looked up through his long greasy bangs at the hairy creature; his fists were balls of death at his sides. The cloud cover was dissipating, revealing Gabryl's shining chariot fully now. The revealing glow showed Kael that the werewolf was nothing more than a man with a wolf hide sewed onto his very skin. A glowering wolf head was stitched with ligament to his very scalp.

The blue moonlight gleaming in Kael's mad eyes turned the wolf man's spine into the same matter now made up his shattered arm.

"Run."

"Wha-what?" the wolf man gasped back at the enraged human. He considered his options for an instant, glancing into the cave. The dark-haired warrior had cleaned his blade on one of the two dead men's backsides and had stood again to witness another death. Without another thought the wolf man launched himself into the diminishing blizzard, disappearing into the flying snow.

Kael stood at the cave entrance, his shoulders drawn back and his head lowered for a fight.

"Better to let nature finish him off," the dark stranger agreed, slowly sheathing his magnificent sword. "Who knows whatever else may lurk in that hellish cold?"

"Truly. Who knows?" Kael nodded with a growl, jumping into the enveloping elements.

The stranger started, and then held himself in check. Only death waited out there, and he was no fool to tempt the evil of this night. Indeed, the death gods were influencing the night with their full glory as the clouds were parting.

Before the tall, dark-haired warrior could move to renew the campfire, a figure broke out of the wind and snow with a stumble and stood at the mouth of the cave. The moonlight shone bright behind the massive form. His hairy right arm hung limp, but his stance spoke of power and victory. The stranger pulled his blade and stepped up to kill his host's murderer when the wolf man fell forward at the warrior's feet.

His back was completely open through to his ribcage.

The stranger looked up to see Kael step out of the whiteness. He held there for a moment then tossed something onto the defeated pseudo-lycanthrope at the dark warrior's feet.

It was the wolf man's spine.

*

Razikyl blew the sweat out of his face with a sputtering huff. His eyes slightly burned from his own sweet perspiration, his thick, dark eyebrows unable to fully dam the flow off of his hairless scalp. He was bare save for his thick work pants. The floor that ran with his cooling water. He stood over his workbench, hands weaving intricate, exact patterns that could abide no mistakes as his gravelly voice breathed phrase after phrase of binding magical language. After eleven hours, the defining moment was now hand.

The entire subterranean cave glowed under the light of nearly seven hundred candles. They intermixed with his counters of potions, vials, and spiraling distilling glasses whose contents lent their own mystic qualities to the hellish light. The very granite of the rocky cave shuddered from the power it housed. It was as if it were the only thing wise enough to fear the energy that was being unleashed.

Razikyl opened his eyes wide as the defining moment materialized.

Continuing to manipulate the energy coursing throughout the cave with one frantic hand, he slipped his other into a pocket of his pants and withdrew a slender, red, porcelain vial. With a flick of his thick thumb, he popped off the cork lid and held the vial's neck in a delicate triangle between his fore and middle fingers and his thumb. He began to match his other hand's movements with the vial holder, albeit more deliberate.

Razikyl inverted the vial and began to scream the mystic words as a command of the very essence and will of God. Roaring defiance to the natural order, the orcen sorcerer drew out the contents of the vial with his own very powerful and incomparable Netsah.

A thick, soupy mist poured out of the vial and covered the body lying on the granite workbench. The fog continued, impossibly for the size of the container, and fell onto the body like a greedy dinner guest. Here and there occasionally a stream or vein would move away from the workbench or try to dissipate into the static-filled air, but Razikyl would not allow it. With a snap of his wrist or fingers the molecules of the mist would congeal again, then begin to feed on the body once more.

Over and over the wizard roared his tongue-tying words, exacting a heavy toll on both the magic he fought to control and his own body. The air was thick with the stink of human sweat and burning wax, all of it mixing with the powerful magic for exactly what the orc sought.

Suddenly, the mist was gone.

Razikyl nearly gasped at the results he had hoped for. Grinning widely, he lowered his voice to a calm, melodic chant, working his hands slowly now, pausing only the instant it took to discard the red vial. He closed his eyes as he continued to smile and speak. Soon, the results of his long work would be fully realized.

Actually, the results proved themselves realized even before he expected, as a thin-fingered hand slipped over his throat and nearly crushed his larynx.

Razikyl opened his eyes in time to see the cave sail by in a blur as he crashed loudly into a row of heavy glass vials. The liquids mixed as they tore free of their cells and erupted into an unexpected explosion of deafening proportions. Razikyl muttered a quick word that doused the flame that rose up to consume him. He hissed another quick phrase and rubbed his forehead and chest, hopefully steeling his body from harm of another such attack.

The figure that rose up to stand on the granite workbench was a form of incomparable beauty and undeniable strength. Standing two hands shy of two paces tall, she had long, amber hair that flowed just past her shoulders. Her pronounced cheekbones, long nose, and full lips fueled the fire in the orc's loins as surely as they had to any other male creature that had ever set eyes upon her. Her build was athletic and her stance sure as she stood fully naked. Her breasts were full and firm, her hips curved and powerful. Her legs and arms were thin and lithe, yet wired with the muscle of a jungle cat. Her eyes fell on Razikyl like a weapon. They were a color of brown that not even nature could match.

"What is all of this?" she quietly asked of the orc, holding up her arm and fist before her. Her entire arm (and body, for that matter) was covered in dark tattoos of runes and symbols of a varied nature. Here was a design of an intricate cross of stone; there was a smattering of geometrical shapes placed in a very precise pattern. She looked down at her body, seeing that the tattoos covered her entire body save for her breasts and nether region. Her pubic hair was shaved clean and when she lifted her foot she saw that even the bottom of that was covered. "Is it on my face?" she wondered aloud, no malice in voice.

"Here," Razikyl tossed her a broken shard of a mirror. She caught it easily and peered into its depths. She saw a single bolt of blue lightning permanently falling from inside her left eye, arcing out and around her cheekbone, ending in a point near her chin. It was the only tattoo that shone of a bright color; all of the others were formed out of dark ink. She saw that the runes ended at her neck, and when she held the mirror properly, she could see her covered back. She tossed the shard to the ground after her inspection. Razikyl was unable to discern if she cared about the tattooing or not. It seemed that she had looked more out of curiosity than concern of appearance.

"Who are you?" she asked, jumping down from the workbench and approaching the orc. Razikyl stepped up and met her halfway across the floor. "Is it you that did this to me?" When they faced, she barely came up to the massive orc's chest, yet she stood with superior confidence, her fists on her seductive hips. "Who am I?"

Razikyl looked down at her and smiled. He ran a finger down her beautiful face, tracing the lightning trail to the tip of her chin. Grasping her softly by the shoulders, the sorcerer turned her gently around. She relented with a raised eyebrow and her gaze followed his pointing finger to the garb that hung on the opposite wall of the deep stone cave.

"That is yours," the orc bent to whisper in her delicate ear. "That and everything else in this universe that you crave."

Alique, who knew nothing of ever having been Alique, heard the underlying meaning beneath the sorcerer's words and began to smile.

*

Jehoel found himself, as always, crouched at the edge of the mouth of the Cave of Kings. His toes touched the edge of the two thousand pace drop-off, his elbows on his knees and wings folded and pointed back behind him. The storm was calming for the moment and the moon was beginning to bathe the snow-covered lands far below. The angel knew the winter was far from over, but this would be a welcome reprieve to the creatures he watched every day.

The night before, Jehoel had seen yet another example of the vileness of these mortals. A band of hobgoblins had invaded a neighboring goblin tribe and murdered half of them in their sleep. By the time the smaller goblins had finally managed to form into some sort of a defensive front with the few that had not fled or been killed, it was too late. The hobgoblins ran through them like electricity through the air. More than forty of the green-skinned, spineless creatures were slaughtered. The remaining fifteen were kept for slaves, either for servitude or torturous pleasure.

Jehoel had watched the entire scene from high above and done nothing. The day before that he had seen that same goblin tribe decimate a small band of wood elves while they gathered around a campfire.

"Who was to be saved?" Jehoel breathed, his words snatched by the surrounding winds that were gathering for another freezing rise. "Who should be mourned? The goblins attacked the elves and ate them. The hobgoblins enslaved the goblins for their own designs. The goblins would surely do the same to others if the opportunity presented itself. The wood elves of the forests renounce violence and choose to flee rather than fight. Does this not mark them as targets to the more feral creatures? Does this not invite violence by those who care little for peace and harmony and more for survival?"

Jehoel ran a hand through his silken blonde hair and hung his head. He felt guilt that he had not defended the helpless elves from their vicious fate. Did that make him like the demons that he strove against? They would have aided the goblins, and then ate the goblins, too. Jehoel's inactivity had brought about much the same result. He wished to oppose the objectives of demons and evil for more reason than just to oppose them. He demanded a rational reason more that just the opposite side of a sword fight. What had the mortals below done to deserve Jehoel's aide?

Then, he thought, what of the goblins? Jehoel saw that these creatures seemed to be made of pure evil. If there was ever a chance for them to take advantage over a neighboring tribe or species, they did. If there was a chance of gathering dead wood for a fire or chopping down a living tree for its flesh, they chopped down the tree. That is, if they weren't too lazy. They lived in their own feces and if they weren't killing something—anything—they were continuously copulating. Jehoel saw why there were so many goblins. If female goblins weren't carrying or having children, they were trying to. Children seemed to serve a lot of roles. Males made the younger ones do everything that they couldn't make the females do, and if scavenging went poorly, they were delectable entrées.

Jehoel stood up and scanned through the clouds to the north. There dwelled the bulk of the scattered, loose hobgoblin tribes. They weren't much different than the goblins except they were twice as big and yellow. One main difference was the fact that hobgoblins did not participate in cannibalism. Past that, they were ever bit the desecrators as their goblin cousins.

Within the woods that the hobgoblins inhabited were the simple wood elves. They shared ideals with the animals and other inhabitants of the forests. They foraged berries, fruits, grasses, and bark where they could and hid from the bigger predators. Occasionally, they would use their wood skill to aid an injured animal, be it hunter or hunted, but inexorably that same kindness would not be shown on their next confrontation with the creature.

Though it seemed silly to Jehoel for these bipedal humanoids to seemingly renounce their higher reasoning and throw themselves back into nature's most basic food chain, it pulled at his emotional heartstrings. He could understand the elves' desire to live a basic and uncomplicated existence. What he could not grasp was the fact that they threw themselves to the mercy of their natural enemies. They seemed to create their own victimization. Did such actions warrant Jehoel's intervention and protection?

Jehoel sighed. He shared a basic phenotypic make-up with these creatures, yet he understood none of them. The fair-winged warrior placed a hand on the enormous handle of the Midnight Blade and turned back into the Cave of Kings. Before him stood the dark warrior that he had met days ago.

"Dark Warrior," the black-garbed figure chuckled, his cape flowing about him as if trying to consume him. "I like that."

Jehoel double gripped the Midnight Blade, drawing it only five inches. The dark steel of the blade matched the night void of the Dark Warrior's clothes. The red of the sash around his waist and shins, and the bucklers at his wrists glinted with the slant jewel eyes of the weapon's cross-guard.

"What are you doing here?" Jehoel stated flatly. He wasn't afraid of this mysterious dark figure, but he wasn't stupid, either. The Dark Warrior before him verily radiated power and the angel respected that.

"What are you doing here?" the dark one returned evenly.

"I live here." Jehoel answered matter-of-factly.

"Do you?" the dark man asked stepping up to circle the fair angel. "Is this where you were born, then?"

"Well, no..." Jehoel began, turning to always face his mysterious guest.

"Oh," the stranger looked down at the gut-wrenching distance below. "You discovered this place." Jehoel didn't say anything this time. He wasn't entirely sure what the dark one was up to. "No? How did you find this place?"

Jehoel sighed. For some reason the dark warrior was looking for a confrontation and the angel wanted nothing of it. He was tired of the posturing and the arrogance that had identified him and the others as WindBearers. As such a hunter he had acted more as a mortal child than a being of power and purpose. Jehoel walked through the dark warrior's circling stalk and into the Cave of Kings.

"I am sorry," a voice came from outside as Jehoel settled down at the base of the grand rock throne. The dark warrior stepped into the mouth of the cave, barely hiding his outline from the glowing moonlight outside. "I only came to question your knowledge of this place."

"My knowledge?" Jehoel raised his hard blue eyes. "I know nothing of this place. It was once the home of Appollyon the bounty master until he was slain by me. When I ran as a leader among the WindBearer hunters it was a place for me to find purpose in my abilities—in my existence. It could not house much power, I suspect, since Appollyon was unable to use it to save his own life."

"You are partly wrong," the dark warrior stated, crossing his arms and leaning back on one foot against the cave wall. "Appollyon never ventured into the darkness beyond. It was beyond even him to harness the power that rages there."

"Then you know what lies in the depths of that darkness?" Jehoel cocked his head, one hand still gripping the Midnight Blade. "What knew you of Appollyon? What know you of the Cave of Kings?"

"There is more knowledge in the universe than any one being can possibly contain, Jehoel," the dark warrior said after a long silence. "Appollyon was a guard. Nothing more. He was put here to protect the Cave of Kings. True, the bounty master was powerful in his own right, but, in the end, he could not stand before the might of an angel wielding a power he was not created to face."

"So," Jehoel nodded, nearly smiling at the seeming confirmation, "I am an angel."

"At least you were. You still may be. I truly don't know."

Jehoel paused at that. It made little sense to him, but he didn't press the point. He knew that his memory was nonexistent and his brain a fog. He was in no position to question the validity of any point, even one that made no sense to him.

"What do you know, dark warrior?" Jehoel stood back to his feet. He cast a quick glance to the bottomless darkness behind him then let his eyes fall again on his guest. "What do you know of what you ask me?"

The dark warrior scratched his chin as if in contemplation, then adjusted his mask and wrist bracers.

"I know you are Jehoel. I know that you wield the Midnight Blade. Perhaps it is my intent to only recruit you as an ally to my cause."

"What is your cause, dark warrior?"

The dark garbed warrior chuckled quietly at that. He pushed away from the cave wall and stood daunting as the moonlight bathed him. His haunting cape billowed as if it were alive, covering him whole one instant, then flowing back to block the outside world.

"You are a valuable warrior, Jehoel. I may again be in need of your varied talents and it is my intent to have them at my disposal."

"Again, you say?" Jehoel wondered aloud. "So I have fought for you before? Is that it? And what will endear my 'varied talents' to your cause this time, dark warrior, if what you imply is true?"

"You are an angel, Jehoel," the dark warrior turned to exit the cave. "You can't help but do the right thing."

Out of the moonlit, cloudy sky descended the dark warrior's ebony steed, lighting down an inch off of the ground. He jumped into the bone saddle, adjusting the huge scimitar at the pommel and the dirk at his thigh beneath his loose pants.

"Take good care of yourself, Jehoel. Don't let those mortals below urge you into something you may not live to regret."

Jehoel stepped out into the cold, night air to see the dark warrior disappear into the cloudbank of the rising storm. Snow began to fall again as he contemplated his meeting with the dark warrior and wondered what was to come. He looked over the cliff edge again to spy through the vapor and falling winter on the mortals below. He knew that the storm that ravaged this land was going to get much worse, and he wondered what role he was destined to play in the drama that seemed to be mounting.

Jehoel didn't think to consider if he would survive or not.

*

"Jyautch," the strange armored warrior stated as he turned. He had put the finishing repairs on the destroyed door, keeping the rising blizzard outside. "My name is Jyautch."

"Kael," he said rising from the ring of rocks to formally shake his guest's hand. He nodded his head at the new door. "We've done a fine job fixing the door. The storm rises again. It'll be the death to this land."

"But not to us, friend," Jyautch smiled, slapping Kael's shoulder heartily. "We'll ride this out in comfort."

"Comfort," Kael snorted, stepping down to the stone ring to work his two flint rocks together again. "We'll freeze solid if I don't get the fire going again."

"Here," Jyautch crouched down and took the flint rocks from Kael. Kael stepped up, not sure whether to be indignant or not. There wasn't enough time to be.

Jyautch held his cupped hands over the small pile of brush, palming the flint. He looked up at Kael's doubting eyes and chuckled. "Just watch, friend." The tall, dark stranger took a deep breath, then let it go slowly. He rubbed his hands together in a blur, for what looked to Kael like two times. It was closer to two thousand. The flint rocks erupted into a tiny shower of sparks and rained down onto the dry brush, igniting it immediately. Jyautch quickly fed the infant flame from their ample stock of firewood and it roared to a healthy blaze.

"How..." Kael stammered wide-eyed at Jyautch's dexterous display of speed. "My flints, the speed. How did you..."

"Same as your Gevurah, friend," the swordsman stated quietly, standing to match Kael's gaze. "Your power over the Gevurah gives you matchless strength. My speed comes from the gate of the Hessed."

"Hessed," Kael whispered quietly, scanning through the catalog of his memory for that familiar word. After a brief second he remembered. He had read about it when he had wielded the Midnight Blade and lived in the Tower of Hosampsich. "Within the tomes that I have read, Hessed had been identified with the emotions of love, mercy, and grace. The very definition of the word was haste."

"True," Jyautch nodded, his eyes still even with his host's. "I cannot confirm that love, mercy, and grace are Hessed's qualities, but speed is. I can move faster than most mortals can possibly see. It is that very ability that makes me a greater swordsman."

Kael nodded, breaking his gaze with Jyautch and letting it fall on the blaze warming the cave as he crouched down. He crossed his arms, resting his elbows on his knees and his chin on his forearm. Jyautch dropped his eyes to the fire as well, sitting down to gather his own knees to his breastplate. Silence reigned for long minutes before the tall, dark-haired swordsman broke it.

"What do you know of your power, Kael?" Jyautch's words were quiet but taut. "And what are these tomes that you have had at your disposal to know so much of the gates of power?"

"You speak as though I am a witless fool."

"No, my friend, you misunderstand," Jyautch quickly backtracked. "Given your heritage, I would think it uncommon for your people to know the written word."

Kael started as if to argue, then chuckled and sighed. There was no point getting upset over the truth.

"Aye," he nodded. "I was taught knowledge of the word when I gained access to the Tower of Hosampsich. There I learned what the tomes would speak. Never before had I beheld a book. They are powerful. Perhaps as powerful as these gates of power. Perhaps more."

"What you say is true. Very nearly more so," Jyautch smiled suddenly, then resumed his seriousness. "You lived in the Tower of Hosampsich? You knew the demon?"

"Yes," Kael started again. "Well, I really didn't know him. He was a scourge to my people. He was the lord of these lands where my people once dwelled. He tried to kill me. I killed him first."

"You killed the demon Hosampsich?" Jyautch was wide-eyed in amazement. "What of his ancient sword?"

"You knew of the Midnight Blade?" Kael queried.

"Everyone knows of that grand weapon, my friend," Jyautch returned. "It is one of the first items ever forged out the heart of God's creation. Hosampsich has held it longer than any historian can remember. Surely it is the original source of your wondrous power."

"Surely," Kael snorted, a tinge of disgust in his voice.

"I mean no disrespect, friend,"

"No," Kael shook his head. "I am sorry. It's me. From the beginning of my life I have been a pawn. It should not surprise me now that even with this grand power, I am still little more."

Jyautch nodded at that and allowed silence again to fill the cave. There was nothing he could say that could possibly console his host, and he was in no real position to refute the statement. Often times he felt the same way. The only sound that filled the air was the popping of wood and the crackle of the flame. It was Kael who finally spoke.

"I know very little of my power. I was born to a people that have inhabited these rolling hills for centuries—the Kelt-Ra. We were a people of hunters and warriors. We lived with the land and for the land. We were its stewards. Nothing entered these hills without the consent and respect of my people. The goblinoid creatures were driven away, disdained for their disrespect of life and the land that provided for them.

"Countless centuries rolled by, I was taught, and we never knew strife. If there was a threat to the land, my people banded together the many tribes to form a grand clan and defeated whatever opposed them. Nothing evil or vile treaded these grassy hills for their entire rule over these lands. My grandfather's great-grandfathers were the last to live and tend to these lands as chieftains, not knowing the terror and death that would befall the Kelt-Ra.

"My grandfather's grandfather was the chieftain when it happened. It was like a swarm of locusts come to destroy the grasslands, only this plague sought humanity. They appeared out of the eastern horizon one day like an approaching storm cloud, but moisture was not what they rained down on the land.

"Demons. Great winged beings that stood a foot taller than any man my people had ever seen. They walked on two legs like a man, had two arms, a head—every one appeared to be like a man, but they were not. They were distortions of men, massive, evil reflections of the very nightmares that men dream. Some were half-animal, half-man; others walked and looked more like beasts. All of them were covered in horns, tusks and had appendages that only an imaginary creature could have.

"They flew from over the eastern mountains and descended on my people without warning. They wielded weapons that looked like swords or spears, but shot fire, ice, and commanded the very elements. My people were decimated. It is said that not one demon was even injured in the attack. My father always said it was because of the suddenness and viciousness of the attack, but I knew better. It was because of the simple fact that no man could stand before the demons' frightening and incredible might."

"You know better now," Jyautch interrupted quietly.

"Yes," Kael nodded in agreement. "I know better now. I also know that the power I wield makes me more than just a man." Jyautch nodded back at that. Both of them knew that their access into the gates of power had raised them over mortal mankind. "Anyway, my long-gone patriarch saw that his people could not stand up to the power of demons, so he looked to leave the lands they had lived in for so long. He took what was left of my clan and hid them beneath the ground. All chieftains had long known about the underground tunnels beneath our land and had kept them a secret in case of any such need. The caves and tunnels were found by one of the first chieftains over a millenium ago and that knowledge was passed down with great care to each heir. It isn't known how or why the caves and tunnels were constructed but all that matters is that my people were able to use them to escape death.

"The chieftain took a scouting party, leaving my people safe beneath the ground, and broke out in search of a new home. Twenty warriors left on that scouting party and only one returned three months later. It was not my great-great-grandfather.

"The lone scout returned malnourished and on the very threshold of death. He had been a mighty warrior, twice the size of any other, and when he returned he weighed barely more than an adolescent. The tale he spoke of was the very definition of Hell. To the north in the vast forests, the goblinoid creatures were enslaved by the demons and putting every living thing to the sword. To them it had appeared that the goblinoids had been under heel for centuries. To the east, in the mountains, the demons swarmed like gnats in a swamp. It was surely the seat of their empire. It was there that the scouting party was first discovered and nearly destroyed. Half of their number, including my great-great-grandfather, was butchered by a wandering band of demonic monsters. From their war cries, the surviving members of our party learned the name of the ruling demon: Hosampsich."

"Hosampsich," Jyautch nodded. "He is a powerful entity."

"Was," Kael corrected, not raising his eyes from the warm fire. "He is no more.

"As terrible as the scene to the north and east was," Kael continued, "It was nothing compared to what raged to the west and south. Past the Border River that represented the outer reaches of the Kelt-Ra's boundaries, there was nothing but fire. Where fertile soil and lush vegetation once thrived, now there was nothing but a continuous blaze. The remnants of the scouting party waited nearly two weeks for the incredible blaze to die down but it never relented. Numerous times they saw demons fly over or into the intense inferno. Not once did they see anything emerge. After another two weeks waiting for the blaze to diminish, a band of demons discovered them and killed them to a man. That remaining man fled death and ran for his life. He didn't stop running until he came back to where the last of his tribe lay in hiding.

"That lone man relayed his story to the tribe and lived barely through one more night. That was the night that my great-grandfather became chieftain and that my people became moles and scavengers."

"But your people survived, that is what mattered," Jyautch stated after a brief quiet. "What more could they do than flee to the safety of hiding?"

"My people are no more," Kael returned, his voice strong but barely above a whisper. "I am the last of my people. Only I remain."

Jyautch sighed. What Kael spoke of was a scenario that had happened to thousands of people in many lands. The dark-haired warrior knew that Kael didn't yet know of the many kinds of people that covered the earth, but the story was very nearly always the same. These people were some of the last to witness the terror, it seemed to Jyautch. His own people had fought demons and devils for over a millennia. Why now did the demons choose to attack peoples they had left alone for countless centuries?

It was inevitable, he reasoned. There was no place in the world that man could escape from the might of demons. This place had lasted longer than any other but in the end it, too, had fallen.

"What then of you?" Jyautch urged. "How did you survive when no others could? How did you come to master the Gevurah?"

“I am hardly a master of anything,” Kael chuckled. “My survival is one of luck, not skill.”

“I beg to differ, friend,” Jyautch returned, his voice bound in seriousness. “I saw what you did to that wolf worshiper. I saw you fight that hobgoblin.”

“You saw that?” Kael jerked his head up to finally meet his new friend’s eyes. “You were there?”

“Yes,” Jyautch nodded, “I saw you fight the gigantic hobgoblin. I have been tracking him and his little troupe for some time. I came through the storm just as you faced off with him and watched from behind the goblin’s ranks. You are a true warrior. The power that the yellow monster wields is based in his beautiful hatchet. It allows him to access the Hessed and move faster than most any other being alive. You faced that power and were on the very cusp of victory. You shouldn’t have lasted ten seconds with him.”

“What can I say,” Kael chuckled, realizing that the words were not meant as an insult. “I’m a resilient bastard.”

“And that,” Jyautch resumed. “I have met tribal people like you before in lands not so very different than this. None of them knew the word resilient.”

Kael laughed out loud at that, nearly doubling over. Jyautch chuckled as well at the shared joke. Both began to feel a kinship for each other, something stronger than just a need of companionship to survive. This was the birth of a friendship.

“My time in the Tower of Hosampsich,” Kael continued, wiping tears of mirth from his eyes. The mention of his time in the arch-demon’s tower sobered the both of them immediately. “I had taken Gevurah from him…”

“What do you mean ‘taken Gevurah from him’?” Jyautch interrupted.

“My mistake,” Kael nodded in correction, “Before I knew any better, I had thought that Gevurah was the weapon’s name. It wasn’t until later I learned that was merely the power it controlled.” Jyautch understood. Often mortals referred to ancient artifacts by their power instead of their name, not realizing anything about the gates of power.

"Anyway, I had taken the Midnight Blade from him," Kael paused for a moment. "Or rather the Midnight Blade had taken me from Hosampsich. In any case, I used the sword to gut Hosampsich and skinned him like a deer."

Jyautch snorted his approval at that. "I thought I recognized the pattern of your kilt and cloak, my friend."

"Yes," Kael breathed grimly, running a hand over the immense cloak he was resting on. "I took his tusks, too, as well as the tusks of every other demon I've destroyed." Jyautch followed Kael's pointing finger to a rock hook on the opposite wall. A kilt and shirt of demon tusks hung there.

"Do you know how powerful those are?" Jyautch gasped, rising to walk over and inspect the articles. They were fitted perfectly, the tusks facing away. The tall warrior looked over many of the tusks carefully and saw that every one was detailed with intricate carvings and runes. Jyautch turned to see Kael regarding him casually. "You did this?"

"I sewed them together with demon gut and ligament and tooled the tusks with runes and power symbols that the Midnight Blade had shown me from the tomes of the tower."

"The weapon spoke to you?" Jyautch could not believe the quality of his host's work. "I have heard of that before."

"The weapon took control of me," Kael returned to staring into the depths of the fire, remembering the long months past. "It suppressed my memories and strove to make me its lackey. I don't know its full designs, but I was nothing but a tool to it. I am sure it chose me over Hosampsich only because it could meet its personal goals with me. The demon's will was probably too powerful to take over. The sword saw its chance and took it. If not me, it would have been somebody else."

"Do not let that dishearten you, friend," Jyautch turned back to the fire. "I can teach you to repel such mind attacks."

"I know now how to fight that," Kael sighed. "When I was finally able to control the power of Gevurah within myself rather than through the Midnight Blade, it was a short trek to breaking free of the sword's control. It is not the slavery to the weapon that fills my heart with sorrow. It's really two things: Foremost, I don't feel as powerful without the weapon. I would be a fool to face anything equipped as I am now. When I held the Midnight Blade, nothing could face me. I laid waste to whole parties of demons. This land was mine again for the taking. Now…who knows what fate holds this land."

"You lost the sword?"

"I became a target of demons and WindBearers alike. They banded together to defeat me. The battle when I lost the Midnight Blade was more intense than I could ever describe. In fact, I don't even remember the end. I remember being injured nearly to death by a hunting party of WindBearers and seeking refuge when the devil Imamiah attacked them. I lost consciousness and awoke some time later. Before the battle it had been late summer. When I woke, snow blanketed the ground as if in the very heart of winter."

"And the Midnight Blade was gone?"

"Gone."

"You're wrong about one thing, friend," Jyautch refuted. "You can face anything with the power you wield within your limbs. Your Gevurah is powerful enough to lay waste to whole troupes of demons, just as you have before. All you need is to be trained properly."

"And you can do that?" Kael narrowed his eyes, looking up at his guest. "You can teach me to face axe swinging demons and kill them barehanded?"

"I can do that and more."

"Why would you?" Kael asked. "What good would it do for you?"

"The good it would do would not be for me, friend. It would be for the good of all."

"All?" Kael didn't see what he meant. "All of who?"

"All of mankind," Jyautch stated plainly, as if obvious to anyone. "Mankind has great need for warriors such as us. You don't know what is going on past the boundaries of your own snow-covered hills, but you will. If not for warriors like us, mankind would exist no more."

Kael looked up at his friend and nodded slowly. It sounded good to him. To learn how to harness this power and to fight against the creatures that had brought destruction and genocide to his people brought a smile to his face. He wanted the demons that had made him the last surviving of the Kelt-Ra clan to disappear. Perhaps all that it took to accomplish that was in the hands of men such as himself.

"Kael," Jyautch interrupted his host's thoughts. "You had said it was two things that gripped your heart in sorrow. What was the other?"

Kael said nothing for a very long time. He was a loner by nature. He had been his whole life, more out of survival than for want. He was hesitant to speak of his greatest heartache. Looking up at Jyautch, Kael saw the sincerity in his newfound friend's face. This man was more than a companion of convenience; this man was a friend.

"I lost my mate."

Jyautch nodded, lowering his eyes in respect.

"She was injured when we were captured by a band of goblins," Kael explained. "I sought aide for her in the Tower of Hosampsich and she was killed when two WindBearers attacked me there."

"I am sorry," Jyautch smiled weakly.

"So am I, friend," Kael whispered softly. "So am I."

Jyautch settled down near the fire, pulling his heavy bison cloak around himself and closing his eyes. He was asleep in minutes, leaving Kael alone to track Gabryl's progress through the small opening at the top of their makeshift door. The storm was strengthening and clouds soon covered what little light the moon could offer. Kael pushed himself down to lay on the heavy tiger-striped demon cloak, wishing those clouds could lend their cover to his memory, if only for the briefest of moments.

In moments, Kael too was asleep. Fortunately, it was a sound sleep, empty of the usual haunting of his past. Instead, it was filled with the hopes of a brighter future, one in which Kael dreamt he had come to terms with what he felt were the mistakes of his past and, finally, forgiven himself.

But in the end, it was only a dream.

*

Alique fingered the two long-bladed dirks that lay on the granite workbench. The table was covered with heavy books and a hundred potions of a hundred varied shades in a hundred different jars. Smoke puffed from two distilling jars that were slowly gelling to some substance that she dared not ask about. The smell was acrid, but hinted at the smallest scent of rose and lilac. Alique smiled at that. Everything about the tall, foreboding half-orc smelled of the trace of lilac.

Her attention was back to the dirks on the table with a dismissive puff of her lips. The weapons were powerful, she knew. She could feel the very energy within them, something within herself rising when she touched them. The handles were made of bone—the femur of a demon, she thought Razikyl had said—and they fit her hands perfectly, the joint ball making a perfect, if gruesome, pommel. The diamond-shaped guards were dragon tusks, fitted through the demon bone and bound by the orcen wizard's powerful magic. The blade was the purest of steel and smooth as a lover's lie. Along the razor sharp double-sided edge ran a tiny clear tube. It looked to be made of glass and was barely the diameter of a hair. It ran up and down both edges, connecting to a thumbnail-sized container at the hilt. Alique had no idea what that was for but surely it served some purpose. It seemed everything that the orcen mage did had purpose.

"Magnificent, aren't they," a deep base voice sounded from behind. Alique didn't even bother to turn to face Razikyl. She had known that he had been coming down the long entrance tunnel to this cave since he first entered. She didn't question how she knew, even though she wanted to very badly. There was a lot that she wanted to question, but had not. It didn't yet seem the right time to do so. First, she had to learn more about this curious half-orcen sorcerer; then she would decide her best course of action.

"Yes," she agreed quietly, still fingering their outline. "The symbols you have carved into the demon bone. Some of them are the same that you tattooed onto my body."

Razikyl nodded from behind her, not offering anything. He was going to be careful with Alique at first. He was unsure how much of her original memory was left and he didn't want her remembering things that he didn't want her to remember. She was going to be the most powerful weapon he could ever possibly have, but not if she didn't want to be.

"They were made for you," the wizard urged, placing his large hands on her delicate shoulders carefully. She was wearing the garment he had constructed for her. It was made of black demon leather and nearly as thin as paper. It consisted of a long, back-less loincloth that dangled to her knees, and an enveloping cloak on her shoulders. The hood was down and the front gathered just enough to cover her breasts. Like the long dirks on the table before her, the clothes were tooled and enchanted. There was power within the fabric.

Alique reached down and grasped the two weapons. She gasped, almost erotically, as she shared a surge of energetic ecstasy with the powerful weapons. Various points on her body burned with a chilling fire of strength, the symbols and tattoos on her body responding to their mystical ability. The feeling was akin to emptiness. It was a feeling that she had never felt before, but she knew was the beginning of a wondrous power.

Razikyl stepped back, allowing Alique to turn around. She did so slowly, the dirks in her hands at her sides. The cloak seemed to move around her hands and the weapons they held, as if to hide them from the orc's view. Razikyl smiled The properties of the clothing were functioning exactly as he had intended.

"What now, orc?" Alique cocked her head slightly, her hair falling forward over her shoulder. Razikyl stunted the erotic desire that he felt nearly burst out of him. Something within Alique let her see into her host's desires for that one moment and a smile slowly spread across her face as she lowered her jaw and looked up through her wavy bangs. She stepped up and turned her back to Razikyl, pushing up against him seductively. She raised her one hand, the magical dagger still held to her palm by her thumb, and traced her extended finger through the open chest of the orc's leather jerkin. Razikyl swallowed hard, knowing exactly what she was doing, but unable, or unwilling, to stop it. "Well, orc? What now?"

"Well," Razikyl stammered. "Now I make you more powerful than you could possibly imagine."

"Ah, yes," Alique turned looking down, Razikyl's gaze following hers. The other dirk's point was hovering a hair's breadth from the wizard's crotch. "An excellent response." Alique pulled the blades back into the depths of her cloak and stepped away.

Razikyl breathed out slowly and wondered if he really knew what he was doing.

*

"Amazing," Jyautch gasped in wonder, his arms crossed before him and a smile wide across his face. "I have seen men use the power of Gevurah before, but never before with so much capability."

Kael nearly smiled at the praise that his friend heaped upon him, but could not. His eyes were shut tight and his concentration focused on the task at hand. He was holding a boulder that weighed more than twenty men in both hands over his head. Every muscle in his body bulged nearly through his skin, his veins pushed to burst. His elbows were locked tight and wavering only the slightest bit. His back and legs were straight and taut.

"Amazing," Jyautch grinned anew. He looked down from where they stood for the briefest of moments, surveying the countryside with an agreeing eye. They were in the foothills of the towering eastern mountains, their cave over twenty miles to the west. They had set out two days ago, primarily in search of more plentiful game, but also to keep mobile after the wolf men's attack a week ago. Neither feared the band of wolf worshipers, but only a fool would underestimate an enemy. There was no telling how many of the mangy fur-wearers had filtered from the southern forests to fill these snow-covered hills. They had taken up the trail of a small band of goats and had paused only a moment at the ledge of one of the many loose, rocky outcroppings for a breath. Jyautch had taken full advantage of the opportunity to help Kael become more aquatinted with his control over his power.

"Now open your eyes, my friend," Jyautch said after Kael had held the rock aloft for the count of a hundred. "Control over the gates of power is easier for a beginner when their eyes are closed. It is simpler to dispel distraction, to concentrate, and to focus. Such action is helpful at first, but many fall back on it when they are in distress. It becomes a crutch for the weak of mind or faint of heart. That is usually their death knell."

Kael nodded and took a very deep breath. Letting it out slowly, he opened his eyes. The light flooded into his brain and for the most scant of moments his limbs nearly faltered. Jyautch grimaced, but remained quiet as Kael recovered.

Kael looked out, not really focusing on anything in particular, but surveying the snowy beauty before him. The storm had relented for the moment and the sun was able to push a glimmer of its power through the heavy cloud cover to reveal the wonderment of the rolling hills of the Kelt-Ra clan. Even under three paces of snow, it was perfection to Kael's eyes.

Jyautch counted another hundred, and then asked Kael to toss down the enormous boulder. Kael shook his head and slowly lowered it to where he had picked it up. As he stood back up he willed the power raging in his limbs to subside and after a moment it complied. For a long moment his left arm retained the queer empty feeling, but then it too closed.

"Excellent, Kael," Jyautch smiled, clapping his friend on the back. "My people have learned much of the ways of the gates of power. The knowledge that I have will hopefully make you a mighty warrior."

"I am indebted to you forever, Jyautch," Kael looked up grasping his friends hand in his own. "Nothing I could ever do would repay you."

"No, my friend," Jyautch shook his head, clasping Kael's hand firmly in both of his own. "Your friendship is my reward. It is up to people like us to reclaim this world for mankind. In a very real sense, it is up to you."

Kael nodded, a smile on his thoughtful face.

"Quickly now," Jyautch laughed, running up the thin goat trail that ran up into the towering reaches of the unmovable mountains. "Our dinner awaits."

Kael grabbed the fold of his demon cloak, flipping it across his shoulder with a laugh, and ran to catch up with his comrade.

*

Alique picked her way carefully through the rugged tunnel from Razikyl's deep, dark laboratory cave. There was no light on the entire hundred-pace trek, but not once did she trigger any of the dangerous traps laid by the orcen wizard. Somehow, even beyond her own reasoning, she knew exactly where to step. Tingling in her feet and fingers kept her from stepping and touching here or there. A tiny sensation at the base of her neck warned her to duck at one point, and then to hug the wall at another. Alique was positive that the power symbols and tattoos that covered her body were the basis of her newfound awareness. She made a mental note to thank the wizard for that if she was unfortunate enough to ever see him again.

As she approached the mouth of the cave Alique moved to pull her revealing black, leather cloak around herself, but the cloak beat her to it. Just as her hands reached for the front of the garment, it pulled itself tightly together, covering her bare flesh. As if sensing her next thoughts, the long, backless loincloth rose up between her legs, covering her posterior and wrapping through itself at her waist. She wore tall black boots that rose to the top of her thighs and housed her two demon-bone dirks. She had finally divined the purpose of the thin tubes at the blade's edge—poison.

Alique tied her shoulder length amber hair back into a ponytail with a bit of string and pulled the cloak hood up as she stepped out into the snowy countryside. She squinted against the unexpected brightness. Though the sun wasn't visible through the clouds, it managed to lend its light, at least for now. The storm was rising again to the north and west and would soon overtake the land.

She smiled, closing her eyes, hugging herself tightly. Her breath condensed immediately after leaving her nose and mouth, and Alique opened her eyes again, ready to escape Razikyl's clutches. Doubt had gripped her just an hour earlier as Razikyl had settled down to sleep. She was unsure in her feelings for the wizard. She knew that he had brought her back from the very brink of death, but everything was very clouded and hazy for her. Alique could remember only bits and pieces about herself and her past, and could recall nothing concrete. If she stayed here before her memory returned, who knew with what garbage Razikyl would fill her head? She wouldn't deny herself her own reality or her own truth.

Vowing to herself to return to Razikyl after she regained the full use of her facilities, Alique stepped out from the cave mouth and into the bright winter day. She took only two steps before a vise gripped her chest and forced the very air from her. She fell into the elbow-deep snow gasping for air and tearing at her chest for any sort of release. She pulled the heavy cloak away from her heaving chest, but the pressure did not relent.

"It is not your cloak," Razikyl's voice sounded as he appeared out of the cave mouth. He cocked his head as he gazed down on Alique's bare chest appreciatively. She could read his thoughts through her squinted eyes, but could do nothing about it. She writhed in absolute pain in the snow, kicking drifts up around herself. Razikyl stepped down beside her and touched her wrinkled forehead with his large left thumb and uttered a quick phrase. Immediately the pressure that was crushing Alique's chest relented.

"Here," Razikyl sighed, helping Alique to her feet. He drew her cloak up and covered her up again, clasping the bone buttons at the front. Alique allowed him, unable to do much more than try to regain her breath. Razikyl placed a finger on her chin and raised her head up to meet her eyes with his. "There is an enchantment on your very soul that will never be erased, Alique. If you ever step beyond one hundred paces from me, you will die. If I ever die, you will die. I am your very tether to this world, your spiritual anchor, in a sense. I brought you back to this world and I will take you back out of it. Do not ever doubt or forget this."

Alique could not speak, could barely think. She managed to nod her agreement and allowed Razikyl to draw her into the folds of his enveloping cloak. He hugged her protectively as she rested her head against his heavy chest with a sigh. Again the familiar scent of lilac flooded her nasal cavity.

"Come," the half-orc urged, stepping outside into the snow. Alique followed carefully, her hand in his, a shadow to his every step. "I think it is time you learned to use the powers I have vested into you. Perhaps that will prove the honesty in my actions."

Alique wasn't sure she agreed with what Razikyl said, but the thought of being able to control these random sensations she had felt appealed to her. Of course, the fact if she wasn't at his side every moment she would die didn't hurt the sorcerer's cause either. Alique was smiling on the inside as they began to make their way to the east. Razikyl's hold over her was overpowering now, but that just might be her only chance. Nothing was a guarantee. After all, hadn't Alique been dead only days ago?

*

Tamagan stopped in his trek for a moment, looking back behind himself. His little tribe of goblins was in single file behind him, many dragging travois carrying what little the motley troupe possessed. Many of the spindly-limbed little creatures wore heavy wolf hides that were too big for their bodies. Tamagan grinned at that. The wolf men beserkers had attacked the goblin's "stronghold" and laid waste to it. The attack had been both a disaster and a boon. Though in the fight the gigantic lean-to was destroyed, Tamagan had made quick work of the wolf men. Not only did their hides now adorn the goblin's forms, but their bodies also filled the goblins' bellies.

With a chuckle and a pat on his hatchet's head, Tamagan turned and began again to trudge through the deepening snow. The storm had retreated to the north and west to regroup and attack again. It had come at an appropriate time for the goblins. Having lost their home and stability to the wolf men, it could have been a true disaster. With the storm relenting for the moment, it gave the small party the opportunity they needed. Tamagan had quickly gathered the goblins for travel and headed for the eastern mountains. The snow was lighter away from the rolling hills as even the game seemed to realize. Housing would be easier found in the caves of the towering mountains, as should food. Most of the mountain-dwelling animals had escaped the ferocity of the winter, finding refuse in the higher elevations, oddly enough.

Tamagan glanced back one more time, making sure everyone was in line, and did it for the first time without wondering why he cared. With a determined clench of his massive jaw he continued to blaze a trail through the hindering snow toward the jagged eastern horizon.

*

Jehoel rested his hands casually on the ornate golden scabbard belt around his waist as he hovered a thousand feet above the Cave of Kings. With his twelve-foot wingspan fully spread, the now-gentle updrafts held him aloft effortlessly. That would change with the approaching renewed vigor of the northern cloudbank, but for now he was content to glide calmly with the eagles.

Like the aquiline hunters around him, Jehoel surveyed the surrounding lands, albeit with a superior eye. While they gazed for the chance passing mouse, cat, or deer, the angel gazed not for food. The objects of his interest were a few steps higher on the food chain…usually.

It made good sense for the various peoples of the hill lands to migrate with the struggling game, but surely there would be some tense confrontation. The mountains were large but the vastness of the rolling hills was more hospitable by far. Despite the rugged mountains' unmatched size, barely a tenth was livable. Most of it was impenetrable snow pack, dense pine forest, or at an angle that a spider couldn't scale. The imposing terrain mixed with the meeting of racial enemies would surely bring an encounter of explosive consequences.

Jehoel brought in his wings as the wind began to rise, slowly drifting down to the ledge of the Cave of Kings. He wondered what he would do when the various peoples met up with each other. Would he fight them? Would he be better off to kill them all? That didn't seem reasonable, especially given his affection toward the humans, but what else could he do? He was safe in these mountains and wouldn't allow them to become a battleground like the hills to the west. Besides that, Jehoel thought as he turned into the Cave of Kings and its mysterious darkness, this place was far too dangerous for any mortal to find.

Jehoel stood at the heavy granite throne and pondered for a long moment. Even though he had never ventured into the cave's darkness, he knew that there was power unimaginable in its depths. Any mortal that stepped into this cave was sure to boldly enter the dark. Mortal curiosity outweighed every emotion in the universe, far greater than any angel's courage.

Jehoel stared for many long hours into the darkness, wishing he had to temerity to discover its power. He decided that he would leave the mortals to their own devices for now. All he would keep them from would be this cave.

The red, slanted, jewel eyes of the Midnight Blade gleamed brightly as Jehoel absently fingered the three-handed, jagged guarded handle, the emptiness of the black matching the fragmented thoughts of his clouded brain.

*

"Focus is the determining factor of power, my dear," Razikyl stated plainly. He stood to the left and just behind Alique, his arms crossed and his right thumb and forefinger pinching his chin thoughtfully. They stood at the top of one of the highest plateaus in the gigantic eastern mountains. "In my capacity as the demon Hosampsich's apprentice, I learned all of what is needed to access the unquenchable energy of the gates of power."

"Hosampsich," Alique nodded imperceptibly, not turning her head. She recognized that name. With that recognition came the image of an eight-foot tall behemoth of terror with the face of a nightmare and wings of a bat from hell.

"Yes," Razikyl returned. "The once-lord of the entire Kelt-Ra hill lands. He was actually the demon lord of everything you see from this lofty vantage. Nothing entered these lands without his consent or knowledge. Even fewer exited."

"Kelt-Ra," Alique muttered in recognition. "My people. I remember darkness and a musty smell." Then, as if a light had brightened in the corner of her brain, "The tunnels." Razikyl nodded carefully. He whispered a choice phrase and entered her consciousness unsuspectingly. Using a fraction of his ample Netsah power, he quickly sorted through the murky depths of her memory and let loose only what he felt she needed. "We lived in the tunnels beneath the land to escape the demons. We had escaped them for so long, but not forever. Hosampsich found out our tunnel entrances at long last and murdered us to a man."

"Yes," Razikyl nodded, still carefully sorting her probing thoughts. "You and another lived."

"Kael," she breathed. Razikyl held his breath at the name. For the week she had been alive since he had brought her back, the orc had taken every night to painstakingly alter her perceptions of what she had seen with her own eyes. Delving into her chemical and electrical subconscious, Razikyl impressed upon the physical tapestry of her brain with his ever-powerful Netsah. Nerve endings were rewired and impulses rerouted, useful knowledge added, as well as useful garbage. Now when she thought of her capture by the goblins those long months ago and being tied to the stake, instead of seeing Kael chained helplessly to a tree, Razikyl allowed her to see no chains. Kael's struggles against the binding vines were seen to Alique instead as an orgasmic dance of nihilistic ecstasy. Where Kael had fought and tore at the very flesh of the goblin tormentors, Alique's melting vision now remembered him grasping them in glee.

"But he was my love," Alique turned now to look at Razikyl. The memories seemed uncomfortable to her feelings. She thought that Kael had been her lover, not her death-cause. She remembered moments stolen together at a nearby grove of ash trees one unforgettable night. "Why would he have done anything bad to me at all?"

"Power," Razikyl sighed. He had thought of the perfect lie to tie everything together some time ago. It was the same one he had used on Kael himself not six months ago. "Kael made a deal with Hosampsich: the sword that the demon wielded for the lives of his people. Betrayal was all that it was."

"But why was I left alive?" Alique pressed, looking down to the ground sightlessly. "Why was I not found in my hiding place?"

"Many reasons, I suppose." Razikyl continued his devilish weaving. "Perhaps Hosampsich wanted you spared for later sport. It appears Kael wanted you for a sacrifice of flesh to the Midnight Blade for even more power. Maybe your survival was pure luck. Maybe your hiding place was just that good. In the end, it didn't matter. Kael ripped your fate out of the Norn's hands and cut your life thread himself. That is the truth."

Razikyl held his breath as Alique turned away once again, drawing her black leather cloak around herself. The breeze was strengthening, as was the cloud cover. It would begin snowing again soon and the duo was still an hour away from Razikyl's mountain hiding place. Despite the weather, though, the wizard knew that this moment was an important one for him. If Alique followed the logic that Razikyl set out for her then his conquest of her would be all but complete. A little chill was more than enough to stand for that.

"Focus," Alique stated at long last. "Focus is the determining factor of power."

"Yes, my dear," Razikyl grinned stepping up beside her. "Raise your hands and let me show you what I mean. Let me help you to begin accessing the all-powerful energy that is the gate of Netsah."

Razikyl reached under her arm and gently grasped the inside of her right thigh. The black-tooled leather of her loincloth seemed to beckon his hand as it grazed the shadow of her inner hip. The cloak on her shoulders billowed back and around him, welcoming the influx of power to come.

Alique's face showed no emotion or thought at all to his petty desire or actions. The tattooed runes and power symbols tingled at the approach of his massive hand and that is what aroused her interests. When he grasped her thigh, circumcising it entirely, emptiness permeated her entire leg and then her body.

"Prepare yourself, my dear," Razikyl whispered into her delicate ear. "Today you become the most powerful mortal weapon in the world." Alique tried to grin at his words, but the shock of their coupling left her unable to do anything but what she needed to.

She was unable to do anything but focus.

*

The dark-garbed warrior stepped down from his mount, his foot gliding out of the bone-white stirrup and onto the ledge of the Cave of Kings. The snow was falling again and the cloud cover had made the day more akin to night. The storm was rising, much to the dark one's liking. His milky-eyed stallion snorted lightly, stamping the rocky ledge with one mirrored, obsidian hoof. The small wings at the side of each hoof twittered quickly, lifting him an inch off of the ground for only a moment, then fell still. The dark one smiled beneath his black turban mask. His mount disliked the Cave of Kings as much as any rational creature should.

Stepping into the cave, the dark warrior's flowing cape glowed bright red then an eerie purple. It shone as if made of pure energy for an instant then again appeared as black cloth. The brief shimmer brightened the cave for a moment and Jehoel turned slowly from where he stood by the granite throne. The Midnight Blade was in his hands and glowing a murderous red. The slant jeweled eyes flared bright at the hilt.

"Please," the dark warrior raised his hands, still slowly advancing. "Don't tell me the sword has taken you over, Jehoel. You were always stronger than that."

"Aye," Jehoel nodded. "I am stronger. I have silenced the weapon's voice. As long as I wield it, it shall remain mute."

"Good," the dark one lowered his hands. Jehoel, on the other hand, did not relent his stance. The dark one crossed his arms and cocked his head ever so slightly. "What seems to be the matter, Jehoel?"

"I do not trust you, dark one," the lithe blonde warrior stated. His wings opened slowly, the Midnight Blade brightening as they did. "Nor do I remember you as you seem to remember me. Perhaps from some long, lost time we knew one another, but no longer. Until I am able to discover the truth of myself and of this place, I have appointed myself its protector. There is power here beyond any being in this realm and I am not about to let any take control of it, for ill means or otherwise."

"True," the dark warrior nodded, raising one hand to cup his masked chin. "There is power within the depths of this cave that few can imagine. Appollyon was actually here more as a guardian than as you WindBearers' precious bounty master. The purpose of the guise was a mystery to all."

"Appollyon is no more, as you already know," Jehoel raised his clenched jaw, his knuckles white in their grasp. "He is no more than dust."

"The fleshy shell he inhabited on this planet is dust, that is true," the dark one agreed with a nod. "But Appollyon himself is as alive, as your brother-in-arms Seraphiel."

"Seraphiel," Jehoel nodded, his gaze looking blankly past the dark one now. "The earliest memories I have are of Appollyon telling us of our purposes and powers in this world. We were born as the equalizers of the mortal realm. We are the hunters and they are the prey. There were, of course, rules. Hunts could only be performed with a permit. The permit was a tiny orb of Tif'eret energy that enabled a WindBearer to easily access that gate of power. With our ability to open the Tif'eret and other gates of power, we knew we were better than those we hunted. Even if we were slain, it was only the death of a body. Our spirit would return to this realm after the passing of time." Jehoel looked up to meet the dark warrior's gaze again. "I know differently now. We are not better than those we hunted, only different. The powers that we wield can just as easily be wielded by a mortal man."

"So, Jehoel," the dark warrior said at last. "If you now know that what Appollyon filled your head with was lies, then what makes you believe any of it at all? Are you sure you live on if you die on this world? Are these gates of power that you claim to wield truly what you believe them to be?"

Jehoel looked puzzled for a moment then sighed. The dark one was right. It was true that the angel had found an inkling of himself and cast off the lies that had ruled his known existence, but he still found himself clinging to the tattered shreds of lies to build his truths. For the first time Jehoel realized that he knew absolutely nothing that was certain. Very simply, every thought he had ever had could be false.

The reality of the truth bit the very reason from Jehoel's brain. His eyes widened and blanked as he twisted the three-handed handle painfully. His arm muscles bulged and his breathing quickened as madness began to roll over him like a tidal wave. Clenching his teeth and flaring his nostrils like a charging bull, the blonde angel raised the Midnight Blade and stepped forward with a lurch.

"Nothing is true then," Jehoel hissed, his words more of a gust of wind than the uttering of a sentence. "There is no reason to existence. There is no plan. There is only pain. We are pawns in the grip of a madman, only there is no madman."

"Something like that," the dark warrior agreed, sidestepping as Jehoel struck at him with the Midnight Blade. The red, shimmering, jagged sword hit the cave floor with a deafening ring, shattering granite. "Or not. To tell the truth, I'm really not sure anymore."

Jehoel spat rage and anger as he turned to swipe again. The dark warrior raised his hand and his gigantic scimitar flew from the scabbard on his stallion's back into his outstretched hand. Twisting his curved blade as he caught it, the dark one parried the jagged sword evenly, holding Jehoel in a lock for the moment.

"See," the black-garbed fighter stated. "I have one, too; a little different, though."

Jehoel pulled away with another scream, the whites of his eyes seemingly trying to consume his pupil and iris. Foam dripped from the corner of his mouth, his straining neck pulling his lips from his gums. The angel's mind was gone, covered in a cloud of rage and denial. Jehoel raised the Midnight Blade again, the slant-eyed jewels flaring brightly, and he allowed the sword's energy to soak his body. The Gevurah power flooded his whole form as he threw himself to attack the dark stranger.

Jehoel's attacks were furious. Down and down came chop after chop. Every thrust was made with the intent of murder and vindication of insanity. Again and again the dark stranger parried every strike.

"Enough," the dark one roared. "Even my patience is not infinite. I will have what I came for." Having said that, he spun deftly, gripping his enormous scimitar with both hands and struck out. He hit Jehoel with colossus might, the flat of his blade spinning the angel completely around. Tossing his weapon to the ground, the dark warrior leapt forward onto Jehoel's back, covering him completely, gripping both of the angel's wrists. "With this weapon and our combined Gevurah, my ends will be easily met."

"W..wh…what do…do you mean?" Jehoel managed to whisper, a sliver of reason breaking through his overpowering stupor. He was completely under the dark one's control. The stifling cape wrapped around both of them entirely, only their arms and heads peeking out of its confines. Jehoel tried to open his wings to fling his attacker back, but they would not respond to his commands. In fact, none of Jehoel's faculties would respond to his commands.

"Watch, my friend. Watch and learn."

Jehoel could only stare as the larger man jerked him forward to stand before the giant, granite throne. He could not understand why, but all he felt was horror when the dark man lifted both of their hands with the Midnight Blade and brought it down onto the stone throne. The jagged, black blade cut through the rock like butter, and energy coursed through the entire cave. Jehoel felt as though he were the conduit of the power and very nearly passed out before he witnessed the entire top of the mountain explode around him. Whiteness blinded him as a hundred thousand million tons of rock was blasted into the stormy air.

The last thing Jehoel heard was the dark warrior.

"Finally. It has been so long."

Then, nothing.

*

The explosion that strove to make a mile-high crater of the Cave of Kings rocked the surrounding terrain with the force of a thousand earthquakes. Tremors of unimaginable power coursed through the land for hundreds of miles, sending trees splaying and causing the very land to buckle and fold. Chasms ripped the mountains wide open; dry creek bed coulees folded in on themselves to the west; and avalanches of snow and rock poured off of every incline. The countless tons of rock that were once the peak of the Cave of Kings mountaintop made the surrounding ten-mile radius an apocalyptic war-zone.

Razikyl and Alique found themselves at the base of the very mountain of the Cave of Kings. When the ground erupted and heaved from the eruption, the orc was barely quick enough to use his arcane power to steady the ground they stood on. With a twist of his hands he bound the magnetic energy of the enormous rock they stood on to the earth's core.

"Quickly!" Razikyl barked to Alique, his hands maintaining the energy that kept them from riding an avalanche of rocks to the valley thousands of feet below. "The words of destruction I taught you! Access the Netsah that I have released within you and save our lives!"

Alique took no time to respond as she looked up to see a thousand ten-ton shards of solid granite falling down onto them. With a deep breath she reached into her inner brain and focused on the connection between her right leg, her mind, and her spirit. Emptiness swelled in all three as she raised her arms with her hands outstretched. As she drew power from the gate of Netsah, the hundreds of tattoos covering her body shone brilliantly, the black demon-blood ink turning purple.

Razikyl, his hands now firmly planted on the ground to maintain the magnetic connection, could scarcely believe how much energy he was pushing into the earth. It was taking everything he had just for them to keep their feet. Whatever it was that had happened had unleashed a power akin to nothing the orcen wizard had ever witnessed.

"Now!" the sorcerer roared. "Blast those boulders or we die!"

Even before the wizard could finish his command, white energy burst out of Alique's hands and struck an oncoming boulder. The Netsah energy hit the fifty-ton hunk of rock and exploded it into a thousand pieces, strewing them harmlessly around the duo as Alique continued to throw blast after blast of overpowering energy into the sky above. Razikyl felt the ground tremors relent slightly and lifted one hand from the ground. Able to maintain his magnetic hold with only his left hand now, the orcen sorcerer lifted his right to form a hemisphere of force around them to deflect any trace shards that remained despite Alique's efforts. It would allow her to continue her attack on the falling boulders and would defend them against any ancillary rocks, those less than a man's weight; still, a direct hit by any of the main boulders would crush the both of them like grapes under a gorilla's step.

Down nearly two thousand paces from Razikyl and Alique's precarious position on the very same mountain were Jyautch and Kael. They were at a point on the mountainside that was sharply angled and covered entirely in loose gravel rock. When the explosion rocked the land, both warriors were thrown into the air and sent skidding down the slippery incline. Kael pivoted, reaching out in opposite directions at the same time just as he was sent over the thousand-pace embankment. With his left hand he grabbed the tip of the ledge, his powerful fingers gouging into the very rock. His right hand grasped Jyautch's outstretched hand.

"Thank you, my friend," Jyautch smiled, reaching up and pulling himself over Kael's dangling body. As he stepped up on the ledge, he hauled up Kael to his side. Before the two could step away from the ledge, the taller, black-haired swordsman looked up, his face aghast. "Look out!"

Grabbing Kael, Jyautch moved with a speed only he could muster and dodged out of the massive boulder's path. They both had an instant to recover as another enormous stone fell onto them. Without a moment to think, Kael reached back and struck out at the hurtling, granite projectile with an arcing punch. His fist struck the boulder with a blinding flash of blue energy and the stone exploded into a million chunks of dusty rock.

"Quickly," Jyautch hissed wide-eyed as he gripped Kael's right arm. Kael winced as his comrade forced open a bond between them that flooded the blonde warrior with emptiness in his entire right arm. The sensation was very nearly exact to the feeling of Gevurah that coursed within his left. With a pointed finger Jyautch yelled, "Look!"

Above them was descending the entire shattered remains of a mountain peak.

"What do…" Kael began but Jyautch cut him off.

"Smash them, Kael!" he roared, kneeling behind the blonde warrior and gripping him around the waist. "With your power and my influx of dexterity, only your fists will save our lives!"

Kael didn't have even a moment to consider his ally's words as the shower of rock pelted them. Kael swung again and again, shattering rock and granite with every punch. Both of his arms glowed bright blue as electricity exploded and thunder clapped with every blow. Jyautch knelt behind his comrade with his eyes tightly shut, concentrating on infusing Kael's entire body with the unmatched speed of the Hessed. Kael moved faster than he had ever even thought of doing before as he punched and tore apart the granite bombs that fell around them.

For a thirty second span that felt like an eternity, the rock fall was relentless. With one final chop, Kael stepped forward and fell to his knees in exhaustion. Jyautch stood over his comrade's side.

"I…I am fine," Kael gasped, his herculean effort draining even his mighty endurance.

"Yes, you are," Jyautch nodded. "Yes, you are." A smile spread across his entire face as he patted his friend's back lightly. Jyautch looked around again, scanning for any other terrible threat that might be falling out of the sky. "What in God's grand name could have caused something like that?"

Kael staggered back to his feet with Jyautch's aid. He looked up over the crest of the enormous mountain they were scaling. "Look."

A column of red, fiery energy was coursing up into the air from where the mountain's peak had once been. The dark, stormy clouds parted before the fire's might, revealing for the first time in months the sky above. It was dusky champagne as night showed to be soon approaching.

"God's name," Jyautch breathed as the fire illuminated the whole mountain range and surrounding countryside in a hellish red hue. "What could that possibly be?"

"Can't you feel it?" Kael whispered, almost reverently, as he too was caught spellbound by the wondrous sight. "I don't know what it is, but it's power unparalleled."

"What do…" Jyautch started but then felt, too, what Kael meant. The emptiness that always accompanied the use of his gate of power was more intense than ever before. Also, there was the fact that neither warrior could willingly shut down their power. It seemed that the gigantic column of energy had completely destroyed any dampers that would attempt to stifle the gates of power.

Jyautch was finally able to pull his eyes from the unimaginable reality before them, and when he did he spied two people scaling the mountain some thousand paces above them.

"Look," the taller swordsmen pointed, drawing Kael's sight to his. "Two men."

"Nay," Kael squinted, raising a hand to shade his struggling eyesight. "One man, one woman."

"What would a man and woman be doing up here?" Jyautch snorted. "And how in the hell did they survive the rock fall?"

"Probably the same way we did," Kael shrugged. "We could ask them."

"Aye, we could," Jyautch answered, his stony visage holding the trace of a smile. "Into a ten-mile high pillar of fire."

Kael looked at his comrade and nodded as if nothing was out of the ordinary, not one thought to the courage of his actions.

"Aye," Jyautch shrugged, stepping up to lead the way. "What in God's name else would we do?"

*

"Look," Alique pointed below them. "Someone follows us up the mountain."

"Aye," Razikyl squinted at the two figures in the distance below them. He opened his Netsah, enabling him to see the two as if from ten feet away. He raised his chin as he saw exactly who it was.

"Who is it?" Alique asked.

Razikyl looked at her, thankful that she didn't realize she had the ability to see exactly as he had.

"Trouble," he answered, his eyebrows cocked in contemplation. He looked up at the nearing column of hellish energy and thought for a moment. If the power coursing above them was what he thought it was, the two figures below would not be any problem. "Come," he urged his female consort. "Quickly. We have little time."

*

Tamagan stepped to his feet precariously and leaned back against a boulder that was as large as most normal hills. From beneath the boulder stuck a spindly green hand, a gooey green puddle of blood pooling below it. The gigantic yellow-hided creature shook his head, trying to still the ringing in his ears and the stars before his eyes. He patted the head of his enchanted hatchet and slid it back into his belt.

Kneeling down Tamagan rested his hand on the smaller green one and held it there for a long minute. The coldness of both the hand and the wind finally compelled him to other boulders. Every one that he came to or tried to overturn revealed the same thing: one or two goblins smashed lifeless by the unstoppable force of millions of tons of falling rock. Not one of Tamagan's small goblin tribe seemed to have survived the unexpected and unrelenting attack.

Tamagan knelt down, weak-kneed at the sight of his adopted people utterly destroyed. When the rock fall had begun, his unmatchable hatchet had lent its power to him to survive. Tamagan had jumped, tumbled, and dodged every boulder. His little clan had dodged nary a one.

Rage rose in Tamagan's gullet and exploded out of his mouth in the form of choking, acidic bile. The eight-foot tall hobgoblin wiped his mouth and spat out the sour taste. He knew that something within him had changed. He had known that ever since he had chosen to help this pitiful little troupe of creatures in the first place. Compassion had sprung in his heart and Tamagan had accepted it. He had never before felt it or needed it, but after being introduced to it, he found it addicting. These little goblins had never had a chance in life and when Tamagan had tried to give them that, they were wiped completely from the face of the earth.

"Enough," Tamagan growled, his voice nearly shaking the ground. He pulled his mighty hatchet from his belt and snarled as he looked up at the billowing column of death from high above. He sensed both naturally and through the slight tremor in his right arm that the fire raging above was the cause of his misery. "Whatever you are, it matters not," the death in the hobgoblin's voice was unmistakable and unnerving.

"Whatever you are," Tamagan seethed, the chill in his voice colder than the snow that was beginning to fall, "you are dead."

*

Alique stepped up beside Razikyl, the heat and wind of the energy before them whipping her thin leather cloak and loin cloth back against their seeming will. Her bare body immediately bubbled with beads of sweat despite the chilling storm building around them, the heat warmer than the hottest day of summer. Razikyl didn't even notice Alique's beautiful form and blatant nudity as he stepped forward, his arms outstretched and his cloak pushed nearly straight back by the power. The duo was rendered completely speechless by the sight before them.

Razikyl had seen the Cave of Kings before; they stood at what had once been the mouth. In what had been the cave, a stone throne of gigantic proportions had once sat. It was currently split into two pieces and both lay on their side, some distance apart from each other. Near it laid the unconscious form of a WindBearer, whom Razikyl recognized as Jehoel, and standing near him, facing the fire column, was a dark-garbed stranger that the orc did not recognize. Beyond them rose the column of fire. Where Razikyl had only ever seen darkness was a pit of blackness that spit forth the very fire of hell into the winter sky. The fire rose beyond the reach of even the clouds, sending the shadowy storm-fluff flying. The intensity seemed greater than even the sun's heat and immediately both the orc and Alique were covered in slippery sweat.

The one thing that truly unnerved the wizard was the fact that despite the terrible wind raging from the hole blasted in the ground, not one stitch of the dark warrior's clothing moved. His large flowing cape swished at his feet of its own accord, completely ignorant that it should be whipping like a flag in a tornado. The dark stranger turned and faced Razikyl and Alique for a moment, then resumed gazing into the fiery pit. Neither saw the stranger's face, it being covered by a black mask from his turban. All they saw were his eyes, the very white-blue of a summer day's sky.

The tall, dark warrior pulled something from one of the thick, red leather bracers at his wrist, gripped whatever it was tightly, and stepped into the raging inferno. He immediately fell into the depths of the fiery pit and disappeared completely.

"Wow," Alique gasped, trying to wipe the sweat from her hands on her loincloth but only succeeding in wetting it thoroughly. She slipped her hands down into the tops of her leather travel boots and withdrew her long, demon-bone dirks, the blue steel reflecting the hell fire radiantly.

"Stay very close to me," Razikyl pulled her behind himself and stepped forward towards Jehoel's unconscious form. The orcen wizard's eyes went wide as he glimpsed the Midnight Blade laying not a foot from the WindBearer's body. Razikyl forgot nearly everything, wiped the sweat streaming down his large bald scalp with a shirtsleeve and staggered forward towards the enormous, void-colored sword.

"I know that weapon," Alique commented, her own grip tightening on her dirks at the sight of the Midnight Blade in Razikyl's hands. "Where do I know that weapon from?"

"Kael," Razikyl blurted without a thought, a maddening smile crossing his face as he looked on the ancient weapon like a child with a new toy. "Your lover and murderer once wielded this weapon. This WindBearer stole it from him."

Alique's brow furrowed as she struggled to remember Kael with the weapon. There was so much of her memory that was still a mystery. She could remember Kael gaining mastery over some grand power, but the recollection was too vague for her to recall correctly. She bit her lower lip, dismissing the thought, and tapped her thumb on the tiny glass container at the dragon-tusk cross-guard. The thick poison within stirred to life, coursing up the hair-sized tube that ran the length of the steel blade. Alique freed her mind of any thoughts of her past for the moment. The demon-blood ink within her skin tingled a warning, as did her Netsah-saturated muscles.

Razikyl no longer felt the tremendous heat or heard the sound of the roaring inferno that blasted unchecked into the darkening sky mere feet away from him. He looked down at the magical sword and smiled evilly. The slant-eyed jewels at the cross guard burned with an intensity and color that rivaled the hell-fire column. The glow that circled the weapon's blade was as red as blood.

"Finally," the large orcen wizard breathed. "No meddling humans; no pestering WindBearers; no more ass-licking apprentice work for anyone. Finally Razikyl wields the ultimate power." The sorcerer lifted the Midnight Blade and reveled in his victory. "Finally Razikyl will command this land, then all others. Razikyl the lord of the rolling hills. Razikyl, the lord of the world."

"Trust me, my little friend, that sword is powerful, but it isn't that powerful." A deep resounding voice laughed. Razikyl and Alique looked up, their muscles tight at the recognition of the all-encompassing evil of the hated voice.

"Hosampsich," Razikyl mouthed, his voice little more than a whisper. The din of the hell-fire column stilled as a behemoth figure emerged. The foul blast of flame parted like a curtain for the gargantuan demon lord.

"Ah," Hosampsich chuckled, the sound grating on both mortals' souls. "It is good to be remembered."

Hosampsich stood as tall as Razikyl's six-and-a-half feet, but was easily twice as wide. He resembled a human save that his head was entirely covered with finger-sized L-shaped tusks, and his skin was patterned like a black and brown tiger. Long canines slipped out of his chapped lips, and enormous, orange bat wings rose out of his back. Between his legs dangled a disfigured dog's penis that slapped sickeningly against his thighs as he stepped forward to stand before his one-time apprentice.

"And you brought me a gift," the demon lord chuckled. "Always the teacher's pet."

"I…" Razikyl began, but before he could finish the thought Hosampsich had ripped the Midnight Blade from his grasp and kicked him full in the stomach. The orc flew back over the destroyed throne and landed heavily. Razikyl rose up slowly and cautiously, drawing his heavy, leather cloak around himself and filling his hands with powerful spell components.

"And who are you, my dear?" Hosampsich stepped forward to stand over Alique. Alique looked up at the demon lord without a trace of emotion and stood her ground confidently. Her shape was pleasing to demons as well as humans. The serpentine tracings of runes and power symbols brought arousal to the demon as he looked down at her. Her bare, white breasts and close-shorn genitalia brought his blood nearly to boil as hot as the pillar of fire behind him. "Now that I am back, I will be in need of companionship."

"Take your companionship with the snakes you share your heritage with, demon," Alique spat, spinning away from the demon's outstretching hand, slicing thin traces down it as she retreated. Hosampsich pulled back his hand and licked the thin line of green ichor.

"Poison," the tusk headed creature smiled. "Always a delightful surprise. Too bad that you must now be punished for such a disloyal display."

Hosampsich stepped forward, bringing the Midnight Blade to bear. Alique crouched, clenched her teeth, and readied her dangerous dirks. The Netsah within her flared, causing the blades of her daggers to shine. The mighty demon smiled as he readied to slice her apart. He never got the chance.

As he stepped forward, a rush of downy whiteness struck Hosampsich full in the face, sending him stumbling across the ravaged mountaintop. The tusk-headed demon spun on his attacker and held his position. A single white feather floated down past the demon's head and fell to rest on his tiger-striped shoulder.

"Back to hell, Hosampsich."

"Ah," the demon nodded. "Jehoel. This must be old home week."

"Drop the sword and return to the pit, fiend. I shan't ask you again."

"Threats, my dear Jehoel? Don't tell me you have fallen as low as me."

Jehoel said nothing. He raised his hand before him and suddenly white energy slowly extended from it. A quarterstaff of pure Netsah energy formed and solidified. Jehoel gripped it with both hands and advanced on his demonic nemesis. Hosampsich brought the Midnight Blade down to cleave Jehoel in half, but was halted by the upraised staff.

"Damn you angels and your cursed sense of goodness," the demon spat. "Why can't you just forget the past like the rest of us?"

"I have forgotten the past, Hosampsich," Jehoel easily held the demon's downward chop. "I am stopping you not because of any remembered past, but because of what I am. I can do nothing else."

"You can die!" Hosampsich roared, kicking the angel away and advancing with sword upraised. "Die!"

Jehoel said nothing else, easily parrying the demon's attacks and managing occasionally to land a strike of his own. Every blow infuriated the demon even more and brought Hosampsich more strength. However, despite his increasing physical power, the demon's swordsmanship did not improve. Jehoel's bludgeoning strikes were more frequent, but had little effect against the thick-skinned horror.

As the fierce battle raged, Alique and Razikyl crouched together behind one half of the broken throne.

"Amazing," Alique breathed, pulling her cloak around herself. "Such raw power from these incredible creatures."

"Yes," Razikyl pouted. "Amazing." He cursed himself again and again. Every time he managed to place his hands on the power of the Midnight Blade, he lost it. Maybe it just wasn't meant to be.

"Look," Alique grabbed Razikyl's heavy shoulder, turning him to face what she saw coming over the mountain's edge. "Two more men."

"Great," the orc wizard cursed. "This just keeps getting better."

*

"Hosampsich," Kael growled as he and Jyautch crested the edge of the mountaintop.

"That is one ugly demon, my friend," the dark-haired warrior admitted, sliding his blue-bladed katana from its sheath. "He'll die."

"I'm not so sure," Kael looked over to his friend. "I've killed him before." Kael pointed over at the two fighters. "And with that very same sword."

"Great," Jyautch said sarcastically. "How hard can it be to kill an invincible demon?"

"We must try, Jyautch," Kael gripped his curved short sword as well as his friend's armored forearm. "This demon killed every member of my clan. He killed and ate every human for hundreds of leagues in every direction of this land. I will not live to see that happen again. Tonight, somehow, that demon dies for the last time."

"We will prevail, my friend," Jyautch nodded with a smile. "You have learned well from me how to use your wondrous power. I am a swordsman unparalleled in any land. We will prevail."

Kael nodded and gripped his short sword tight.

"Together then."

The duo rose up and sprinted for the fighting angel and demon, both roaring their war cry, battle lust boiling within their blood.

*

"Who the hell?" Alique hissed at the two new members to this fast, unfolding drama.

"Kael and someone I do not recognize," Razikyl returned with a squint. Had he seen the human's companion before, he wondered as they remained crouched behind the fallen, granite throne. "Kael still wears the kilt and cloak of Hosampsich's hide, as well as a shirt and kilt of mail, only that it's made of demon tusks rather than metal. The stranger's armor betrays him as a member of a far-eastern sect of warriors called Zymuari. His odd armor is made of dragon bone and scales. These two came to fight."

"That is Kael?" Alique managed, her eyes glossed over completely. "He was the one who caused my death?"

"Yes, yes," Razikyl muttered, diving behind the thick throne-half to dodge a stray bolt of killing energy, pulling Alique with him. "Get your damn head down. By Gabryl's chariot, I figured you had more sense than that. Let them kill each other and the survivor will be ours to fell."

"Kael," she whispered, spinning from behind the throne and standing. She caught the rushing duo of Kael and Jyautch and began to walk toward them. As she did, she slipped her dirks back into their boot sheaths. Razikyl didn't see her until it was too late. He peeked over the top of the rock throne to witness what kind of disaster was about to unfold.

*

Kael and Jyautch were only yards away when a side-glance caught their attention and brought them to a screeching halt. A beautiful woman approached them, her perfect form accentuated by a glossy film of sweat and the radiance of the hell-fire roaring nearby. Her breasts and face were all that could clearly be seen before the rippling waves of her black, leather cloak and loin-cloth.

"What the hell…" Jyautch began.

"Alique," Kael gasped. He felt as if the mountain itself had fallen on him. His chest tightened and his breath became short as she approached. Jyautch glanced at the two supernatural fighters, then back again at the gorgeous tattooed woman.

"She is your lost love?" the tall swordsman reasoned. "I thought she was dead."

"So did I," Kael whispered, lowering his weapon and walking toward Alique. "Alique," he reached out with an outstretched hand. "My love. You live. All I know…"

Kael had no time to finish his words as white-hot Netsah energy exploded from her hands and blasted full into his tuskmailed chest. The force of the blow lifted him full off of his feet and sent him flying across the mountaintop. His short sword went clattering as Jyautch ducked to keep from being carried off with him. Kael's short flight ended when he struck Jehoel from behind and sent both of them sprawling.

Both Kael and Jehoel's attackers took full advantage of the moment.

Alique had followed her bolt of energy and drawn her demon-bone dirks. Tapping the poison containers, she dove under Kael's lifted arms as he rose back to his feet and slashed him twice on his unprotected inner arms. In passing, she struck out at the felled angel as well, dealing Jehoel two long, poison-filled wounds between his downy wings. Alique came to stop at the lip of the hell-fire pit, crouched and ready to deal another deadly blow.

The poison worked immediately and Kael gripped his stomach as the vicious combination of neuro- and hemo-toxins went to work in his system. Jehoel, too, felt the effects of the poison and could not stop his body from throwing itself in a writhing convulsion to the ground. That one moment was all that Hosampsich needed, and he took full advantage.

The human that he recognized was too far away to kill, but Jehoel had landed right at the demon's feet. He brought the Midnight Blade back and around in a viscous, circling attack, carrying it down to bear on Jehoel. The angel was wounded, but not incapacitated. Seeing the evil reflection of the hell-fire before him, he spun to escape what ever it was that was coming. He did not spin away fast enough.

The Midnight Blade's jagged edge sliced clean through the bases of Jehoel's wings and severed them utterly. The scream of pure pain and anguish that erupted from Jehoel's throat froze the blood of all, even Hosampsich. The crippled angel felt nothing but fire burn through his veins and mind, shimmering blue energy bursting out of his eyes. Curled into a fetal position, shimmering blue energy burst from every orifice on his body, blasting away his white, silken kilt.

Hosampsich backed away carefully, the Midnight Blade drawn up before him protectively. Alique reached forward, horrified and sure that it was she that had caused this beautiful creature so much pain, but could not coax her legs to push ahead. Kael was frozen in pain of his own, convulsions rippling through his muscles and organs, shutting down everything that was alive within him. Still, he kept his feet, his arms wrapped around his torso as he roared in pain.

If the pain had broken him enough that he had fallen prone or at least to his knees, Kael would not have been in the direct line of what was about to occur.

Jehoel, insane with agony, gathered every molecule of his angelic essence and bound it to his natural ability to access the gate of Tif'eret. Binding the two energies together and drawing more from the Tif'eret than he thought possible, Jehoel forced out the poison through the very pores of his flesh. With the toxins expelled, Jehoel's body proved unable to hold the combined power of his angelic essence and the all-healing Tif'eret. The energy sought and found the easiest escape route: the bloody stumps of his severed wings. The stumps glowed clear blue and pulsated with force. White-blue energy exploded out like lances of light.

The twin spears of energy penetrated Kael's mailed chest effortlessly, raising him up into the air nearly ten feet. Kael's eyes flared open, as did his mouth. Glowing blood burst outward. He hung limply, lifelessly, his arms and legs dangling like broken tree limbs in the wind. Still, his eyes were wide open and his chest heaved, every pump of his heart pouring blood out of his nose and mouth.

Jyautch roared in blood-curdling rage and fell onto the angel with a speed unrivaled. He slashed through the spears of energy that had emerged from Jehoel's back, the solid blue light dissipating at the tall swordsman's strikes. Kael, no longer supported by the pseudo wing-lances, fell to Jyautch's waiting arms. The warrior eased his comrade to the ground, checked to see that he remained breathing, then stood straddling his limp form, both hands on the handle of his blue-steel katana.

Seeing Jehoel dazed and trying to struggle out of a fetal position, Jyautch kicked out, striking the angel square in the rear and sending him flying head over heels off the edge of the mountaintop. Without warning Hosampsich and Alique attacked the dark-haired swordsman. Alique struck first, shooting out white Netsah energy from splay-fingered hands. Hosampsich raised the Midnight Blade and stepped to cleave both mortal men in twain.

Jyautch ducked under the demon lord's arcing swipe, angling his own blue katana to refract Alique's Netsah. The double blast of the sorceress' energy glanced off the gleaming blade and struck Hosampsich full in the chest, sending him back a step and drawing a grunt from the bat-winged beast. Jyautch saw the advantage and pounced on it like a jungle cat. Drawing from his seemingly infinite pool of Hessed, the tall, dark swordsman attacked with a fervor unmatched. Hosampsich was unable to recover from the single lost step dealt him by the witch's misguided attack and Jyautch did not relent. Slashes trailed under the demon's guard and sword strikes jabbed him with blinding speed.

Hosampsich roared in futility, willing open the gate of Gevurah and drawing more power. The demon pushed back against the katana-wielding warrior, bringing the Midnight Blade up in a dazzling display of prowess. Every thrust, swipe, and arc showered blasts of granite, barely missing their mark, but miss their mark they did. Jyautch gave the demon every advance he wanted and dodged every attack by only an inch, sometimes less.

When the tall swordsman's heels touched the vertigo-inducing mountain ledge, Hosampsich grinned and thrust out. Jyautch leaped through the air over the demon's attack, somersaulting and landing behind the gigantic horror. The swordsman slipped the entire length of his blade into the demon's kidneys and pounded his shoulder behind it. Hosampsich roared in terrible pain, his back arced like a hissing cat's, and fell limply from the cliff edge.

Before Jyautch could turn around, a thick blast of white energy struck him full in the back and hurled him from the mountaintop as well.

"No," Kael groaned, still writhing nearby in excruciating pain. The emptiness that always accompanied his access of the Gevurah had taken over his entire left arm and seemed to be seeping into his torso. Kael looked down, his eyelids nearly too heavy to keep up. With every heave of his chest and expulsion of breath, bright blue liquid squirted out of the two long gashes in his chest and back. It felt like his heart was pumping his blood directly out of his chest with every queasy breath, but the blue glowing liquid was obviously something else.

Kael looked up and began to drag himself to the ledge from which Jyautch had just been thrust when two sets of feet flanked him. He struggled against his rebelling muscles to push himself on his side and look up. The orc wizard and Alique stood there, the sorcerer with his hands on his hips and a look of satisfaction on his face. Alique's face was one of stone.

"Alique..." Kael could barely sigh. The feeling he had was as indescribable as the pain he felt. Sure that he was dying, Kael tried to smile. At least he would get to see his life's love one last time. Still, as his head dropped and bloody drool poured out of the corner of his mouth, he couldn't understand what was going on. What was Alique doing with the orcen wizard? Why was she covered in tattoos? They were questions that Kael was sure he would never have answered.

"Never speak to me again, murderer," Alique snarled, her hard visage dropping to reveal her deep, internal pain. Razikyl smiled at her reaction. Both of them opened their hands over Kael's struggling form. White energy began to permeate and hiss. "Never again."

Raging, white energy roared out of both of the wizards' hands and bathed Kael completely. They finally stopped after nearly a full minute and stepped away. All that remained of Kael's body was a charred and burning mass of flesh. His hairs were wisps in the air and his eyes were melted onto his exposed cheekbones. Still, the thick blue liquid was pumping methodically out of the two, long gashes through his chest.

"He...he...he's dead," Alique gasped, looking up at Razikyl. "He's dead, isn't he?" Razikyl nodded, pulling a small vial out of his cloak and catching a drop of the thick blue liquid out of Kael's chest. He capped the vial stoically and slipped it back into his cloak.

Alique looked down on Kael's burnt remains, her breath ragged and quick, unable to catch her elusive wind. She gripped her cloak and pulled it around herself as tears involuntarily poured out of her eyes. Suddenly, she realized that despite what she could remember of Kael, what she had done was so very wrong. Regardless of the memories that she could manage to piece together, this man that lay dead before her had loved her like no other; and she had loved him. What her brain had told her could not stand against the fact that her heart screamed at her betrayal of him. Whimpering and sobbing, Alique bit her fist and let the tears flow more than ever before.

Razikyl looked up and knew exactly what was going on inside the head of his ever-powerful female weapon; he knew that there wasn't a thing he could about what she was going through. If her spirit managed to survive this, she would truly be his forever. Razikyl stepped beside her, taking her in his arms to comfort her when he saw an odd sight.

Up over the ledge from which Alique had blasted the Zymuari warrior stepped the biggest hobgoblin that Razikyl had ever seen. Over his shoulder was the dark-haired swordsman, unconscious and limp. The enormous yellow-skinned beast set the swordsman carefully beside Kael's charred remains, laying the brilliant katana at his side. He looked at the burned figure for a moment, and then lifted his pumpkin-shaped head to level on Razikyl.

Both sorcerers gasped at the creature's size. Razikyl was six-and-a-half feet tall and he barely came to the creature's bear-sized chest. Without another thought, the orc ripped open his Netsah energy and tore into the hobgoblin. Alique spun away from Razikyl and half-heartedly added her own power to his incredible attack.

The hobgoblin's speed was awe-inspiring. In a thought he pulled a gleaming steel-headed hatchet from his belt and smashed the Netsah blast down like a felled bird. Again and again Razikyl shot blast after blast at the enormous creature and again and again the being knocked down every attack.

"Impossible!" Razikyl roared in rage, still throwing ball after ball of energy. Alique quit her pitiful attempt to help the orc and stepped back to fall to her knees behind him, tears still flowing from her face. "Who are you?"

"I am Tamagan," the hobgoblin screamed with a taunting laugh. The massive creature knew that his name meant nothing to the orc and the irony of why it should made him laugh even harder. "You can just call me Orc's Death."

"I'll call you that when I drink wine from your rotten skull!"

"I like that," Tamagan roared with a smile, pressing into the wizard's attack.

"Get up and help me!" Razikyl cried at Alique's sobbing form, energy arcing across his teeth as he did. "This foul beast is going to kill us!"

Unable to argue, Alique stood up at the orc's command, wiping the tears from her face. She stepped in front of Razikyl's now-continuous stream of Netsah, allowing the power to flow through and around her toward the hobgoblin. She lifted her hands and uttered a long, arcane power word. Her energy, added by the bathing of the orc's, erupted like a geyser and struck Tamagan as an avalanche. The hobgoblin tried to block the stream, but it was just too much. He was tossed like a leaf across the mountaintop, coming to rest just before the cliff's ledge.

"Not bad," Tamagan spat, rising back to his feet with effort. His thick hide was burnt to pink and steam rose off his cooking form. He gripped his wondrous hatchet in both hands and took a single step forward. "But all you done is piss me off. And bad."

"I've just started, beast," Alique growled through clenched teeth. This was a perfect chance for her to release the anguish she felt from Kael's death, and she would not be beaten now, perhaps not ever.

Tamagan felt the very truth of her words and braced himself for it. He had fought a thousand battles and something told him this was probably his last; but something had changed in the hobgoblin. He didn't know what it was, but he had embraced it. He was determined to die like a true warrior. He was determined to die with honor.

"Bring it on then, bitch," Tamagan growled through grit teeth.

Alique did just that, uttering her power word ten quick times and folding the Netsah within her hands to strengthen it. With a cry that mixed rage, strength, uncertainty, and doubt, Alique let forth her most powerful effort of killing death.

Tamagan closed his eyes for his final blow…and it never came.

The hobgoblin looked up and saw an amazing sight: the blonde, human warrior that he had fought nearly two weeks ago stood in front of the death strike of Netsah and took the entire discharge. He stood before the incredible force of Alique's attack with his stance wide and his form unmoving. After a full minute, Alique was forced to relent, her energy entirely depleted. She looked up to see what remained of the yellow-hided beast and cried out in amazement at the sight before her.

Kael stood where she had let the full fury of her power strike. No longer was he a charred corpse, burnt beyond recognition. He had discarded his leather tiger-striped cloak as well as his rent demon-tusk scale armor, and his sandals had burned right off of his feet. He stood bare-chested, wearing only his kilt. Two long gashes still ran the length of his torso and they still pumped blue liquid, but the thick, shiny ichor now coated his entire body and glowed mystically in the red-hued darkness.

"Again!" Razikyl screamed, stepping up beside Alique.

"I...I've nothing left," she mouthed, unbelieving that her once-love stood alive before her. Something within her rebelled against the past and thanked whatever gods there were that he wasn't dead. Despite everything that she seemed to remember, she knew that she still felt something indescribable for him.

"The hell you don't!" Razikyl roared in rage, gripping her roughly with his right hand. "I didn't make you so that you could just lay down and die again! You are my greatest weapon!" The orcen wizard yelled out one of his many arcane phrases and forced Alique to her knees in pain. Willing open their spirits and binding their access to the Netsah, Razikyl combined their might and redoubled their strength. Gripping Alique's shoulder tight, he turned to Kael's glowing form. "Now, human! Now you die! Nothing can defeat Razikyl the Wizard Lord!"

Raising his hand, the wizard shot forth an energy he was sure no mortal had ever before controlled, showering the entire force onto Kael's blue, shimmering body. Kael lowered his head and, bracing his bare feet against the granite mountaintop, he stepped into the Netsah energy and advanced inch by inch.

Alique screamed in pain, her eyes wholly white from the draining outflow of power. She writhed in the orc's grasp but could not deny his strength. His grip on her was unbreakable. She fell limp, whimpering at Razikyl's feet, her energy melding with his to rain death on her former love.

Kael opened his own power of the Gevurah to aid his advance and he slowly gained ground into the deadly onslaught. It was not enough, though, and Kael looked down to see flakes of his thick, filmy blue coating chip away and dissipate. The tiny cracks in his "armor" allowed the wizard's energy in to hit Kael full and the pain was incomprehensible. Still, the blonde warrior continued, despite his full realization that he would not reach the wizard before the Netsah energy incinerated him.

"Alique," Kael managed to whisper, white Netsah burning his mouth and lungs as he did. She lifted her head, unable to open her eyes, and smiled, unable to speak. Kael fell forward onto his hands and knees, smiling as well. He knew that she knew. He loved her.

Razikyl's attack was unrelenting. Drawing from Alique's very soul, he increased his attack on Kael's fallen form, laughing in sadistic glee.

"Now, human!" the orc screamed, stepping up to finish off Kael. "You are the last between me and my rule over this land!"

"No!" a deep bass resounded.

Razikyl looked up just in time to see what his ears had already heard as a terrifying beat of force against the air. An enormous blue-headed hatchet buried itself into the wizard's shoulder, flinging him through the air to the edge of the cliff. Razikyl was lucky that the axe had first spun through his own Netsah attack. If it hadn't, it would have tore his upper quarter completely from his body.

Kael staggered to his feet with the aid of a gigantic, yellow, clawed hand and leaned on Tamagan for support. He looked over to see Jyautch recovering his senses and sitting up, katana in hand. Kael smiled at that and looked up at who had picked him up. Tamagan returned the human's glance with one of peace but uncertainty.

"Thank you," Kael stated, standing with the hobgoblin's help.

"Thank you," Tamagan returned quietly, watching in wonder as the flecks of blue coating that had burnt away from the Netsah assault sealed up once again. He looked down and saw that none of the liquid had rubbed off on his hands at all.

"How fare you, Jyautch?" Kael shouted across the mountain-top.

"Well enough, friend," Jyautch returned, stumbling to his feet, sword gripped tight in both hands despite his waning strength. "How fares our newfound comrade?"

"Well," Tamagan nodded to both. He offered his hand to Kael. "Kael, we meet again. I am Tamagan."

"I remember," Kael returned, allowing the massive creature's hand to envelope his own. "That is Jyautch." Tamagan and the swordsman nodded to one another. Kael slowly made his way over to Alique and painfully kneeled at her side. He brushed away her hair from her face as he pulled her cloak back over her gorgeous form for modesty.

"She is truly beautiful," Tamagan whispered, keeping his distance regardless of his words. "Why does she want you dead?"

"I don't know," Kael returned quietly, tracing a finger around her delicate face just as he had done a thousand times before. It seemed that the last time he had done this was a thousand worlds away. Kael nodded towards Razikyl's still form. "I am sure that he would know."

"Aye," Tamagan growled, walking over to the still orc. He put a foot on the wizard's chest and pulled out his blue-headed hatchet with a tug. The hobgoblin's eyes widened as the wound beneath the rent cloak sealed shut. Dried blood still coated the orc's shoulder and chest, but the sorcerer was slowly breathing and still very much alive. Tamagan shook his head, his hands still white-knuckled around his weapon's handle. Magic was indeed a formidable adversary.

The hobgoblin looked down then over to his newfound human friends. Something in his brain told him he should decapitate the orc immediately; but something in his heart stayed his hand. Where selfishness and pettiness had once reigned, now ruled pity and mercy. Tamagan looked down at the still wizard one more time, then walked back to the three humans.

"Dead?" Jyautch asked Tamagan.

"No," the hobgoblin returned. "But very worse for the wear." He gestured toward Alique, Kael still holding her unconscious form. Her breathing was erratic and short. "And her? What are we to do with her?"

"If she lives, she seems a little dangerous to keep around," Jyautch began, drawing a steely glance from Kael. Shrugging weakly he returned, "Consider, friend. It isn't as if we can tie her up. She houses more power than I've ever seen before. If she learns how to use it, we all may be in for it."

"Look!" Kael gasped. Tamagan and Jyautch shared his amazement with slack jaws. The filmy blue liquid that covered his body was congealing and running off. What could, drained off his arms and onto Alique's, quickly disappearing. What pooled underneath him slowly ran into the crevices and cracks of the newborn plateau top. Still, Kael had the long gashes, now sealed, on his heavy chest and back. The gashes had already scarred over and glimmered sapphire in the hell-fire light. As the blue liquid dissolved, Alique's breathing improved immediately and she seemed to fall into a deep and restful slumber.

Kael stood up and walked over to retrieve his long dirk and garb. He returned to his comrades, pulling on his demon-tusk scale shirt and heavy, leather cloak. The three stood for a long moment, considering their next move. Their eyes looked from Razikyl to Alique to the unrelenting column of hellish fire rising into the winter's night sky. They could think of nothing to calm the infernal discharge of fire, wondering if it could be staunched at all. Their thoughts were answered as Tamagan pointed toward the lip of the hell column chasm and barked for Kael and Jyautch's attention.

"No," the two hissed at source of the hobgoblin's urging.

"Ah, yes, my little morsels," Hosampsich chuckled as he stood before the spewing pit. In his hands still was the enormous Midnight Blade, its glassy black depths amplifying the abyssal inferno. His jagged fanged smile spread, as did his enormous bat wings, orange hell-glow in unrelenting fury as he bathed in the doom-fire that rose to the sky. He slipped a hand from the massive sword's handle, grasped his sharp, unsheathed sex organ and waggled it sickeningly. "I'll eat your very brains while I have my fill of your ass."

Kael took one step forward, swept his cloak over one shoulder and clenched tight his short sword as he did. Jyautch blinked away his dizziness, holding his shining katana before himself as he flanked his shorter comrade to the right. Tamagan took his cue and stepped to Kael's left, spinning his hatchet like a baton for a quick second, then grasping it aloft tightly in both hands, his elbows bent for the attack. All three were at the very limit of their mighty endurances. Jyautch had fought the witch and demon to a short-lived and painful victory already; the hobgoblin had taken both of the wizards' full fiery attacks, his hide most probably permanently blistered red; Kael had seen death's doorstep twice in the span of ten minutes. The trio was fighting against their very bodies and minds now. They were fighting for the chance to fight.

"You mortals are fools," Hosampsich chuckled, extending back his wings to allow them to fully soak in the rising shower of flame. The licking fire encompassed the demon's whole form, circling around his tiger-striped body and tusk-covered skull. "Have no doubts. You will all die this night."

"In that case," Tamagan growled, his burnt hide still drawing winces from his still booming breath. "I hope you choke on my giant bones." The three launched themselves forward as one.

From behind Hosampsich, out of the towering inferno, leapt eight grotesque figures, lighting down between the demon lord and the attacking mortals. All eight figures were short of two paces tall and thin as skeletons. Their thick red skin was pulled tight against their wiry bodies; black, eyeless sockets stared out of grinning skull-faces. Short and seemingly useless bat-wings sprouted from their shoulder blades, beating the wind only when one of the fiends jumped into the air.

"Here, my meals," Hosampsich chuckled. "A little warm-up for you so you are ready for me."

The three were wordless. Six clawing, screaming fiends rushed for both Tamagan and Jyautch, the remaining two falling upon Kael. The hobgoblin and dark-haired swordsman gritted their teeth against the tide of exhaustion that sought to consume them and spun into the hellish banshees. Kael somersaulted forward, pulling his cloak around himself as he did. The two red-skinned demons clawed at him but could not penetrate the tiger-striped cloak. Kael stood up between them, summoning open his pool of Gevurah as he did. Both of his fists punched through the demons' chest cavities and tore them completely in two. They fell to the stony ground, motionless, as Kael walked forward.

"Impressive," Hosampsich mused, gripping the Midnight Blade in both hands. Neither Tamagan nor Jyautch saw Kael's display, so intent were they with their own struggles. Both warriors weaved a dazzling display of stealth and steel that would have sent any other opponents to the hereafter, even in their weakened conditions. As it was they were just able to stay a step, sometimes only a half one, ahead of death's clammy grip.

"Quickly!" Jyautch spat at himself quietly, ducking under two raking claws and spinning away, leaving deep gashes in two of his opponents. The tall warrior knew, somehow, that he had to end this quickly to get to Kael's side in time. Drawing on his reservoir of Hessed, he leapt into the midst of the demons again.

Claws and teeth snapped at the dark-haired warrior's form as he pushed into the depth of the three demons. Jyautch's Hessed-soaked muscles pushed and pulled, his actions a dancing loom spinning only death. The thick, square dragon bone on his arms cracked under the demon's attack as he ducked under their swipes. Jyautch twirled on the ground, bringing his gleaming blade like an ocean wave under each of the demon's pelvises. Jyautch stood and took not a moment to regard his work as he sprinted to help his blond comrade. The three demons that had opposed him lay squalling in the dirt, their legs sliced cleanly from their bodies. They strove to drag themselves back to the roaring pit, shamed that they had been humbled so by a mere mortal.

Jyautch ran past the three horrors that Tamagan strove against, cleanly hamstringing all three as he did. As they turned to swipe at their unseen attack and react to their loss of mobility, a shimmering, blue-headed streak of steel decapitated each of them. Their twisted energies were expelled from their earthy flesh and sped back into the depths of hell, banished in dishonor.

Tamagan joined Jyautch as they ran to aid Kael in his final confrontation with the demon lord Hosampsich. Sprinting only twenty feet from their comrade, both were suddenly frozen in place, inertia hurling their guts and souls painfully against their flesh. Jyautch painfully twisted one eyeball to its peripheral, tears gushing at the only movement his entire body could muster. At the edge of the mountaintop plateau stood Razikyl, his hands and concentration holding the dark-haired warrior and his hobgoblin comrade immobile.

"It is just you and I, mortal," Hosampsich grinned, leaning back against the force of hell that bathed him amorously. "If I remember correctly, it was a situation just like this that allowed you to pick yourself up out of the sty of feces that your clan wallowed in for a century. Tell me honestly. Can you truly bring yourself to battle the being that granted you your near-godhood?"

Hosampsich's answer was a resounding ring as the Midnight Blade just parried the human's arcing attack. The demon bounced away from the vast rushing pit, shrugging off his cocky smile, his bat-like wings unfurling above him like a boxer's defense. Kael spat at him, crouching low as he skirted the hell-gate. The slight blue shimmering across his skin and the emptiness in his stomach warned him of the fire's unquestioning power. Kael gritted his teeth and spun his dirk into an inverted grasp.

"You are mine, demon." He advanced careful and sure. "Tonight, at long last, this earth is rid of you."

Hosampsich leapt at Kael, roaring a sound that shook the very mountain and the spines of every mortal for a hundred miles. Kael met that war cry with one of his own, equally as fierce and horrid, and jumped to meet the hurtling demon lord in mid-air.

Kael ripped open the vast gate of Gevurah within himself, his reason gone with the force of his rage. Any mortal or civilized dampers that had ever existed were torn asunder in his reach of unfettered power. His arms were wide, soaked in unparalleled might, ready for the attack.

Yet, Hosampsich, too, was a master of the might of Gevurah. Utilizing the Midnight Blade as a conduit, he empowered himself with an energy equal to the mortal's—superior, he hoped, due to his demon flesh. The gleaming void of his sword whirled hypnotically as it was raised above head to bring forth a deathblow.

An ear-shattering clash drew blood from Kael's ears as his dirk met the unrelenting steel of the Midnight Blade and shattered into shards like glass before a stone. Hosampsich nearly had enough time to smile as his body smashed bone-crushingly into Kael's. Air rushed from the mortal's lungs as they met and the demon's larger mass bore them down. Still, the blade of the giant ebony sword rushed to meet with Kael's throat as the breathless warrior was thrown to the stony ground.

But Kael had a card to play that the demon lord could never have suspected: Kael had tasted the succulent swift fruit of the power of the Hessed thanks to his strange-armored comrade from the east. With the barriers and defenses that his mortality had erected against the use of such cosmic force now battered down, his essence grasped for whatever weapon it could to survive. It latched onto the gate opening of Hessed and ripped it apart.

Reality itself slowed to a snail's pace as Kael felt the twin emptiness within each of his arms and shoulders swell to bursting and encompass his whole being. He cocked his head ever so slightly as his perspective of the world spun and then sharpened. Kael's grasp focused and his eyes narrowed. His actions were a blur even to the supernatural senses of Hosampsich.

Kael bent his neck and angled his head into the descending arc of the Midnight Blade. The invisibly sharp edge of the weapon shore the ends of a pinch of matted, blond hair as it missed its mark. Kael twisted clockwise, pulling his right shoulder and arm out of the sword's path as well, allowing the missed opportunity to spin the demon in the air. With a quick hand-over-hand action, Kael found himself now atop the demon's plummeting form, his right hand and knee against a tiger-striped shoulder and his left hand grasping a futilely beating bat-wing. They struck the ground hard, Kael adding to the fall with his Gevurah force, driving Hosampsich's head into and through the rocky ground.

Kael stepped under a swiping bat-wing easily and met its next swoop with a sickening chop of his hand. The wing was severed clean and the demon lord howled in pain, pulling himself up from the stone. He crouched in wrath, death and evil personified as blood poured from his tear ducts and from between his teeth. He screamed a dragon's cry, again drawing blood from Kael's ears. The mortal stood impassive before the demon's impending attack, his legs bent and his arms raised lazily in sure defense. Hosampsich roared again, and blood and pus oozed out of the pores of his heavy hide. Tamagan and Jyautch winced in pain, unable to cover their ears from the banshee wail. If Razikyl's spell would relent, they would have curled to the ground and wailed like children.

"You cannot defeat me, demon," Kael stated as the enormous creature finished his keen. Acidic blood and ichor steamed at the demon's feet, burning the very foundation of their footing. "There is nothing left to say. Nothing else remains to be written of you. After tonight, you are a thankfully forgotten dream."

"Maybe, mortal," Hosampsich growled. "Be not too confident in your uttering! I have tasted death at your hands before and here I stand again to face you!"

"Hosampsich..." Kael began, but blood poured out of his mouth as he tried to continue. A deadening pain opened in his back as his strength ebbed, then fell, releasing the emptiness from his arms and soul, replacing it with an emptiness of life. Kael turned, thick redness pouring down his lips and back. He knew that it was a dirk that had defiled him. He was positive that it had a handle of demon bone and dragon tusk and he saw that it was Alique that had thrust it into him.

"W...w…wh...wh…" was all that he could manage as his eyelids became more and more impossible to support. His form came to feel as his eyelids did, and Kael stumbled forward to his knees before Alique. He forced open his eyes and looked up to see that his lover's were closed tight. Her head and arms were limp, her legs barely supporting her. She looked like a marionette at the beck of a quick-fingered puppeteer. Kael managed to drop his head, looking sideways to see Razikyl waving his hands from across the mountaintop. In effect, it was he that had struck the deathblow, not Alique. Razikyl finished his spell and Alique fell to the ground again, unconscious as ever, a rag-doll tossed aside after boredom sets in.

"Ever the dutiful apprentice, orc," Hosampsich laughed, stepping forward and raising the Midnight Blade. "Tonight, human, it is you that is forgotten. Just as is your entire race."

Jyautch and Tamagan stood still frozen twenty feet away, trapped in their attacking stances like statues. Jyautch was nearly unconscious from his futile attempt to break free, but Tamagan's inhuman constitution raged away. He held his enchanted hatchet high above his head and he struggled to tear the weapon from his own hand and hurl it through the air. Again and again he pressed his near-animal will against the unrelenting power of Razikyl's Netsah. As Hosampsich raised the Midnight Blade above his head to smite Kael, the hobgoblin choked his very soul into action. Razikyl's Netsah could not diminish the newfound love of life that had sprung from the depths of a creature of wanton evil. That very love broke through the trappings of magic, and as the hobgoblin fell to the ground, his unmatched physical power hurtled the enchanted hatchet across the mountaintop just as the tiger demon was bringing down the Midnight Blade.

Unfortunately, Tamagan's aim was guided by emotion rather than skill and the hatchet sailed just wide of its target. The tiger demon's void-colored sword arced swiftly through the winter's night air to finally claim Kael's head; but was stopped clean in mid-air. The smile on Hosampsich's face was wiped just as clean at what he saw. Though the hatchet had not found its target, Kael had plucked the spinning projectile from the air and caught the demon's deathblow beneath the blue, shimmering head of the magnificent axe.

Another roar of rage bellowed out of the demon lord as he swept Kael to the ground with his free hand. The mortal fell to his side as if he were no more than a sack of meal. His eyelids began to rise and fall with the pumping of his life-blood out of his back, as he lay sideways, face-to-face with the sleeping love of his life. He smiled as Hosampsich began to raise his enormous weapon again. Kael knew nothing of it and cared even less. Euphoria entered his brain as the blood was leaving and comfort was finally his, as he felt reunited with the only mate he had ever wanted or needed.

Hosampsich was never able to raise the sword again, though, as Tamagan grasped him roughly from behind and clubbed the demon heavily across the head with both hands. The demon fell over Kael's dying form and that of his slumbering mate. Tamagan followed, lighting into the tiger-skinned behemoth with every ounce of energy left in his heavy arms. Again and again the hobgoblin's coconut-sized fists hammered onto the back of the demon lord's skull. The gigantic yellow-skinned creature's Hessed-drenched limbs struck faster and harder than eyes could follow, dealing damage most thought nigh impossible. Hosampsich reeled from the flurry as he felt the incredibly long fingers of his attacker wrap around his thick, muscled neck.

Was it possible? The demon's ragged thoughts spun as oxygen drained from his mind. Could he die at the very hands of a mortal? Fortunately for Hosampsich, the answer did not come at that moment. Lightning arced out of the sky and tore into the eight-foot tall hobgoblin. Tamagan flew from his quarry like a leaf in a tornado. Again and again lightning came down from the skies and up from the very mountain. Electricity wreaked havoc across and around the goblinoid's form, rising him up off of the ground, turned and spun by the killing forces of the electron. Razikyl raised his hand again, bringing yet another bolt of white-hot death, amplified by the Netsah of his spirit.

"Die, hobgoblin!" Razikyl seethed, jerking the energy out of the air with the slightest flick of his finger. "Nothing shall stop the ascension of Razikyl to Wizard King!"

Suddenly the energy and Netsah was halted and Tamagan fell to the ground, his skin blistered to black, smoke rising from his entire, listless form. Razikyl looked down and saw a gleaming length of shimmering blue steel sticking over a foot out of his solar plexus. Bile rose, clogging his throat as he turned to look into the hard, unyielding visage of Jyautch.

"Die, orc," Jyautch whispered, his taut voice an unbreakable wire. "You shall rule nothing more than worms and maggots. Razikyl, the King of Dirt and Shit."

Razikyl opened his mouth, his tongue lolling out of his mouth despite his intent to speak. Jyautch pushed him away and stepped over the orc mage as the dark-garbed figure slid down to the ground. The tall, dark-haired warrior held back his tears as he passed by Tamagan's ravaged body and stood before Kael's nearly still form. The blond warrior's body was white as bone, blood still seeping from around the steel protruding from his back. His breath was short and erratic. Alique lay directly beside him, her forehead to his, her consciousness adrift. They lay dead or dying, peace with them finally as the final bell poised, ready to toll.

Jyautch looked up, no weapon left to hold, his armor cracked and broken, his endurance spent. Across from him Hosampsich stood up, drawing again the void-like length of the Midnight Blade. One wing was severed, the other mangled and hanging worthless behind him, but the grand demon lord still towered over Jyautch's lean six-and a half foot frame.

"You fought valiantly, mortal," the Tiger Demon acknowledged with a shake of his head. "I have never seen more powerful souls in mortal clay."

"I care not, demon."

"Care or not, mortal, now you die."

"No, Hosampsich," a powerful, soothing voice flooded across the mountaintop's length. "No more. It ends now. It must end now." Hosampsich and Jyautch both looked to the very ledge of the towering plateau and saw Jehoel crest the edge and touch down lightly on the rocky soil.

The wiry, angelic form shone brightly, radiant in power. His long blond hair glowed golden from his own iridescence. His garb was clean and pure as if just tailored: the silken kilt and white, virginal leather sandals. His downy dove-like feathers had regenerated wholly already and spread full in warm white energy. He wore no sword, no scabbard, no belt. None of this drew the attention of the eastern warrior and the demon. It was the gigantic, inner, second set of wings that rose from the angel's shoulder blades. They spread twice as far and larger than the feathered, bird-like wings, easily a span of twenty-five feet. They were made of another substance other than physical matter like that of feathers and bone. They were ectoplasmic and glistening, blue in color save for the surging veins and threading streams of white. They seemed to float with a mind of their own, akin to a sheet given to soft high winds.

"How the f…" Hosampsich nearly said. He didn't get it out of his mouth as Jehoel's enormous will-o-the-wisp wings cracked forward like a whip sending blue-hot energy full into the demon's chest. Hosampsich was sent flying back into the very depths of the inferno, Jyautch hurtled across the mountaintop with Kael and Alique's unconscious forms. The dark-haired warrior scrambled to pull the barely living Kael into his arms. He looked up to witness Hosampsich disappear into the fiery depths, and Jehoel walking forth toward the rising column of horror. The angel paid no regard to the mortals around him as he came to a halt a few paces before the yawning pit. He cocked his head as if in anticipation. Yellow flames flared for an instant, mingling with the powerful red as a dark figure leapt out of the hell-gate. He carried an enormous form over one arm.

The figure, tossed to the ground once they touched down, was a groveling Hosampsich.

"Please, don't slay me," the demon lord bawled, head in his hands as he sat on his hands and elbows. "I must exist!"

"Shhh," the dark warrior raised a black-gloved finger to his masked mouth. "Be silent and you just may."

The tall turbaned warrior laid one hand on his gigantic scimitar and hooked the thumb of the other into his red, silken sash about his waist. His sky-white eyes mirrored both the heat of the fire column and the cool pulse of the angel's protoplasmic inner wings.

"This is all your cause," Jehoel spoke, his hands at his sides. "To what end?"

The Dark Warrior pulled a demon tusk from under the red leather bracer around his left wrist and held it before Hosampsich. He waved a quick pattern in the air and whispered a single word and the tiger-skinned demon lord was pulled shrinking and screaming into the tusk's very depths. Hosampsich saw as the world whirled and grew around him that the tusk that was to be his prison was from his own previous body, slain by the blond mortal many months ago. The skull-tooth pulsed for an instant, then dimmed, and the Dark Warrior slipped it back under his bracer.

"For that?" Jehoel asked, his voice a mix of inability to understand and an unwillingness to try just now. "All of this suffering and battle. This destruction of life was for you to trap one worthless demon?"

The Dark One stepped near Jehoel and picked up the Midnight Blade. Both warriors stood silent for a long moment. Finally, the dark one stepped before the hell-gate and struck at it double-handed with the gigantic sword. The void blade struck the plane of the opening and it shuddered as if a pool of water. Transparent ripples rose and rushed to the stony edges. As they struck the lip of the pit, they rushed back to the center, pulling the mountain together as they did. With a deafening rush of air that stole the very breath from Jyautch as he watched, the hell-gate shut. Where it had opened now was flat, smooth rock, the Midnight Blade half-buried, rising like a crucifix out of the ground.

"I have no answers for you now, Jehoel," the Dark Warrior returned at last. He turned again to face the warrior angel. "But answers will one day come. Have faith in that. I do."

And with that the dark one's steed dropped out the sky like a whisper. He mounted as easy as a breeze, and was gone as if only a dream.

Jehoel stood for only a moment, pondering the Dark Warrior's words. He regarded Jyautch and the others with sympathy, then spread both sets of his majestic wings and lifted into the heavy clouds of the winter night.

Jyautch watched the angel fly into the depths of the mounting storm, then looked away. He pulled the limp form of his friend closer to himself, pressed his lips to the top of Kael's head and let the pain and anguish finally take over. For one of the only times in his life, a single tear poured from his eye and ran down his face into Kael's.

For long hours, Jyautch was silent.

*

Razikyl was barely able to pull himself up to his knees, clear fluid running from his hanging lip. His gaze was blank as he reached back behind himself and gripped the leatherbound handle of the long, blue-hued katana. The mage pulled at the sword's handle with one hand as he pushed at the blade itself with his other. Pain coursed through his whole body as he inched the weapon out of his torso. Stars erupted against the darkness of his vision as, after what felt like an eternity, the orc pulled the sword out of his body. Blood and bile forced up out of his throat as he clenched his belly to hold his intestines into his body. Life force poured out of the gaping wound in his back as he staggered to his feet.

Razikyl tried to survey his surroundings but his brain refused to assimilate the information that his hazy eyes were collecting. Something other than his vision sparked for a moment as the orcen mage sensed the aura of his human weapon—Alique. He stumbled toward the essence that he felt and fell to the side of Alique's unconscious form. He pulled out a small vial that held a single drop of Tif'eret and uncapped it with his teeth. The wizard inhaled the contents of the vial and slipped it back into the reaches of his cloak.

His mind cleared for a nanosecond, but it was enough. Grasping Alique's right leg, he whispered a spell of teleportation, and the two disappeared with a flash of light. All that remained was the ever-so-slight scent of lilac in the air.

*

Kael dreamed of opening his eyes and returning to life. He turned his head and saw Jyautch complete a long burial pyre. At the head of the pyre rose the Midnight Blade, as if it were a headstone. Kael turned his head back and saw snow begin to fall ever so lightly. He almost managed a chuckle. It would be good to be alive, again.

Kael closed his eyes and the dream faded to black.

*

Kael opened his eyes slowly and took a deep breath. Pain coursed through his entire body as life-giving air did the same. His eyes clamped shut as he tensed from the hurt. He held his breath, then cautiously took another attempt. This time a long deep breath caused only a bearable amount of pain.

Kael sat up, shifting to lean against a thick, smooth rock. He brought his arms together, his elbows against his sides. He had a heavy bison hide on, which slid down from his torso as he sat up. Looking down, Kael saw that the entire right half of his abdomen was covered in a thick, red mudpack. He moved to touch it, then reconsidered. He really didn't want to know.

"Hai," a familiar voice spoke. Kael looked over to see Jyautch kneeling over a cook-fire, a thick leg of meat sizzling from a spit. He wasn't wearing his foreign armor or sword, and was garbed only in his simple brown long-sleeved shirt, pants, and tall leather boots. "Welcome back to the land of the living."

"Am I?" Kael grimaced as he pulled the blanket up to re-cover himself to his neck. He looked around again, recognizing his old cave. The makeshift door was in place, a storm howling behind it. At the space at the top of the door where it failed to reach the cave's roof, a snowdrift licked at the warm interior of the rocky opening. "The storm?"

"Aye," Jyautch nodded, "You've been out of it for days—nearly a week—and the storm has worsened each day. I pray it lets up soon. Game is getting more scarce every day."

Kael nodded. With only one man hunting, it would be even more difficult. Still, he didn't feel any hunger. When he questioned his dark-haired comrade about being fed, Jyautch shook his head.

"I've managed only water down your gullet, as hard as I've tried."

Kael nodded again, falling into silence. The snap and pop of the fire was the only sound for long minutes, while both warriors sat in deep reflection.

"What was accomplished?" Kael whispered after some time. Neither warrior met the other's gaze. "Did you see anything that was accomplished?"

"I saw a majestic Saracen warrior step out of the very pit of hell and take Hosampsich's whole form into the depths of a finger-sized tusk. He rode away on a devil stallion. I saw an angel with four wings—one set of a dove and the other of pure, blue energy. When I awoke after the conflict, the orcen wizard was gone, as was your lover. All that remained of the scene was the Midnight Blade sticking out of the stone where the hell-pit had rose, and the charred remains of Tamagan the Hobgoblin."

"I saw your pyre for him," Kael breathed, honor in his tone.

"The least I could do for a creature so valiant."

"So that was all that was accomplished," Kael sighed. "Powerful beings that we know nothing of grew even more powerful, and a creature that transcended his environment to bring honor into his own heart was destroyed."

"Aye," Jyautch nodded, walking over to sit near his friend. "Those things happened, but something else great also happened."

"What's that?"

"Men stood forward to defend what they felt was right. You and I survived a fight against powers that should have torn us asunder without a second thought. You survived death three times in a single night. Those were great things."

Kael nodded slightly.

"It was so chaotic," he stated at last. "There was no method—no reason at all to any of it."

"Aye, and we still survived," Jyautch said. "We survived, but did we learn anything?"

"We learned of our own power," Kael returned, looking up to meet Jyautch's eyes. "I learned that this world can be ours again. We can wield the same power that they do. We can overthrow the demonic lock on this land."

"Aye," Jyautch grinned, extending his hand to his comrade's. "Together, then, my friend. Together, we can turn the tide back. Together, we can make whole this fractured land."

"Together, then." Kael grasped the dark-haired warrior's hand tightly.

The duo's bodies filled with the familiar emptiness of power that always accompanied the access into the Gates of Power, and their hearts filled with a not-so-familiar sensation that verily outshone any other they could have experienced: hope.

Jyautch released Kael's grip and stepped over to cut the cooking meat. Kael accepted the food with a nod and quietly ate at it. Even the movement of his jaw made his whole being ache, but he continued. Kael cocked his head at his own thoughts as he ate. He still felt no hunger, but his mind told him he needed the nourishment, despite what his stomach felt. He looked down at the long blue-red scars that ran up his chest. All of his tissue and muscle was sound, but the scar tissue was there never the less. Kael thought of the healing abilities that had obviously come from the binding of his and the Wind Bearer's energies. That energy now flowed through his veins and had kept him alive twice during the incredible fight on the top of the mountain. He knew that given time, he would be able to access that power as he accessed the Gevurah through the meeting of his soul and body, but would it spell his doom?

Kael looked over at Jyautch and thought of the power that they had shared when they had first ascended the mountain in search of game. It was the power of the gate of Hessed. Kael knew that he would someday be able to access that power, too, like the Gevurah. Looking over at his comrade, Kael wondered if the dark-haired warrior could access the Gevurah. Had Jyautch benefited from their coupling during the rock fall? Would either be able to survive the strength of both gates of power?

Exhaustion swept over Kael again. How long had he been awake? Only five minutes and he could barely keep his eyes open. Sighing, Kael closed his eyes, completely trusting Jyautch's ability to keep the both of them alive while the blonde warrior slept. Dreams came quick to his rest, visions of summer and peace in the lands of the Kelt-Ra clan filled his mind. Kael stood again with Alique at his side and the land was restored to its luscious vitality. Outside, unknown to the inhabitants of the snow-covered cave, a stream of sunlight peeked out the vast, foreboding clouds and the intensity of the fierce storm began to slacken; and Kael continued to dream.